SPEAKERS OF THE DEAD

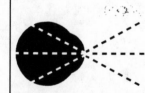

This Large Print Book carries the
Seal of Approval of N.A.V.H.

Speakers of the Dead

J. Aaron Sanders

THORNDIKE PRESS

A part of Gale, Cengage Learning

GALE
CENGAGE Learning·

Farmington Hills, Mich • San Francisco • New York • Waterville, Maine
Meriden, Conn • Mason, Ohio • Chicago

GALE
CENGAGE Learning®

Thorndike Press® Large Print Historical Fiction.
The text of this Large Print edition is unabridged.
Other aspects of the book may vary from the original edition.
Set in 16 pt. Plantin.

LIBRARY OF CONGRESS CATALOGING-IN-PUBLICATION DATA

Names: Sanders, J. Aaron, author.
Title: Speakers of the dead : a Walt Whitman mystery / by J Aaron Sanders.
Description: Large print edition. | Waterville, Maine : Thorndike Press, 2016. | © 2016 | Series: Thorndike Press large print historical fiction | Include bibliographical references
Identifiers: LCCN 2016014291| ISBN 9781410491091 (hardcover) | ISBN 1410491099 (hardcover)
Subjects: LCSH: Whitman, Walt, 1819-1892—Fiction. | Murder—Investigation—Fiction. | Body snatching—Fiction. | Large type books. | GSAFD: Mystery fiction. | Historical fiction.
Classification: LCC PS3619.A5265 S64 2016b | DDC 813/.6—dc23
LC record available at http://lccn.loc.gov/2016014291

Published in 2016 by arrangement with Plume, an imprint of Penguin Publishing Group, a division of Penguin Random House LLC

Printed in Mexico
1 2 3 4 5 6 7 20 19 18 17 16

For Gareth and Eliot:
Missing me one place search another,
I stop somewhere waiting for you.

When I read the book,
the biography famous,
And is this then (said I) what the
author calls a man's life?
And so will some one when I am dead
and gone write my life?
(As if any man really knew
aught of my life,
Why even I myself I often think know
little or nothing of my real life,
Only a few hints, a few diffused
faint clews and indirections
I seek for my own use to
trace out here.)
— Walt Whitman

During the nineteenth century public out-
rage over dissection continued. There
were dozens of riots or ransackings in
protest against medical school dissections
and/or grave robbing. In 1807 in Baltimore

a mob burned down the anatomy hall at the University of Maryland. In 1824 mobs rioted every night for a week against barricaded Yale medical students after a purloined body was found at the medical school. Rioters destroyed medical school buildings at Worthington Medical College in Ohio (1839), McDowell Medical College in Missouri (1844), and Willoughby Medical College in Ohio (1847). In short, the detested scourge of body snatching plagued every state with a medical school at some point during the period from 1807 to 1890 and often produced an outraged public reaction.

— Norman L. Cantor
After We Die: The Life and Times of the Human Cadaver

■ ■ ■ ■

NEW YORK, 1843

■ ■ ■ ■

PROLOGUE

In the dream, Elizabeth Blackwell sits opposite Jane Avery's deathbed. She dabs Jane's furrowed forehead with a wet cloth and whispers that all will be well. Jane tilts her head toward Elizabeth and tries to speak through her cracked lips caked in muck. Then Jane slips into an irreversible coughing fit —

And that's when a noise wakes Elizabeth.

She opens her eyes, relieved. She hates that recurring dream, the helpless feeling of watching her friend die. It's been six years since Jane Avery's death, and not a day goes by that Elizabeth doesn't believe she might have saved her had she been properly trained as a physician.

The noise sounds again.

Around her, in the dormitory of the Women's Medical College of Manhattan, the other four students do not stir. Perhaps it was nothing.

She closes her eyes and summons the image of Jane in her prime, her long, elegant frame and creamy skin. After Latin class at the Cincinnati English and French Academy for Young Ladies, Jane is cleaning the blackboard. She erases the word *mulier.* She senses Elizabeth watching, turns and smiles —

There it is again. A metallic banging this time.

Elizabeth reaches for her robe and slippers. She lights a candle, waking Miss Zacky in the bed next to hers.

"Lizzy." Miss Zacky checks her pocket watch. "It's three in the morning, and Abraham's trial begins at nine."

Abraham Stowe, cofounder of the women's college and a married man, has been accused of manslaughter, the result of a botched abortion performed on Mary Rogers, with whom he admitted having a love affair. In his defense, and for the sake of Abraham's wife and college cofounder, Lena, the students stayed up late preparing anatomical diagrams outlining the effects of abortion on a woman's body. The diagrams would be compared with the Mary Rogers autopsy report, which Lena and Elizabeth believed had been altered to implicate Abraham.

"Be that as it may, I heard a noise downstairs. I should have a look."

Miss Zacky groans. "You know that means I have to accompany you."

"I also know that you are capable of making your own decisions."

The two women skulk across the room into the stairwell, closing the dormitory door behind them. They make their way down the stairs past the third-floor maternity ward, all silent, then to the second-floor infirmary.

Inside, the patient nearest the door, Mrs. Cook, sleeps soundly. Mrs. Stephens, a few beds over, also lies still. Mrs. Dowd, in the bed next to the window, shifts at the sound of their entrance. She sits up straight, struggles to breathe through the dehydration associated with the cholera-like symptoms that landed her in the sickroom the day before.

Elizabeth props Mrs. Dowd with a pillow while Miss Zacky goes for laudanum.

"There, there, Mrs. Dowd," Elizabeth says. "Take your time."

But Mrs. Dowd's deep, panicked breath can't catch up to itself, and suffocation is closing in. Elizabeth keeps talking, rubbing her back. "You can do it," she says.

Mrs. Dowd's eyes roll back, and she heaves.

Elizabeth doesn't hesitate. She slides onto the bed and wraps her arms around her patient. She finds the sternum and pushes hard. Nothing happens, and so she repeats the move. This time, Mrs. Dowd coughs up a bite of meat, which lands on the white sheet at the end of the bed. Elizabeth holds the woman until she catches her breath. "Didn't quite finish our supper, did we?"

While Elizabeth holds her upright, Miss Zacky raises the glass to Mrs. Dowd's mouth. She struggles to swallow at first, but then works it down.

When the laudanum takes effect, the results are swift. Mrs. Dowd's body weight collapses into Elizabeth's lap. She looks at Miss Zacky, who mouths the words *Her eyes have closed.*

Relief washes over Elizabeth. She has the fleeting thought that healing is what God put her on earth to do. She eases out from behind her patient, tucking the blanket under the sleeping woman's chin.

Back in the stairwell, Miss Zacky whispers, "You're going to be an excellent doctor, Lizzy." Elizabeth smiles in response.

In the dormitory now, Elizabeth observes the rise and fall of the sleeping bodies and contemplates the miracle that is a medical college for women. *And it's all thanks to Abraham and Lena Stowe.* Later this morning, they'll begin the work of proving Abraham's innocence, and the college can return to its primary mission: to advance the welfare of women through medicine and education. Slipping beneath the covers, she lays her head on the straw pillow and closes her eyes to dream of Jane once again.

Suddenly, loud and chaotic noises, a string of grunts and screams, ascend from the first floor.

She glances at Miss Zacky, eyes wide. The other students pop up, one after another: Karina Emsbury, Olive Perschon, Patricia Onderdonk. *What is it?* they want to know, and Elizabeth bids them *Wait here.*

She and Miss Zacky hurry down the stairs to the dissection room on the first floor. Elizabeth puts her ear to the door. Nothing.

From behind her, Miss Zacky whispers, "The body snatchers . . . ?"

A scream sounds.

Elizabeth throws open the door, searching for signs of the fearsome resurrection men who dig up fresh graves and sell the corpses to medical colleges like this one. A single candle on the back wall illuminates the familiar sight of a large central table ringed

15

by shelves and counters. A lone figure hunches over a body, laid out as if for dissection.

It's Lena Stowe, gazing down at her dead husband. His eyes and mouth are open, and his chest has been split apart, his rib cage sawed in two. Blood is everywhere. On Abraham. On Lena. On the table and floor.

Elizabeth wraps her arms around a sobbing Lena, and while they cry together, she can't help but stare at the monstrous carnage.

It's not yet morning on February 12, 1843.

■ ■ ■ ■

Two Weeks Later

■ ■ ■ ■

CHAPTER 1

They are going to kill her.

Walt Whitman, reporter for the *New York Aurora,* is standing in the courtyard of the Tombs, with several hundred New Yorkers who have crushed past his cold, aching body for a glimpse of the execution.

The sun is at the halfway point on its short cycle through the winter sky, and its low angle casts long shadows from west to east, shadows that cover all but the east wall of the prison. It is on this wall that Lena's large and lonely shadow is cast as if by stage light.

The noose dances in the harsh winter wind, and below the gallows, a layer of frost blankets the dirt. Walt pushes his way to the front of the crowd, the ice crystals crunching beneath his boots. They are all waiting for Sheriff Jack Harris to return from his meeting with Mayor Morris about whether or not to grant Mrs. Stowe a stay on her execution because of her pregnancy. Walt worries that the decision to deny the stay is a fait accompli, which is why he brought with him a sheaf of testimonials from Lena's medical students in which they argue that the fetus has quickened, a legal problem for the city, because if the fetus has begun to move, New York would be executing two of its citizens instead of one.

The sheriff's coach, a new yellow phaeton, rumbles through the prison gates, around the crowd, and skids to a stop. Jack Harris's silver hair is stuffed under a top hat, his bearded face deceptively slight compared to his stout body. By reputation, he is a man who sometimes puts instinct before protocol.

Whitman calls out to the sheriff, and when he tries to follow the lawman, two guards block his way. He scurries back around to the front of the gallows for a better view. The arrest and trial were rushed affairs, rigged against her from the beginning, it seemed, and her defense never gained real traction with anyone but those closest to her. The students know Lena and Abraham. They spent time with them every day for months, and they saw what Walt saw: a couple who, despite their problems, had become closer. None of them even considered Lena as a suspect until Sheriff Harris arrested her.

At the sheriff's appearance atop the gallows, the crowd quiets.

The silence presses down on Walt, and he fights back feelings of despair. The woman who treated him like a son is beautiful and haggard, still wearing the medical school–issued black dress and white apron stained with her husband's blood, having refused to change since her arrest. Her long black hair ribbons stream in the wind, and her dark eyes are red and swollen. His heart aches to see her suffer like this.

The sheriff approaches the condemned woman, her body quivering, and he whispers in her ear.

There is a moment of nothingness —

— and then she reels backward, emitting a preternatural scream that convulses Walt's soul.

Lena flails until the wiry priest powerfully grips her shoulder. "And God hath both raised up the Lord," he calls out in his baritone voice, "and will also raise you up by his own power."

"But the baby!"

Whitman rushes the stairway but is again blocked by the two guards. He shuffles backward, stands on his tiptoes. Behind him, the bloodthirsty crowd stirs.

Harris pauses for a moment, then nods to the jailer, Little Joe, who holds Lena fast while the sheriff ties her hands behind her back.

Walt's heart races.

This time Whitman charges, using his large frame to knock one guard to the side, the other to the ground, before ascending the staircase, two steps at a time.

On the hanging platform, half a dozen coppers line the back end. There's the priest, wide-eyed and hunched over. There's Little Joe, twice as big as any other man in the city, and there's Sheriff Harris. Walt holds up the leather-bound sheaf. "These medical testimonies demonstrate that Mrs. Stowe is quick with child."

The sheriff shakes his head. "Mr. Whitman, our medical expert reached a different conclusion."

A few feet away, Lena's sobs are muted by the wind.

Walt takes a step toward the sheriff, and two policemen meet him. "Mrs. Stowe's colleagues disagree."

"Those women are not doctors."

The sheriff turns away, but Whitman catches him on his shoulder. "You're a good man. I saw how you restored order after the cigar girl was murdered."

"The law is the law."

Whitman pushes a little harder. "This city does not need another controversy."

At the delay the crowd jitters, the kind of tottering that precedes a mob action.

The sheriff briefly looks Walt in the eye, then gestures to two of his men, and they promptly take Walt into custody.

"Her death will be on your watch," Whitman shouts.

Knowing that Walt has failed, Lena resumes her struggle to get free. She rolls toward the edge of the platform and nearly goes over —

But Little Joe grabs her from behind and lifts her to her feet.

During the commotion, Walt wrestles away, but a third man kicks him in the stomach, and the other two retake him. The pain is searing. He rolls to the side. The watchmen have the platform covered, and there are more of them on the ground for crowd control and even more at the gate. He is surrounded.

The sheriff slips the black hood over Lena's head and reaches for the noose, and that's when the men holding Whitman loosen their grip just enough —

He wiggles free, dodges Harris, and scoops up Lena, black hood and all. She is heavy in his arms, but the adrenaline drives him to brave the blockade of six men, their Colt pistols drawn, their faces blank. He charges through them, and miraculously sees daylight between him and the stairway. If he can only make it down —

— and then the space closes, and the men are upon him. Walt clings to Lena with all his might until she whispers, her voice strong and deliberate from beneath the hood, "It's over, Walt. You did your best."

He holds back his tears. "But you're innocent."

"Keep the college going so our deaths are not in vain."

He holds her tighter.

It takes four men to hold Whitman, and two more to pry Lena away from him. The men push him to the ground and cuff him, the metal cutting into his wrists. Walt screams, curses, thrashes about, mad with rage over what is about to happen.

He watches as the sheriff slips the noose over Lena's head, positions her over the trapdoor, and addresses those who condemned her to this fate: "For the murder of Abraham Stowe," he bellows, "you have been sentenced to death by hanging, after which your body will be dissected at the Women's Medical College of Manhattan."

The crowd roars.

Walt breathes in.

The sheriff claps three times, the lever is pulled, and the floor falls away —

Lena's body drops.

— her neck breaks.

— and Walt Whitman collapses on the platform, sobbing now, and waits for his friend and her unborn child to die.

Chapter 2

Whitman's wrists sting where the skin has abraded, and his spirit is raw. He wants to look away from the gruesome scene, but out of respect for Lena's wishes, he will bear witness. Before him, her body twitches, and two men with pistols stand guard over him. He watches until she stops moving altogether, her last prayer smothered in its utterance.

At that moment, Coroner Barclay, a tiny excuse for a man, creeps onto the scene and pronounces Lena dead. Little Joe cuts the rope suspending her body midair, and she drops into the back of the coroner's wagon. Barclay tosses a tarp over her, and drives away.

As Walt stands, restrained, the sheriff finishes up interviews with James Gordon Bennett from the *New York Herald* and Horace Greeley from the *New York Tribune.* The fact that Greeley and Bennett, both with readerships in the twenty thousands, are in attendance illustrates the enormity of what has happened, and Walt will add his own account to the *Aurora* as soon as he can. Before joining the *Aurora,* with its five thousand readers, he worked as a printer for Park Benjamin at the *New World.* While there, several of his short stories were published by Benjamin, who later hired him to write the novel *Franklin Evans,* despite their public disagreements that led to his departure from the *New World.*

The meeting disbands, and Harris approaches. Walt holds out his hands to be released.

"Sorry, Mr. Whitman. You'll be coming with me." He tugs at the heavy metal cuffs. "The newspapers are about to run wild with your antics."

"But I have an appointment to transport Mrs. Stowe's body from the coroner's to the women's college today."

"That is the coroner's responsibility."

"I promised Miss Blackwell, and Dr. Barclay agreed."

"Perhaps you should have had this in mind before you attempted to halt the execution."

The watch house jail stinks like an outhouse,

and is as dark. Walt squints to see better but has to rely on sounds — the shuffling, scraping, and breathing of confined men.

The sheriff leads him to a cell near the back of the hallway. With a key larger than his hand, Harris unlocks the door and uses his full body weight to push it open. He nudges Whitman into the cell, where a freckle-faced boy with bright red hair sits on the cell's one cot. Dressed in socks but no shoes, tattered pantaloons, and a ripped white shirt, he can't be more than thirteen years old.

"This is for your own protection," Harris says as he swings the cell door shut.

"Do those words ease your conscience?"

"You rushed the gallows," Harris says. "You assaulted my men. You should be grateful I don't lock you up for a year."

Whitman stands strong and tall until the sheriff is out of sight, then doubles over in grief. He is surrounded by stone and one window, less than a square foot in size and set above eye level, the only break.

The boy catches him eyeing the window. "There's no way out," he says. "Believe me, I've tried."

Walt sinks to the floor. He cannot escape this situation, nor his own grief. Lena is gone forever from this world, and he'll never sit across the table from her or Abraham — no more conversing into the late hours of the night, no more comparing their readings of Emerson, or listening to Abraham and Lena discuss Oliver Wendell Holmes's latest précis on hygiene and disease.

The boy asks, "You tried to stop the hanging?"

"Of an innocent woman."

"No offense, mister, but she had good reason to kill her husband after what he did to the cigar girl."

The boy's version of events matches popular opinion: Abraham Stowe had an affair with Mary Rogers, the pretty cigar store clerk. She became pregnant, Abraham botched the abortion, and Rogers died. Abraham panicked and tossed her body in the river. Lena found out about the affair and abortion, and killed him. The State of New York executed her. Done.

"I know what has been said about this matter, but the City of New York has made a terrible error."

The boy leans forward. "You couldn't find proof that she didn't kill her husband, could you?"

"It's an eventuality."

"But she's dead. Why not leave her be?"

Walt locks eyes with the boy. "The truth

29

always matters."

The boy does not pursue the topic further. Instead, he confesses his own crime. "I was arrested for grave robbery." The boy pauses, then continues. "I tried to dig up the body of my neighbor, Mrs. Abernathy."

Whitman tries to ignore him, but the boy persists. "Have you ever dug a grave, mister?"

He shakes his head. "Of course not."

"It ain't as easy as you might think. The ground is frozen solid, and it took me two hours to break up the dirt." The boy stands, pretends to dig. His movements are pained, but he perseveres. "I'm shoveling and shoveling. *How far down is she?* I'm in the hole about waist deep when I finally reach the casket. *I'll chip the lid off the casket and slide her out that way.* If I'm still at it by sunrise, I know I'll end up" — he flashes his biggest smile — "I know I'll end up in jail."

"The sheriff arrested you before you could sell the corpse?" Walt presses, warming to his subject. He knows about the resurrection men and their grisly trade in dead bodies.

The boy shakes his head. "Mrs. Abernathy's brothers were standing guard, looking out for folks like me. They'd slipped away for a couple of pops, and when they returned, I had her nearly out."

Walt understands this too about body snatching: The burden is on the families to guard their loved ones' bodies — whether by armed guard or by technology. The Patent Coffin, for one, is made out of wrought iron and lined with spring catches so the lid won't open. There are cages, straps, or even *dead houses* — places where loved ones can leave the bodies safely until they are no longer good for dissection. Or, as in this case, the family itself might stand guard —

Suddenly, Walt is concerned about the boy. His face shows no sign of injury, but the way he moves — "And they roughed you up?"

The boy coughs.

Whitman joins the boy on the cot and reaches for his shirt. The boy resists at first, but Walt reassures him with a soft look and a nod. The bruises, deep browns and purples, cover his chest and back.

"Where are your parents?"

He pauses. "Dead, sir."

Maybe Walt can give the boy a chance, bring him to the women's college, where they'll look after him until he's recovered.

"I'm sorry for your loss, mister."

Memories of Lena come unbidden, and

Walt is flooded with the awe he felt observing her medical lectures, Abraham always in attendance. Her distinguished beauty matched her quick wit. Her strong, confident voice would fill the room, and when the students' questions inevitably came, she fielded them with a generous tone and a precise logic.

And now he's crying.

The boy slides close and wraps his scrawny arm around Walt's neck. "It's okay, mister. My mother used to tell me that death is not the end but a start to something better, something glorious. Do you believe that too?"

Whitman considers himself a deist with Quaker leanings, a man who believes that death is a curvature of the ringed self, all part of a larger cycle of comings and goings, that the mind and soul are eternal. But the tragedy of Lena's and Abraham's untimely deaths has undercut these beliefs. For now, he will have to rely on the boy's faith. "I do believe that," Walt says. "Absolutely."

"We're all right, then, the two of us," the boy says.

A clatter of footsteps sounds in the hallway. The key clanks, the chamber turns, and the heavy iron cell door opens to reveal a young man whose sculpted cheekbones and square jawline are framed by dark shoulder-length hair. His low-crown top hat tilts rakishly toward a wilted pink boutonniere on his lapel.

"Henry?" Walt faces his past.

"You look terrible, Mr. Whitman."

After a short courtship, the men had parted a few years earlier — Henry bound to his family farm in northern Manhattan, and Walt to teach school in Brooklyn. They had promised to write letters, and while Walt had written several, Henry had written none.

"What are you doing here?"

"I'm your new boss at the *Aurora,*" Henry says, leaning on his chestnut walking stick. "And Mr. Ropes sent me here to bail you out."

Walt rises to shake Henry Saunders's hand — his skin is soft and his grip strong. "I'm grateful," he says, "but the only way I'm coming with you is if you bail out my friend here, Mr. —" He turns to the boy.

"Smith." The boy stands despite the pain. "Azariah Smith."

CHAPTER 3

Walt follows the coroner, Dr. Kenneth Barclay, down a long white hallway that opens up to a makeshift morgue. Once inside, Dr. Barclay removes the sheet with all the flair of P. T. Barnum revealing an exhibition.

Walt gulps back tears.

Lena's dark eyes are open, her mouth twisted halfway between a smile and a scream. Walt attempts to close both her eyes and jaw — her skin is cold and greasy — but they won't stay shut.

"I'm afraid that's physically impossible." Barclay places his hand on Walt's. "I could have had the body delivered to spare you this sight."

Whitman backs away. "I made a promise."

"Very well. I'll need just a moment with her."

The coroner reviews the autopsy report, comparing his notes to the body, spending most of his time in the neck area. "I knew the Stowes well." Barclay breaks the silence. "Abe was my colleague at NYU. He and Lena invited me to dine with them several times. I admired them greatly."

Barclay waits for Walt to respond. He doesn't.

"I could have never imagined it, Lena killing Abraham." Barclay glances up from his work. "But after what he did to Mary Rogers —"

"They are innocent."

"Innocent? Oh, Mr. Whitman, we must face the truth."

"What do you know about the truth?"

"I saw Abe with Mary Rogers," Barclay says. "And she was only one of many women Abe seduced, his students among them." Barclay forces eye contact. "What Lena did breached morality, but she was driven to the brink. Abe betrayed her with woman after woman, and then the Mary Rogers affair?"

"She *didn't* kill him." Walt gathers himself, recalling Lena's vow to preserve her marriage in spite of her husband's infidelity: *We are stronger now than before.*

Barclay folds the autopsy folder shut, puts his finger to his chin. "Jealously is powerful motivation." He packs his pipe with tobacco, lights it, takes a puff. "At first, Mr. Whitman, I too believed she was innocent." Pipe smoke laces the frigid air. "But I examined the evidence. Abraham becomes involved with this Mary Rogers. She gets pregnant. He administers the abortion. Something goes wrong and she dies. So what does he do? He bludgeons her body to make it look like murder and dumps her in the river." Barclay takes another puff, then blows the sweet tobacco smoke in Walt's face. "Gruesome."

Whitman stanches the verbal assault: "Abraham did not kill Mary Rogers, and Lena did not kill Abraham, and I will prove it."

Barclay scoffs. "*You* will prove it? What can you possibly know that the sheriff has not already investigated?"

Walt shoots back, "The sheriff is not infallible."

"How do you explain the arsenic found on Lena, the same arsenic that killed Abraham?"

"Obviously, I cannot, or she wouldn't be dead on your table."

"Crimes," Barclay says, placing his hand on Lena's shoulder, "are not sensible. That quality is for writers like Mr. Poe to explore in his stories. Poor, poor Lena." The coroner traces his finger along her stomach. "And her poor child."

"That is enough!" Walt grabs Barclay by the collar and lifts him off the ground. "Is Mrs. Stowe's body ready?"

Barclay nods, a twinge of fear in his eyes.

"Good." Whitman drops the coroner to the floor. "Because I wish to take leave of this place."

CHAPTER 4

Walt Whitman drives the horse-pulled flatbed freight wagon he borrowed from Dr. Liston, Abraham Stowe's colleague at New York University, through the hundreds of New Yorkers who have lined the route to the Women's Medical College of Manhattan. Men, women, and children of all social classes, craning for a glimpse of the body. They are eerily silent now, and Walt fights back the urge to tell them they are partially responsible for his friend's death.

He directs the horses onto Centre Street, leaving the white light of the gas lamps and the parade of New Yorkers behind. Poorer streets like these are marked by the absence of light. And sound. The Broadway omnibuses are barely audible from a few streets over, the drivers preferring to remain where the money flows.

The Women's Medical College of Manhattan comes into view, and along with it the protestors. A group of twenty or so gathered in front of the college the day after Abraham's murder and has since grown into the hundreds. Their leader, the antidissectionist Father Allen, stretches his arms toward the sky like some Old Testament prophet: "Dissection stops the resurrection!"

Whitman has met the opportunist priest before, and has observed his skill at wielding human vulnerability, drawing on the fear of a public that believes a dissected corpse cannot rise from the dead. Walt assesses the mood of the crowd, recalling that only a month ago, a mob in New Haven burned down the medical school lab and lynched one of the young medical students.

The college is housed in a black-shingled granite-slab building accessible by a wooden staircase that leads to a porch. Just over the second-floor door, a single window stares like an eyeball. He recalls his first visit to the college a year earlier for an article in the *New World,* and how he got along with the Stowes straight away. They welcomed him in like family, and it was as if he had known them for years. He half expects Abraham and Lena to emerge in the entryway right now, holding hands, as they always did.

Walt steers the wagon right into the midst

of the protestors, and stops in front of the stairs.

With Lena in his arms, Whitman keeps an eye on the priest, who at the crucial moment gestures his followers to remove their hats, bow their heads, and make way for him. A sliver of humanity in the madness.

Walt nods his gratitude as he passes.

Once inside the college, his eyes adjust to the gaslight shining from each corner of what was once a dining room. Anatomical drawings on butcher paper hang from the walls over rows of chairs and desks.

He carries Lena past the bar turned lectern, the chalkboard behind it, and the dangling skeleton. To get into the dissection room, he has to walk underneath the sign painted in blue script: *She must mangle the living, if she has not operated on the dead.*

Walt lays Lena on the very dissection table where only two weeks earlier Abraham was murdered. He straightens the tarp so that it covers her from the shoulders down. A wave of emotion hits him, and he wipes his eyes with a handkerchief. He needs to be strong for the students.

Upstairs the students begin to stir. Whitman can't bear the thought of them seeing their instructor's lifeless body. They appear on the landing, one by one, each of them wearing the same black dress and white apron as Lena. They approach, place a hand lovingly on their teacher, their faces haggard and raw.

He knows each of them by name. Marie Zakrzewska, or Miss Zacky as the other students call her, is from Berlin. An ethereal redhead, she escaped a pogrom that killed her parents, two sisters, and three brothers, then she studied medicine in Europe and, as a midwife, ran a maternity ward in Switzerland. It was her dream to learn from the Stowes.

Blond-haired and blue-eyed Karina Emsbury, from Hartford, was disowned by her pastor father for studying medicine, then connected to Abraham and Lena through her school's headmistress and Abraham's cousin, Harriet Beecher Stowe. Olive Perschon, short and mousy, from Philadelphia, is the daughter of abolitionist parents supportive of her medical aspirations. And Patricia Onderdonk, a tall, powerful woman from the Netherlands who claims to have been orphaned in a coastal flood.

Elizabeth Blackwell, the Stowes' most loyal supporter and handpicked successor, breaks the silent procession. "This is madness." She shakes her head, squeezes her hands into fists, her British heritage evident

41

in every syllable. "How could they?" She clenches her square jaw and thin lips. Her dark hair is pulled in a tight bun at the back of her head. Miss Blackwell will display her determination but never her devastation in front of her students.

Walt and Miss Blackwell will keep the medical college going. The students need Elizabeth to be strong. So Whitman takes her by the hand, and they form a prayer circle around the body. *Our Father who art in heaven,* he begins, and for once he lets someone else's words do what his own simply cannot.

When the last of the *amen*s has echoed through the chamber, he steps back. Watching grief seize their young faces and shatter their confidence, he vows to honor the family circle Abraham and Lena provided for them here at the college.

As they had done for him.

He wants to stand on the table, call them to arms. *We will fix this injustice, we will storm the city, crash their homes, shout from the rooftops.* His army, these strong young women and their new leader, Elizabeth Blackwell. But now is not the time. He will stand down, he will let them cry, and he too will cry.

Miss Blackwell joins him at the back of

the room. "Your friend, young Mr. Smith, is resting upstairs," she says. "We blocked off a corner for him."

"Thank you," Whitman says. "How are his injuries?"

"I'm afraid his internal organs may be severely damaged," Elizabeth says. "I gave him a dose of laudanum to help him rest."

Walt says, "I'll look in on him later."

"He said he has no family."

Whitman nods.

Elizabeth shakes her head. "Poor dear."

Behind them, a distraught Karina Emsbury throws herself across Lena. The other students blanch at this naked display of grief.

Amidst the jumble of emotion, Miss Zacky approaches Walt. "Your wrists." She takes his hands into hers. "They're bleeding." She slides up his coat sleeves and examines the long scrapes from the handcuffs, rubbed raw and bleeding. "We need to clean and dress these." Miss Zakrzewska has become Elizabeth's most reliable help, though their styles of practice diverge. She touches where Elizabeth withdraws from physical contact. She knows the power of her beauty, bewitching others with her penetrating gaze.

Walt says, "I tried to save her —" Flashes

43

of Lena on the platform intervene, the hood, the noose, the floor dropping away, and he grits his teeth in agony.

"We know." Miss Zacky pulls him close, wraps her arms around his neck. It feels good to be held like this, as Henry used to hold him, and in that moment he needs her, and so he presses up against her even more, holding tight.

CHAPTER 5

The cracked plaster on the bedroom ceiling extends like a spiderweb. The last time Walt was in this room, he was helping Abraham Stowe move an armoire, a gift to Lena for their anniversary. At one point, Abe's foot became stuck between the armoire and the doorjamb. To get loose, he had to take off his boot, sending Walt and Lena into fits of laughter.

He sits up on the bed and returns to sorting through the Stowes' possessions. Inside the armoire he finds clothing, jewelry, a Bible belonging to Lena's mother, and an old anatomy book inscribed to her by Abraham. *To my darling doctor. Yours forever in science and love, Abraham.* Lena's clothing will be distributed among the students according to their need, and the rest will be used for patients. Abraham's clothing will be donated to one of the immigrant shelters. Walt makes two piles of clothing, a third pile for non-clothing items, and a fourth for Lena's family.

Miss Blackwell knocks on the door. "May I come in?"

"Please."

She sits down on the dressing chair in front of the mirror. On her lap is the brown leather-bound ledger for the college's finances. "Mr. Whitman."

"Call me Walt."

"*Walt,* then. No one would blame you if we have to close the school. I know Lena asked you to live here, to help me run the college, but you can return to the newspaper full-time, and I'll forge ahead with my plans to get into a proper medical school. The students will return to their families, start again somewhere else."

He shakes his head. "We have to keep the college open."

"We have money for a few months, at the most," she says. "One of the problems is only half the students pay any tuition. I spoke with Miss Zacky about this, and she confirmed my suspicions: Abraham accepted students who could not pay, telling them to repay the tuition once they began earning money as doctors."

Whitman knows this too. "Abraham was terrible with money," he says. "No sense at all." This causes him to laugh, and it's nice to remember his friend this way.

Elizabeth smiles. "Apparently." Her British accent muted now. "You know, they thought of you like a son."

"The feeling was mutual." He felt comfortable around the Stowes as he never had in his own home. "Where will you go, Miss Blackwell?"

"Pardon?"

"If we have to close the college," Walt says. "Where will you go?"

She thinks for a moment. "It wouldn't be the first time I had to leave New York."

"May I ask why?"

She looks at the wall before answering. "My father's New York sugar refinery burned down in 1836, and we relocated to Ohio, where he might rebuild his business using sugar beets instead of sugar cane." She looks at Walt. "You see, we learned that sugar cane relies on the slave trade, and my father was an abolitionist." She begins to cry, but catches herself. "He died three weeks later."

Walt says, "That must have been difficult."

"My sisters and I moved to Ohio to start the Cincinnati English and French Academy for Young Ladies. We were forced to close by those who feared our ideology was too revolutionary. That's what women are up against, Mr. Whitman. Even when no other alternative exists, we are expected to mind our places."

"I left Manhattan in 1836 too."

"Oh?"

"I moved to the city from Brooklyn to work as a compositor, and I fell in love. New York City was an exciting, dangerous place." He pauses. "I had never seen such. One night at the Bowery Theatre, an English actor appeared on stage, and a riot broke out that left the building badly damaged."

"Because he was British?"

"We're Americans, Miss Blackwell." Walt smiles. "We have long memories."

"Why did you leave the city?"

"Same reason you did. Work was scant after the 1836 printing district fire. I moved home to Hempstead, where I began teaching at a country school in East Norwich. I've been back and forth a few times."

"You were a teacher?"

"A poor one for sure."

"Nonsense."

"You'll have to take my word, Miss Blackwell. I do not have the temperament," Whitman says. "So would you try again with the school for young ladies?"

Miss Blackwell sighs. "That's the kicker,

isn't it? I decided to be a doctor after I watched Jane, my close friend, die a painful death. I realized that her doctor, a man, didn't understand Jane's body, and after she passed, it came to me like a revelation from God. Women need women doctors."

Walt nods in agreement.

"Then I saw the advertisement in the newspaper for the Women's Medical College of Manhattan, and when I saw Abraham Stowe's name attached to it, I knew it was another sign from God. You see, one of my acquaintances in Ohio was Harriet Beecher, and she was married to Abraham's cousin, Calvin Ellis Stowe." She looks lost in herself now. "For all that Abraham and Lena sacrificed — we have to keep the college going."

She hands the ledger to him.

"And we do have another problem to contend with," Miss Blackwell says. "Turn to the last page."

There he finds the name James Warren and a series of check marks. The name rings familiar, but he can't place it. "Who is it?"

"I don't know," Elizabeth says. "Probably a sack-'em-up. Dr. Stowe kept that part of the college private."

Walt nods. "He detested working with the resurrectionists."

"That's why he was so grateful for your help with the Bone Bill."

Abraham had asked Walt to help him draft a new version of the Bone Bill, legislation that would provide a legal way for medical colleges to acquire cadavers. Up until now, medical students and their instructors had to rely on the illegal trade of cadavers. The Bone Bill, short for An Appeal to the People of the State of New York to Legalize the Dissection of the Dead, had failed to pass several times, due in large part to the real belief that a dissected body cannot be resurrected.

Abraham approached Walt for help a few weeks after they met, having rightly guessed that Walt had reported on the increase in grave robberies. That reporting taught him that the resurrection men, once a motley group of ruffians, had become more organized and efficient than ever before, their network stretching beyond the city to Brooklyn and Long Island, even up into Connecticut and over to Pennsylvania.

Walt says, "And you think Abraham's murder has something to do with the body snatchers?"

"Abraham became an enemy the moment he publicly supported the Bone Bill," she

50

says. "It would end a very lucrative business."

"I'll let you know what I find out about this James Warren," Walt says.

Miss Blackwell surveys the room, her gaze lingering at Lena's belongings piled on the bed. "I really thought she'd come home." Her voice cracks.

He takes her hand. "So did I."

Walt Whitman sits next to Azariah Smith while he sleeps. He feels a kinship with the boy who has been forced by circumstances to grow up too fast. Walt himself left home at twelve to work and was expected to send home what he earned to his father, a drunkard and a spendthrift.

Azariah opens his eyes. "Ah, Mr. Whitman."

"So how is the treatment here?"

"Well." Azariah takes his time. "I have three beautiful women who tend to me. I'm warm and fed. Drugged with good laudanum. How lucky am I?" He pushes himself upward until the pain becomes too much.

Walt pushes gently on Azariah's shoulder. "You are lucky indeed, Mr. Smith. But your job now is to rest."

The boy relaxes into the bed.

"I wondered if you might help me," Walt says.

"Me, help you?" The boy smiles. "Sure."

"The name James Warren," Whitman says. "Does it mean anything to you?"

He's frowning now. "We all know Warren."

"A body snatcher?"

The boy considers the question. "I spend my time avoiding people like Warren," Azariah says. "If you're smart, you will too."

Walt places his hand on the boy's forehead. He's got a fever now. "Shall I tell those three beautiful women that you need a bath?"

The boy smiles again. "Tell 'em I need three."

Walt cracks a grin. "Posthaste."

"And, mister," Azariah says. "Be careful. Them resurrectionists ain't nothing to fool with."

"Rest up, and I'll check on you again."

Azariah nods, then closes his eyes.

Walt returns to the Stowes' old bedroom, where he writes a note to Henry. *Meet me at the Pewter Mug in two hours, and in the meantime, find out what you can about James Warren.* Then, while he waits for the courier to arrive, he stares out the back window across the street and watches the sun as it slips behind the grog house roof.

CHAPTER 6

The omnibus driver, Broadway Ike, scatters the crowd when he hits the brake just short of the sidewalk, plunging Walt into the coach's plush velvet door. He is the only passenger in the eight-seat vehicle, painted white with red trim, and stenciled SOUTHERN BROADWAY.

"That's us, Mr. Whitman," Ike shouts from his driver's seat. He is a short, round man in a captain's hat, with a shiny nose and a slouch. They're a colorful lot, the omnibus drivers, with names like the Dressmaker, Balky Bill, and Old Elephant, and their knowledge of the city is encyclopedic.

Walt's trust in Ike is quickly rewarded. "Oh, I know Warren, the cunt," he says, making a fist. Turns out Warren owes Ike a lot of money for transporting a couple of stiffs to New York University a while back, and he's waiting for him to show up in his bus again. Whitman lets it be known that he has a little unfinished business with the cunt himself. Then he steps out into the night air, biting and cold. The omnibus speeds away, leaving a clear view of the tavern where he is to meet Henry.

He has often daydreamed about their reunion. A few years ago, their friendship had developed quickly, and when it became something more, both men were surprised. Walt celebrated, but Henry hid.

Inside the Pewter Mug, Henry Saunders has already secured a table near the back. The two men acknowledge each other with a nod, then Whitman stops at the bar for a gin cocktail. The barkeep, Tony, takes the money, wishes him a good evening, and Walt strides across the tavern, scanning the clientele. He sees a few familiar faces, mostly Tammany politicians, but no notables. At the table, Walt stands up straight, makes eye contact, and smiles. "Mr. Saunders, how nice to see you."

"Mr. Whitman." Henry is clean-shaven and smells of citrus cologne. "I trust that Mr. Smith is resting comfortably."

Walt begins to answer, then stops. He has a question of his own. "Did you get my letters?"

"I think of you very often, dearest Henry, and I don't know what I should do if I hadn't

you to think of and look forward to . . . They were lovely."

"You might have sent even a single response."

Saunders shifts in his seat. "You're right."

"Why didn't you?"

"Walt."

"Just because the world doesn't recognize what we have doesn't mean we cannot enjoy it."

"It's not only that."

Walt braces himself for Henry's next words.

"I'm sorry, but things can't be the way they were."

"And how were they?"

"Walt."

"Why did you come back, then?"

"My parents need money to keep the farm. Mr. Ropes knew me from my work on the *Plebeian,* and when he contacted me about the *Aurora* editorship, I couldn't refuse."

The two men sit in silence.

"Mr. Ropes wants me to steer you away from the Stowe story," Henry says. "He thinks you're too personally invested."

"But they're my family."

"Precisely his concern."

"I am objective."

Henry sighs.

"How are the students doing?" Henry finally says.

"They're strong people," Walt says. "But they're heartbroken."

"And you?"

He stifles the truth. Images of Abraham and Lena spool through his mind, their late-night dinner conversations, their support of his writing, their encouragement to mend his own fractured relationship with his father. *Family is everything, Walt,* Abraham said to him one evening. *Life is too brief to give up on it.*

At a table near the door, a shouting match breaks out over the Mary Rogers murder case. Whitman recognizes one of the combatants as Edgar Poe, an odd-looking fellow: thin, gaunt, deep-set eyes, and the author of a recently published serial, "The Mystery of Marie Rogêt," in Snowden's *Ladies' Companion.* These stories comprise Mr. Poe's thinly veiled fictional attempt to solve the cigar-girl murder case, an attempt made instantly irrelevant by the court case against Abraham Stowe.

The barkeep, barrel-chested and unflappable Tony, easily pushes Poe and the other man out the door, to the applause of the tavern dwellers.

Walt says, "Mr. Poe is the only person who shares my beliefs in Abraham's and Lena's innocence. That is a shame."

Saunders lets a moment pass. "James Warren is known for his grave-robbing exploits *and* as one of Isaiah Rynders's men."

"Rynders? That is unfortunate." Like everyone else in New York City, Walt knows plenty about Isaiah Rynders: Tammany boss of the Sixth Ward, gangster, politician. Rynders recently opened the Empire Club on Park Row and was rumored to have more power than the police — the only person with enough power in New York City to start and stop a mob. One story had it that he ripped a man's cheek off with his forefinger just because the man owed him a few dollars. Another story had him chasing a man from a card game with a red-hot poker, and the scar across his forehead confirmed his reputation as a knife fighter. Still, Rynders is a gentleman. That is his power — he is as comfortable with the mayor as he is with, say, a grave robber.

"Did you not have a run-in with the man yourself?"

"More than one, I'm afraid," Whitman says. "When he attempted to break up a meeting with Mr. Emerson in the Tabernacle a few months ago, I may have broken the man's nose."

"Did he draw his pistol?"

Walt shakes his head. "He attempted to land a blow on me, but I easily dodged it. He realized he was overmatched, stormed off, and the meeting resumed. Mr. Emerson gave a most fascinating oration on the role of the poet —"

"Mr. Rynders is a gangster and a thug!"

Walt looks into Henry's eyes. "I will not be bullied."

Saunders claps him on the shoulder. "You're very brave, Mr. Whitman."

Walt gets the joke. "Only when the fate of humanity is at stake."

The two men catch each other staring. He has missed Henry more than he knew.

Henry breaks the moment. "You said you had more than one run-in with Rynders?"

"I may have denounced him publicly in the *Aurora.*"

"Holy Christ, Walt. It's a wonder you are still alive." Henry leans closer. "It's a good thing I returned, so I can keep an eye on you."

"I'm terribly glad to see you." Walt feels awkward saying so, and he worries about becoming a public spectacle. But around them, the men of the Pewter Mug remain blissfully unaware.

"Now tell me again," Henry says, "why all the interest in Warren?"

"I believe Abraham bought cadavers from the man."

"And?"

"He may have a connection to Abraham's death."

"But how?"

"You've heard of the Bone Bill?"

"The proposed law that would allow medical schools to legally acquire cadavers? The one that won't pass?"

"I was helping Abraham draft a new version that he was sure would pass," Walt says. "His suppliers were furious. Elizabeth Blackwell confirmed as much to me only this afternoon. And it was she who discovered James Warren's name in the ledger."

"And in your mind, that's motivation for Warren to kill Abraham? To protect his body-snatching business?"

"A man who kills to protect his livelihood? Certainly."

Henry says, "I guess we need to find Warren."

"We?"

"Given your past with Rynders, you need a lookout."

Walt smiles. "I certainly would not want

to deprive you of the experience."

The next morning at nine o'clock, Walt Whitman and Henry Saunders arrive at the New York University Medical College, a formal three-story building with Ionic columns. Dozens of medical students in white aprons and bowler hats file in and out the front entrance. All are men.

A nurse called Mrs. Huxley directs them to the white-haired Dr. Liston. "Welcome," he says. "Please come inside." He leads the duo through the back door and down a long hallway to his office, a spacious corner room bright with natural light. "Mrs. Huxley?" he calls into the hallway, "tea, please?" He invites them to sit.

"On behalf of everyone at the Women's Medical College of Manhattan," Whitman says, "thank you for the use of your wagon."

"Glad I could be of service," Liston says. "In your message, you said you wanted to discuss another matter?"

Before Walt can answer, there's a knock at the door.

Mrs. Huxley appears with tea. She's a sturdy woman with a puckered face. "Oh, and, Doctor?"

"What is it, Mrs. Huxley?"

"They are waiting for you in surgery."

60

"I'll be there presently."

Mrs. Huxley nods and recedes.

Liston waits for the door to close. "You were about to say."

"Do you know James Warren?"

"He is one of the few men who supply bodies to us."

"How does that work exactly?"

"He's a businessman," Liston says. "We let him know what we need, and he acquires it."

"But grave robbing is illegal."

"We prefer to say that the body business is just shy of legal."

"Did Abraham Stowe know James Warren?"

"We all know him."

Walt sips his tea. "What would someone like Mr. Warren think of Abraham Stowe's support of the Bone Bill?"

Liston is quick to answer. "I cannot imagine Mr. Warren even knows what the Bone Bill is."

Saunders says, "Do you think Lena killed Abraham, Dr. Liston?"

Liston looks away. "I knew Abraham before he met Lena, and her worries were justified."

"Enough to kill him?" Henry says.

"One never knows what compels one

person to kill another."

Whitman says, "How can we find Warren?"

"It should not be difficult," Liston says. "Grave robbers search the obituaries, and they go to the source. I find these dealings distasteful, but we must have bodies."

Walt presses. "How do you contact him?"

"Sorry, Mr. Whitman."

"Where does he operate?"

Liston shakes his head. "I don't know."

"A name. A street. Anything."

"These men may be criminals, but they provide invaluable resources to medicine, and I have to protect that." Liston stands.

"But the Stowes were innocent."

"My advice to you: Let Abraham and Lena rest in peace. Now if you'll excuse me."

Walt and Henry buy a *Tribune* and return to the women's college. In the dining room, they review the obituaries. From the dissection room, Whitman can hear the students' voices as they deconstruct Lena's corpse. That they speak in calm tones in spite of the grievous circumstances reveals the depth of their trust in Elizabeth, a sentiment he shares. Yet he still has not been able to look at Lena's eviscerated body. He cannot bear the thought, even if it was her wish.

He and Mr. Saunders concentrate on three obituaries in today's *Tribune:* thirty-five-year-old Roberto Palmero, crushed by a fire engine; nineteen-year-old Angela Pasqualini, who died in childbirth; and Maggie Runkel, a fourteen-year-old cholera victim.

Henry says, "Which one will the body snatchers dig up, do you suppose?"

Whitman doesn't know exactly. It might be any of the three; it might be none of them. There are twenty more obituaries too, all of which are as remarkable or unremarkable as the next. "Perhaps we should ask Miss Blackwell." He hopes Henry will volunteer so he does not have to see what they've done to Lena.

Saunders anticipates this. "You need to look, Walt. She was your friend."

"That she was." Whitman stands, takes a deep breath. "Miss Blackwell?" he calls.

He beckons her to the dining room, where they present her with their analysis of the obituaries.

"You were right about James Warren," Walt says, "and we need to find him."

"And you need me to identify which of these bodies is the most medically desirable."

Saunders points out the three to her.

She reads the notices. "All of them are useful, for different reasons."

"But if you can select only one," Henry says.

"The pregnant woman buried with her infant would bring the highest price."

Saunders says, "But what doctor would dissect an infant?"

Miss Blackwell smiles. "Which one wouldn't, Mr. Saunders?"

Walt says, "We will stake out the woman's grave, and wait for Mr. Warren."

She continues reading. "Of course, Mr. Palmero's lower body has been demolished by the fire engine, and who knows what we might learn from that?"

"So Mr. Palmero, then?"

"Then again," she says, pointing to Maggie Runkel's obituary, "what kills more people in New York than fires or childbirth?"

"Cholera," Walt says.

"And she who cures cholera," Elizabeth says, "shall rule the medical world."

CHAPTER 7

Maggie Runkel is buried near the back of the St. Patrick's Old Cathedral graveyard at Mulberry and Prince Streets. Walt Whitman and Henry Saunders have set up watch behind a graveside tree, which affords no shelter from the swirling wind that slashes through Walt's clothing. He cannot remember ever feeling so cold in all his life, and his father's words come tumbling back to him: *The worst is yet to come.* His father the optimist.

The cemetery surrounds the cathedral — headstones jut like crooked teeth out of the gray, unyielding ground. The cathedral itself is dark and quiet, the priest having locked up and retired to the rectory hours ago.

Henry wants to go home, return tomorrow night better equipped for the weather, but Walt refuses to leave. "I need to see this through."

"By catching our death of cold?" Saunders

says. "Let's go back to the Pewter Mug and drink."

Walt reaches into his pocket and produces a flask of whiskey. "Be my guest."

Henry takes the flask, tips it back. "How well did you really know Abraham and Lena?"

"Well enough."

"Is it possible she killed him?"

Whitman glares at Saunders.

"A fair question, I believe, given our undertaking."

"I can understand how she might appear guilty to an outsider, but you have to trust me."

"I'm here, aren't I?"

The cemetery descends into silence, and Walt can't help but think of the deceased beneath their feet, how each of them lived as he lives, full of hopes and aspirations, and now dead and gone.

"No. She didn't kill him." Whitman blows in his hands. Maybe they should call it a night, try again tomorrow.

Saunders says, "I read your stories in the *Democratic Review*."

"Have you now?"

"And your novel, *Franklin Evans*, in the *New World*."

Franklin Evans has sold thousands of copies so far and has earned him seventy-five dollars, with another fifty to come.

"I'm gratified to be published in the same periodical as Charles Dickens, William Cullen Bryant, Edgar Allan Poe, and Nathaniel Hawthorne."

"It is quite a feat indeed."

Whitman continues. "And the first two chapters to my next novel, *The Madman,* were recently published in the *Washingtonian.*"

"Impressive."

"I'm determined to be a writer of note," Walt says, fully aware that he is trying to impress Henry. "I make it a point to write every morning, first thing. The entire manuscript for *The Madman* will soon be complete."

"What about your work at the *Aurora?*"

"That work I begin midafternoon after my walk."

"Yes," Saunders says, "your walks are the subject of much discussion around the office."

"Mr. Ropes does not like them," Whitman says. "But they are part of my process, and I get my work done."

"Indeed, nobody knows how."

Whitman is not unaware of the discussions he provokes, but he is surprised by

Mr. Saunders's seeming complicity in them. Walt's methods are unconventional for sure, but the results speak for themselves. Indeed, on any given day, he authors the lion's share of what the *Aurora*'s readers have come to expect six days a week. Where there is no problem, no such complaint should exist.

The two men sit in silence until Walt can no longer bear it. "And what did you think of *Franklin Evans*?"

"I love your poems."

Henry's ambivalence toward his novel cuts deep.

Whitman wants to ask Saunders to clarify, when he hears the noises — a click first, then whinnying and clomping tumbling on the wind toward them — voices, wheels scraping, and hooves hammering away at the thick silence of the night. A freight wagon pulled by a team of two horses creaks up to the cemetery gate.

Two men head for the freshly dug grave. The shorter of the two hauls a large bundle on his shoulder and drops it in the dirt. His face is concealed by the brim of his hat and a mustache. He unwraps the white bundle and spreads the canvas upon the ground, while the other man, much taller, broad-shouldered and muscular, picks up the two shovels and pickax wrapped inside. Their actions signal a mundane attitude toward the work, as if digging up a corpse is the most normal task in the world.

Walt turns to Henry, whispers: "Which one is Warren?"

"The shorter one."

"Who is the other guy?"

Henry shrugs. "No idea."

The two men start digging. The taller man breaks up the ground with the pickax while Warren scoops up the dirt with his shovel. They make fast progress, benefiting not only from their obvious experience but also from the loose dirt used to bury the girl earlier that same day. And the deeper they go, the easier the digging, or at least that's how it appears from where Whitman sits.

"What's your plan?" Saunders whispers.

"When they remove the body," Walt says. "I'll approach them."

"No offense," says Henry, "but that's not much of a plan."

"What's yours?"

"I thought we'd approach him before they dig up the body."

Whitman whispers, "That's your idea of a *better* plan?"

It doesn't take long for the body snatchers to reach the coffin, and when they do, Walt scuttles in for a better view. His knees and back are sore from crouching, and his fingers and toes sting from the cold. He finds a good vantage point from behind a tree near the disinterred grave, a spot raised by the tree's roots.

The tall man sits on the edge of the grave, chipping away at the casket lid with the pickax, when Warren joins him with the lamp.

". . . that's what impressed me," the tall man is saying. "It wasn't just a dead body. What Abraham Stowe did to Mary Rogers was artistic." He holds up the pickax. "He created the scene like a painter might do on a canvas."

Warren says, "I saw the body, and it was horrible."

"You're a philistine, Snuffy. You have no sense of beauty. In life or in death."

Snuffy? Walt looks back at Henry, who can only shrug again.

The man continues: "That corpse was an artistic masterpiece worthy of the pen of Mr. Poe. His most recent work is not his best, but 'The Murders in the Rue Morgue'? My God, what a story." He swings the pickax, and the tip sinks deep in the wood. "And Stowe's wife is equally worthy of a Poe story. The way she killed her husband was elegant and well thought out."

"Jesus," Warren says, "watch the head. They love the head."

"I goddamned well know they like the head." The tall man chisels off a square piece of the coffin lid, tosses it aside. "Now shine that lamp here."

James Warren leans over, and the lamp illuminates the young woman's face: her black hair, white skin, sunken eyes —

The sight of her lifeless face takes Walt Whitman's breath. The poor girl. So young, and now dead. His thoughts turn to his sisters, Hannah and Mary. What if it were they who had died only to have their bodies stolen?

"I don't pay you to stand there, Snuffy," the tall man says. "Now get the fucking hook."

Warren trudges to the wagon. *Get the fucking hook,* he mimics.

When Warren returns, the tall man takes the enormous hook from him and slips the tip into the skin just under the girl's chin, pulling the hook upward so that it lodges between her neck and jaw. He tugs the rope to make sure the hook is secure, her teeth clacking together, and then he climbs out of the grave, tosses the other end of the rope over a low-hanging tree branch — not the same tree Walt stands behind but near

71

enough to unnerve him — and pulls downward with his whole strength.

But the girl doesn't move.

"Come on, darlin'," the tall man says, "rise and shine." He yanks the rope again as if ringing a massive church tower bell, and this time the corpse does move, rising up out of the coffin, standing upright for only a moment as if resurrected, before flopping onto the ground.

"She's a real cherry." An animated Warren unwraps the shroud like a child opening a gift. "And she's mine!" He lifts the white dress over her head, then lowers himself on top of her.

And that's when Whitman has seen enough. He charges Warren and kicks him in the side. "Have you no respect?" He kicks him again, and when the man attempts to stand up, Walt knocks him down with a forearm to the chest.

"I was only joking," Warren manages to say. At the sight of Walt, he seems confused, and in the middle of coughing, he spits out, "Who the fuck are you?"

Whitman thinks about kicking him again but holds back. "You should be ashamed of yourself."

"I am," Warren says, "most of the time."

It isn't that Walt has forgotten about the

tall man, but the adrenaline of the moment has taken over, and he stands over Warren in the afterglow of his attack. When he hears a click, Whitman turns around to find a shotgun pointed at his chest.

"I'm with Snuffy," the tall man says. "I'd like to know who the fuck you are."

Walt stands up straight, reaches out his hand. "Walt Whitman. Reporter with the *Aurora*. And I'm doing a story on the glorious underworld of body snatching."

The tall man doesn't shake his hand. "Who sent you?"

"No one *sent* me."

The tall man aims his shotgun at Walt's chest. "I see it on your face. Tell me."

But before Walt can respond, the man strikes him in the head with the butt of his gun. A bolt of pain bursts from his nose to the back of his neck, and his eyes water.

"Now, how does that help anything?" Whitman says. "Nobody sent me —"

The man raises his gun again.

"I came on my own, as I said, to do a story on body snatching."

The tall man lowers the gun. "You're really a goddamned reporter?"

Walt nods. Blood trickles out of his nose, over his lips, and into his beard. He bends over to catch his breath. The pain is thick and heavy. He wipes his nose with his sleeve. "Did you have to hit me?"

"Spying on folks in the middle of the night is a dangerous business," the man says.

Whitman hears Warren stir behind him, but it is already too late. Warren tackles him and comes to rest on top of him. "You son of a bitch." He raises his fist.

"Snuffy," the tall man interjects. "Get off the poor gentleman."

"But —"

"No, your actions were highly inappropriate and this man had every right to kick the shit out of you. It's something I've been meaning to get to myself."

Warren reluctantly releases Walt, curses under his breath. *"I'll kick the shit out of you."*

"Now, sir," the tall man says, "let me help you to your feet so we can do this interview for your newspaper." He reaches out his hand. "I'm a reader myself; just read this amazing book that changed my life, and I am more than happy to help a reporter get his story, contribute to society and what-not. I see it more as an opportunity than a duty, really —"

Whitman reaches for his outstretched hand, but doesn't see the butt of the shotgun rushing toward him until it connects with his jaw. The pain is searing, but quick. A flash of light before the blackness.

CHAPTER 8

The blackness slips into images of the Long
Island home where Walt was born: the two-
story clapboard colonial with green shutters
and white doors, the red barn next to it,
and the large oak tree between the corral
and house. It is the same oak tree Walt used
to sit under when he needed a break from
working in the fields. Sometimes he read,
sometimes he wrote, and sometimes he
wandered around in his own head. Each
musing ended the same way, with his father
standing over him, face red and fists
clenched.

The voice comes from another room.
"Walter Junior?" He turns around but sees
no one. *"Junior."* He spins around to find
his father standing next to him, clean-
shaven, eyes tucked beneath his brow, and
his white hair sticking straight up. "How
many times do I have to tell you? It's time
to work."

He opens his eyes to see the face of a young woman, and it takes him a moment to realize that she is dead. Her skin is not pale as much as colorless. And she stinks. Like Lena Stowe now, she is defined by both absence and presence — the life in her given over to tissue upon tissue upon tissue.

The freight wagon turns right, rolling the corpse into him. He pushes her away, then peels back the corner of the tarp to see outside.

The tall man sits in the driver's seat, James "Snuffy" Warren next to him. They're arguing, but Walt can't make out the words for the wind.

Warren glances over his shoulder. "He's awake!"

The tall man turns. "Get under there, you, and stay quiet."

Whitman folds down the tarp and looks at the body again. He imagines the girl before her death: She looks through the front window, her mouth open, her eyes lost, her brown hair hanging in her eyes, her hands pressed up against the glass. The shadows from inside the building reflect off her palms and turn them black. The sun shines down over her shoulder, and on her right is a building that might be the Old Brewery. From where she stands, she can hear the noises of Five Points, the noises that never stop: the fighting, the playing, the poor taking from the poor.

He feels compassion not only for the young girl but also for the family. They will be devastated to learn that their daughter's body has been taken. Perhaps he can buy the body himself and return it to them. *Stop,* he tells himself. *You've been taken too. You've got to get away, and fast.* He wonders where Henry Saunders is, if he's followed behind or gone for help.

The wagon slows to a stop. Sounds of water lapping up against the piers, voices dancing on what has to be the East River, laughter, yelling, the smell of salt water — Walt guesses they are near the Fulton Ferry.

Without warning, the tarp lifts to reveal the tall man hovering over him. His black hair stands on end, his green eyes blaze, and his nose is sharp. He wears dungarees and a wool sweater under his unbuttoned Albert overcoat. "Watch yourself. Business first, then you and I will talk."

From across the way, another wagon rolls into view, the driver visible only from the orange burn of his cigar. He calls the tall man by name, Clement, and questions his lateness.

Clement insists that he's delivered the

body per their agreement.

Clement looks at Warren. "Do I have to tell you how to do your work?"

Warren jumps into the back of the wagon, signals to Walt for help.

"Who is that?" the driver says, shrugging at Whitman.

"New guy," Clement says. "With business the way it is, I need the help."

Clement wants to keep him alive, Walt thinks. He shudders at the vision of his own body splayed open and eviscerated on the dissection table.

Whitman and Warren carry the girl's body from one wagon to the other. They swing it twice before tossing it in back.

"Careful," the man says. "Jesus."

Warren slows down, pretends to handle the body with care as he shoves her in far enough so the door will close.

"Cover her up with straw, goddammit."

Warren does, but he's obviously irritated.

"You sure can pick 'em, Clement," the man says. "A whole city of people out of work, and you find the idiots."

"Are we finished?" Clement says.

"I suppose," the man says. "I'll send word about the next drop through the usual means." He flips the reins, and his horses stomp the ground. "Next time, don't be late." The wagon picks up speed, turns the corner, and is gone.

"Next time?" Sheriff Harris steps out of the shadows.

Walt Whitman's first instinct is to call to the sheriff for help — but he decides to wait and see why Harris is here.

"And what is the sheriff doing out so late?" Clement says. "Isn't it past your bedtime?"

"I certainly prefer sleep to chasing down shitheads like you."

"My, my," Clement says. "Such language."

Harris says, "I came to arrest you."

"Arrest me, Sheriff? Whatever for?"

"Mary Rogers's murder."

Clement steps down from the wagon. He ambles toward the sheriff, a grin on his face. His right hand rests on the handle of his pistol. "I know we've had our differences, Sheriff, but *this,* where is this coming from?"

The sheriff flips back his overcoat to display his own gun. "Our differences, as you put it, come from the fact that you're a criminal."

"A criminal? Really? Can we not come up with a better word than that?"

"How about an opportunist without a clear sense of right and wrong?"

"Opportunist." Clement says the word as if he's trying it on. "I like that a whole lot better."

"It's time to set this right," Harris says.

"We both know Miss Rogers died during a medical procedure."

"We both know an innocent man took the blame, and now he's dead. His wife too."

The piers are silent except for the waves crashing against the stone barricades, and faint piano music from a few streets over.

"You sure about that, Sheriff?"

"I have to arrest you."

The two men stare each other down. Harris fidgets nervously.

The gunshot rings out like thunder, and for a moment they all stand there, waiting. Then Sheriff Harris drops. Whitman starts toward him, but Clement waves him off with a pistol.

Harris writhes.

Walt hesitates, expecting the sheriff's men to emerge from the shadows. When no one does, Walt sidesteps toward the sheriff, careful to see that Clement does not become skittish enough to shoot him. At the sight of Whitman, the sheriff tries and fails to speak. Walt unbuttons the sheriff's coat — the gunshot is just inches above the heart — and he turns to Clement. "We can still save

81

him." He presses his handkerchief against the wound.

"Are you sure?" Clement steps toward them.

Walt can see what is about to happen. "But why kill him?"

"Why not?" Clement takes another step toward the sheriff.

Whitman looks at Harris. The sheriff's eyes are following Clement now. His whole body shakes in terror, and despite what happened with the Stowes, Walt feels for the man. Walt stands to meet Clement, but Clement is quick —

He shoots Harris in the head, and the sheriff's body goes limp.

Clement turns to Whitman now, smoking pistol raised. "Now why don't you tell me how you knew I would be here tonight."

Whitman steps back.

"And while you're at it, why did the sheriff recognize you?"

Clement can see the surprise on his face.

"You didn't think I would notice," Clement says, "did you? Well, I'm not a dumb criminal — I'm an opportunist without morals, remember?"

Whitman takes another step backward, but Clement takes a step too.

"Did you kill Mary Rogers?" Walt says.

Clement smiles. "You believed that?"

"Why not confess before you kill me?"

"You do think I'm stupid," Clement says. "Like everyone else, I was deeply saddened by the tragedy."

"That doesn't mean you didn't kill her," Walt says. "You're going to kill me, and you don't know me."

Clement says, "I didn't intend to kill you until this little complication arose. That should count for something."

"What if I promise not to testify against you?"

Clement laughs. "I'm sure that will work out well for me."

"Will you toss my body in the East River too?"

"Nah. I'll sell you off to some doctor. You're a young, healthy specimen, worth at least twenty-five dollars. Just think: You might be instrumental in finding a cure for cholera."

Whitman continues to inch backward. He hopes to keep Clement talking — if he can create only a little more distance between them, then he thinks he can get away.

"I know you worked with Abraham Stowe," Walt says.

"So what if I knew him? He bought bodies from me just like they all do. They think they're better than we are, but they depend on us to do their work. They're hypocrites, but we'll still take their money."

"Did you kill him?"

Clement hesitates, and Walt knows this is his best chance, so he turns and runs, the first shot hitting the ground behind him, shooting sparks into the dark. He sprints to the corner and makes the turn before the next shot ricochets off the corner of a brick building.

"Snuffy!" Clement yells.

Walt's long legs stretch into stride, and his body warms up even while James Warren keeps pace behind him. He'll go to Five Points, not too far from here, where he can disappear into one of the many beer halls or brothels and wait it out until it's safe to report the sheriff's murder and try to find Henry Saunders. At the next turn, he casts a glance over his shoulder at the man chasing him: Warren has already slowed to a jog.

Walt continues onto Orange Street toward an enormous bi-level dance hall called Almack's, determined to lose himself among the thousand or so patrons who flock here every night and stay until they run out of money, are arrested, or pass out. Five cents buys a mug of beer and a chance to listen to piano music, or play dice, dominoes, and cards. Sometimes patrons will catch a glimpse of Pete Williams, the colored owner, performing his own juba dance on the second floor.

Walt sits at a corner table with a view of the door. As he tries to catch his breath, the thick cloud of tobacco smoke burns his lungs. His jaw throbs. He removes his coat and hat, then takes out his green notebook to record the details of the sheriff's murder.

"What'll it be, mister?" The girl speaks in a fake Southern drawl and wears too much perfume. Though she looks to be twelve, she carries herself like an eighteen-year-old. She wears a short white dress and red-topped boots with bells sewn into the tassels, the tinkling a constant noise among the chatter, yelling, and laughter. The tightness of her dress presses her breasts together in such a way that make them look bigger than they are.

"Whiskey, please."

At the table nearest him, six men play poker. All of them blind drunk.

The girl returns with the drink, and Walt pays her five cents. He must figure out what happened to Henry after he was knocked out. If the grave robbers had other men staked out around the cemetery, then they might have taken Henry. Or worse.

His only option is to go to the watch house.

"You haven't touched your drink." The girl is back.

Whitman picks up the glass and drains it. "There."

"You look upset." She puts her hands on his shoulders.

He shrugs them off. "Long night."

"I specialize in men who have had rough nights." She rubs his shoulders again, and this time, he lets her for a short moment. "Anything else I can get for you?" The girl leans over to make her breasts visible, and this is when he hears the voice from the front.

"There you are." It's Warren, and he's got a rifle pointed in Whitman's direction. He saunters across the wooden floor, his boots dragging and clomping, the noise capturing the attention of the entire first floor, and even the gamblers pause their game to watch. "Gambling debts," Warren says so everyone can hear.

One of the men laughs. "Then you'll need to take Hank here. He owes everyone in this room at least one dollar."

Walt stands, moves in front of the barmaid. "You go on back to the bar," he says.

She obeys.

Warren comes close enough for Whitman to see the dirt streaks on his cheek. He's an odd-looking sort of man — a combination of strength and awkwardness. His protruding stomach and large head belie his agility and experience. He found Walt in no time, after all.

"Let's go," Warren says.

Walt puts on his coat and hat, and starts toward the exit. He can see the confidence and satisfaction in Warren's face. He's rash, less than intelligent, and eager to impress, Whitman intuits, and then in one quick movement, he knocks Warren to the floor —

But Warren surprises Walt by being stronger and more agile, and the two men wrestle on the floor, bang into a table, and knock off the empty glasses. They shatter, the noise drawing even more attention to the scene. The bar patrons circle the men and cheer them on, and when Warren comes to rest on top of Walt, they rain down applause.

They both scramble for the rifle a few feet away, but Whitman reaches it first. "Now then, Mr. Warren. Where were we?"

Walt pulls Warren to his feet and leads him out of the beer hall and into the night amidst the continuing applause of the patrons. They don't care who won; they just had a hell of a show. He presses the rifle tip into Warren's back as if to tell himself that he needs to be ready to pull the trigger, that he *will* in fact pull the trigger if need be. He wonders where he would shoot the man. He would not kill him. The leg, he decides, he will shoot him in the leg.

"So which is it?" Walt says, "Warren or Snuffy?"

But the man refuses to answer.

Walt gives him a moment before he says, "Snuffy it is, Mr. Warren."

Still nothing. No matter. Their next stop is the watch house.

CHAPTER 9

By day, Mulberry Street streams with people, wagons, and animals, but this night it is completely dark except for the bright light of the watch house halfway down.

Snuffy slows down, and Walt Whitman grips the rifle tight. "They'll blame me for the sheriff's death, you know."

"But I saw it," Walt says. "You didn't pull the trigger."

"You don't understand the people we work for," Snuffy says. "You don't know Samuel Clement." And now he turns around. His face is red and sweaty. "They'll hang me and be done with it." The look on Snuffy's face tells Walt more than his words. He's terrified.

"I'll see to it that you're not blamed for the murder," Walt says even though he's not sure he believes it himself.

"You could let me go," Snuffy says. "I'm a grave robber, not a murderer."

"You didn't kill the sheriff, but what about Abraham Stowe? What do you know about his death?"

Snuffy shakes his head. "You know I hate that fucker Clement, the things he does. And now he will do it to me. You watch."

"What happened to Dr. Stowe?"

Snuffy says nothing. He shuffles to the watch house entrance, opens the door, and goes inside.

Screams and laughter ring out of every corner, and everybody present needs a shave and a change of clothing. In a row of chairs against the back wall sit men in handcuffs, a few of them passed out, a few more of them the belligerent sort that might spontaneously explode. The guard, a tall, broad man, watches over them with his gun raised. He's the kind who will not hesitate to beat any one of these men senseless, and they all know it.

The guard turns to Walt. "Can I help you?"

"I need to see the deputy."

"Back there, then," the guard says. "But you'll have to wait your turn." He looks Snuffy up and down. "Who is the asshole with you?"

"Now, why would you go and say that?" Snuffy says. "Maybe he's the asshole."

"My money is on you," the guard says.

"I'd prefer to discuss *Mr. Warren* with Deputy Petty now," Walt says. "It can't wait."

"Go on, then," the guard says. "You can approach him. If it's urgent like you say."

Walt nudges Snuffy forward, the two of them near the corner desk where Petty is deep in conversation with a man sitting with his back to them. At the sight of Whitman with Snuffy in tow, both men stop talking, and the man turns.

"Walt?" Henry Saunders says. "I was just reporting you missing."

"That saves me some paperwork, then," Petty says.

"I'm afraid not," Walt says. "Sheriff Harris has been shot."

Petty jumps out of his seat. "Where?"

"Near the Fulton Ferry," he says. "Someone called Clement shot Harris, and then he sent this man, James Warren, after me, and well, that didn't quite work out."

The deputy stands still for a moment, contemplating his move, and then maneuvers around the desk. He knocks Snuffy to the ground with his forearm, puts his knee in Snuffy's back, and cuffs him.

"They're too tight," Snuffy says.

"Better get used to it." Petty lifts the man

to his feet and pushes him toward the back door leading to the jail. "That noose gets pretty tight when the trapdoor opens." Petty glances behind him at Walt and Henry. "Excuse me, gentlemen."

Whitman lets the deputy past him, and the deputy's voice can be heard in the next room, first commanding Warren to get into the cell and then calling his men to the ready. The sound of boots scuffling on wood, rifles being removed from the wall racks, and then the pack of them burst through the door, past Whitman and Saunders and into the night.

Henry turns to Walt. "How did you get away?"

Walt tells him about the selling of the body, Jack Harris's surprise appearance, and the shooting. When Walt is finished, Henry embraces him.

"I'm so relieved." Henry releases Walt, steps back. "You have no idea how worried I was."

"So what now?" Whitman says. "Is the deputy coming back?"

"I don't know." Henry touches Walt's swollen cheek. "Does it hurt?"

It does, but Walt doesn't want him to stop. "It hurts some."

"I thought you were dead."

"What do you think of the deputy? Can we trust him?"

"I don't have a read on him yet," Henry says, "but my sources say he's a good man not yet corrupted."

The mustachioed deputy returns, limping as if his left leg is shorter than his right, and sits across the desk from them. "I've sent my best men to see if they can find Harris, and they'll move Warren to the Tombs in the morning. "How about a drink?" Petty stands and retrieves a bottle of whiskey from the cupboard behind his desk and pours three glasses.

"Thank you." Whitman picks up the glass and drinks. The warmth comes quickly, easing the pain in his head.

"So there was another man?" The deputy takes his chair again.

"Yes," Walt says, "the one who pulled the trigger."

"Did you get the name?"

"As I said, it's Samuel Clement."

"Clement, eh?" The deputy takes up his pencil and records the name, then puts down the pencil and rubs his forehead. "And you saw him pull the trigger?"

Walt nods.

The deputy takes up his pencil and writes a bit more. "Now tell me: Why were you two at the graveyard?"

The two men look at each other.

"It will come out sooner or later," Saunders says, looking at Whitman. "I'm the editor of the *Aurora* newspaper, and we are doing a story on the resurrection men."

Petty says, "So you decided to stake out the graveyard and see how these people operate?"

Walt nods. "We believe there's a connection between Abraham Stowe's death and the resurrection men."

"Harris told me about you," Petty says, "and I thought we were past all this nonsense. What happened was surely tragic, but —" He sets his pencil down again and looks first at Saunders, then at Whitman. "Now, I'm only going to say this once. You two are putting your noses where they don't belong."

"But, sir —" Walt says.

"No, let me finish. The Stowe investigation was conducted by our best people. They found the same arsenic on Mrs. Stowe as they did in her husband's body." He pauses. "And we found a clear motive."

Whitman puts his elbow on the desk. "You mean Abraham's affair with the cigar girl?"

"That's none of your goddamn business." Petty takes a drink. "Then you go after these body snatchers, and I don't think I have to tell you what went wrong there. Dangerous bunch with nothing to lose." He takes a deep breath. "You're very lucky to be alive, mister."

"I just hand-delivered one of the men involved in the sheriff's murder," Walt says. "You could show some gratitude."

"Keep your nose out of our business and mind what you write. Folks here get mighty irritated when reporters publish wild accusations to promote their own careers."

Whitman says, "That sounds like a threat."

Deputy Petty sits back, leans his elbows on the desk, and puts his hands under his chin. "If what you say is true, then we lost one of our own tonight. A good man, Jack Harris, and I'll have to tell his wife he's dead. Imagine that." He shakes his head and wipes his eyes. "Forgive me." He reads over the report, makes a few notes, and slides it across the desk. "Read this over and if you have no changes, sign it."

Walt reads the report, and he worries that Snuffy was right after all. If they can't get Clement, they may just let Snuffy take the fall for all of them, and he says so to the deputy.

The deputy looks as if he's going to jump across the desk at Walt.

Henry intervenes. "Thank you, Deputy."

"Look," Deputy Petty says, "I don't want to sound ungrateful. What happened tonight is a tragedy, and your testimony will help us arrest the man responsible. For that we thank you, but you'll understand if I don't get too excited about a couple of reporters who think we botched a murder investigation."

Walt can't help himself. "What if Mrs. Stowe didn't kill her husband?"

Petty folds his hands and leans over the table. "What if she did?"

The two men stare at each other until Henry taps Walt on the shoulder.

"Sign this so we can leave."

Walt feels Petty's eyes on him while he reads the report, which is accurate. Still, he thinks, the deputy is withholding something.

Henry squeezes his shoulder. "Just sign it."

Walt does and passes the sheet across the desk.

"Thank you," Petty says. "We'll be in touch."

Walt stands. "So will we."

CHAPTER 10

On the way back to the women's college, Walt's head swirls, and more than once, Henry has to pull him back from the gates, or lampposts, or whatever he bumps into as they walk. The whiskey has worn off, and the pain has spread from his jaw to his entire head. Henry speaks to him along the way, but Walt feels as if he is outside his body. Words like *fortunate* and *cautious* he understands — the words in between sound more a low-pitched growl than nouns and verbs.

They arrive at the college, and Henry helps him inside.

The classroom is silent and cold. From upstairs come the muffled sounds of intermittent footsteps, but most of the students are likely in bed. With Walt's arm over Henry's shoulder, they shuffle into the bedroom.

Henry lights the candle on the table, and

Walt's face appears in the mirror. His cheek is puffy and dried blood cakes his beard.

"Okay?" Henry stands behind him.

"My head still hurts."

Henry wipes Walt's forehead with his sleeve. "You need a doctor."

"I'm in the right place for that," Walt says. "But I'd rather have a drink. There's a bottle in the armoire."

Henry finds the bottle and a glass, and pours.

Walt drinks down the whole glass, and Henry pours him another.

"Better?" Henry says.

"A little."

"Here" — Henry takes his arm and moves him toward the bed — "you should lie down." Henry eases Walt onto the bed, props him against the headboard. "Good?"

Walt smiles. "Much better, thank you." And it's true. He feels better. Relieved. Safe. Waves of exhaustion wash over him, and he knows that if he closes his eyes, he will quickly drift off to sleep. He also knows that if he does sleep, Henry will leave, so he fights it.

Walt thinks about the cemetery again. He's bending over the sheriff, trying to stop the bleeding, pleading with Clement to save Harris, and then knowing in the moments before, just as Harris himself did, that they were both dead men. It's a miracle Walt survived.

The deputy had better get Clement, or he'll come after Walt again.

Next to the bed, Henry keeps an eye on Walt from Lena's old wooden chair. When Walt makes eye contact, Henry smiles.

It's rather unbelievable, Walt thinks. *The new editor I didn't want, the new editor I can't do without.* He smiles at the sentiment.

"What is it?" Saunders says.

"I was only thinking how glad I am that you are here."

Henry says, "That makes two of us."

"I was also thinking how strange it is that I almost died tonight," Walt says. "Clement tried to kill me. In fact, I'm not sure how I got away. It was an easy shot." He pauses. "In any case, he missed me."

"For which we are grateful," Henry says.

"And why Clement sent Snuffy after me, I'll never understand."

"Snuffy?"

"Warren goes by Snuffy."

"That's confusing," Henry says. "And stupid."

Walt shrugs. "I'm fortunate it was he and not Clement who found me in Almack's."

Saunders thinks for a moment. "You really

took his gun? I can't imagine how." He stops. "So how did you?"

"I've read one too many adventure novels, I suppose. I used misdirection. Distract him and take the gun. Very basic. And he didn't expect it." Whitman drops the bravado. "To be honest, I was lucky. And desperate."

Henry pours Walt another whiskey.

Walt sips it this time, and several minutes pass before he says, "You know what he said to me?"

"Who?"

"Snuffy."

"What did he say?"

"He said that they'll blame him for Harris's death."

Henry says, "But you saw Clement do it."

"That's what I told him."

"Are you worried?"

"There's no call for that," Walt says even though he doesn't believe it. "I wish I knew more about Silas Petty."

Henry says, "I thought I was going to have to bail you out again."

Walt smiles. "Petty knows more than he let on."

"And that surprises you?" Henry says. "Why would he tell a couple of reporters everything he knows?"

Walt takes Henry's point. "But why was

Harris alone tonight? You're going to arrest someone for the most well-known murder case in recent years, and you go alone?"

"You didn't tell me," Henry says. "Harris was there to arrest Clement for murder? Whose murder?"

"Mary Rogers."

Henry reaches for Walt's glass. "May I?"

Walt passes the drink.

Henry takes a sip. "As far as the law is concerned, Abraham Stowe killed Mary Rogers. Harris must have uncovered new evidence?" He takes another drink, returns the glass. "What I do know is you've got a hell of a story for tomorrow's edition."

Walt nods. "Yes, *we* do."

Henry takes Walt's hand. "I think we are going to work well together."

Walt stares at their entwined hands, Henry's skin warm against his own. He shivers. He does not want to frighten Henry away.

They sit like this until a noise sounds upstairs. The moment is broken, and they let go.

Walt's head is throbbing again. He runs his fingers along his swollen face, traces the swelling from beneath his left eye, down his face, and across his mouth.

"You should get some rest," Henry says.

Walt doesn't want Henry to leave, but he is tired. "I need strength to write that article."

The two men fidget in silence. Walt can see himself in the mirror, his swollen face and prematurely graying hair, and that's when he catches Henry looking at him.

"Stay awhile, if you like," Walt says.

"Oh?"

"Only if you want to."

"Sure," Henry says. "Then I can keep an eye on you."

Henry drops a cloth in the water basin, wrings it out, and then Walt feels the water on his skin. He shivers. In the mirror, he watches as Henry gently cleans his neck, forehead, and face. Henry helps Walt remove his coat and shirt. Henry soaks the rag, wrings it out again, and returns, wiping Walt's back, then his chest. Walt's head throbs, but the pain dissipates.

"Do you miss home?" Henry says.

Walt nods. Thoughts of home cause him to feel bereft. He corresponds with George, Hannah, Jeff, and his mother, but they live day-to-day without him. He is an outsider. That is the price he had to pay to get away from his father.

"What about you?" Walt says. "Do you miss your family?"

"I'm the only living child," Henry says. "My younger brother, Phillip, died in the last cholera outbreak, and my mother has not been able to conceive again."

"I'm sorry about your brother," Walt says.

"I miss my parents very much," Henry says. "But they need me to contribute to the farm or they'll lose it, and the best way is to send them money from afar."

Henry looks at the floor, then at Walt again. "When I was a boy, Phillip and I loved watching our mother write letters to her mother in Ireland. We would sit next to her and pretend to write ourselves, and when we would ask her what we'd said in our letters, she would hold them up to the light and make up beautiful things."

"She sounds like a generous person."

"She is, and my father too," Henry says. "Terrible farmer, but a decent man."

"Your father a bad farmer?" Walt smiles. "Somehow that sounds familiar."

They lean in closer, their faces so close Walt can feel Henry's breath on his cheek.

"It's difficult being so far from family," Henry says.

"We all need people we can trust," Walt says.

Now they say nothing. They rest their heads together, and Walt enjoys the closeness, something he hasn't felt for some time —

— and then they're kissing on the bed, pressing their bodies against each other, rolling back and forth, until Henry comes to rest on top of Walt. Henry smiles, turns gentle, and kisses him softly on the lips, then forehead, then cheek. "Well, Mr. Walt Whitman," Henry says, "what have we here?"

Later, Walt lies with his eyes open, staring at the spiderweb crack in the ceiling again. *Did that just happen?* he asks himself, and then, if he needs more evidence, all he has to do is look in the bed next to him, where Henry sleeps.

His romantic life up to this point has been intermittent at best. Given that he's been working since he was twelve, he's matured in many ways, but he's also been able to avoid relationships as such. Sure, like many young men his age, he's frequented the many brothels around the city, but he's never met anyone like Henry, someone to whom he feels connected in a way that is beyond any trite aphorism — though trite aphorisms are all that come to mind.

His eyes ache, and his muscles are sore. The whiskey has dulled the pain in his head, so he decides to take advantage of the respite. He grabs the green notebook from his coat pocket and forces himself to write the story of what happened that evening. He glances at Henry, who is in deep sleep now; the sound of his breathing comforts Walt as he works.

Once he sketches out the narrative using the notes he made at Almack's, he focuses on impressions. The sound of shovels. Metal against dirt. The sheer material of the shroud, wrapped around the girl's body. The resurrection men. The gun pointed at his head. And time passes. He writes until he is no longer conscious of writing, until his hand moves in concert with the phrases that flow into his head. Until all he has to do is keep up.

CHAPTER 11

When Walt wakes, Henry is gone, and he worries that what happened between them frightened Henry away again. He touches the indent left by Henry on the straw mattress. Still warm. He checks his pocket watch, which lies on the small table next to the bed. Almost four.

At the thought of Henry, he can't help smiling. And then worrying. Why hadn't he said good-bye?

Whitman rolls over and tries to sleep, but his face, thick and swollen like a mask, is throbbing again from his altercation with Clement. The next thought that takes hold is that if he doesn't print the Harris murder story first, his eyewitness account will be drowned out by the larger dailies, a problem not only for the *Aurora*'s ledger, or his writing career, but one of accuracy: A story such as this can turn sensationalist awfully fast.

He sits up, swings his legs to the floor,

and takes a moment to gather himself before standing. He lights the lamp next to his bed, goes to the armoire for a set of clean clothing.

While he's dressing, he hears footsteps. Is that Henry? He puts on socks and slips quietly into the classroom. The sight of the small form in the darkness tells him straight away that it's not Henry at all but Azariah Smith, hobbling to the front door of the women's college.

"And where do you think you're going?" Walt's voice carves into the silence.

Azariah turns, and when he sees Walt standing there, he shrugs. "You caught me."

"Is something the matter?"

Azariah thinks before he speaks. "I appreciate all you done for me, I really do, but I don't belong here. All these women fawning over me. I need to get back to my people."

"But you're not well."

"I'm well enough," Azariah says.

Even in the dark, Walt can see the grimace on the boy's face and, from the way he stands tilted to the left side, that he's protecting himself from the pain. No, he can't let the boy leave. Azariah's best chance is to be here, and then Walt has an idea. "Mr. Smith?"

The boy smiles at this. "Yes, Mr. Whitman?"

"I could use some more help. Are you up to it?"

Azariah shifts his weight from his left foot to his right. He looks up at the ceiling while he considers the question. Finally, he says, "I think I am."

"Good," Whitman says, "I'll grab my coat."

And so Walt Whitman and Azariah Smith trudge to the *Aurora* offices together. Next to Walt, Azariah shuffles more than he walks. The boy should be in bed, recovering, and yet Walt would prefer to supervise him than have him out on the streets alone. The twenty-minute walk passes quickly, and when Walt unlocks the *Aurora*'s front door, it is only minutes before five.

In the front office stands Henry's tidy new desk, paper stacked neatly in one corner, a tray of pencils in the other. Walt's own desk is a mound of paper — old newspapers mixed with ripped sheets full of his own scribbles. *Where is Henry?*

Walt locks the door behind him and leads Azariah through the office to the composition room. The large table in the center is where they do most of their work, and the printing press sits heavy next to it. Azariah explores the room with wide eyes. He stops in front of the press, runs his hands along the metal. "Will you teach me?"

Whitman looks up.

"I'm not without ambition," Azariah says. "You should know that by now."

Walt smiles. "You can help by starting a fire in the stove there, and I'll light the lamps."

While Walt lights the three lamps, he keeps an eye on the boy. Azariah has set the kindling up properly, but he's overloaded his pyramid, suffocating the flame. Whitman remembers his own father teaching him how to light a fire, how he lovingly guided him step by step, and for a fleeting moment Walt again feels connected to his father.

Whitman joins Azariah at the woodstove. "You're smothering the fire before it has a chance to burn."

Azariah shoots back, "I know what the hell I'm doing."

Walt shifts the wood, adds more newspaper, and hands Azariah another match. "See if that works better."

Azariah scrapes the match on the brick underneath the oven, waits for the flame to catch, and lights the newspaper.

"Leave the door open for a few minutes," Walt says, exactly how his father said it to him. "Give it a chance to burn."

The two of them watch as the kindling catches fire.

"Well done."

Azariah smiles. "What's next?"

"You are going to help me typeset tomorrow's edition."

"Typeset?"

"Here. Watch." Whitman sets up the trays on the composition table, showing Azariah how he will transpose his article from the green notebook to the print tray. "I learned to set type when I was about your age."

Azariah says, "What should I do?"

"Mr. Hartshorne called it *following the letters.*"

"Following the what?"

"The letters. I have to find each of these letters in type" — he points to his script in the notebook — "and assemble the blocks in the tray so they can be run through the printing press. I work fast, but along the way I make a lot of errors." Walt stops. "Your job is to tell me when I do."

"Okay." Azariah kneels on the table and is ready.

But Walt is stuck in his own history. "Back then, I worked at the *Long Island Patriot,* and I was Mr. Hartshorne's apprentice. He was from Philadelphia, and while we set the daily edition, he used to tell me about meeting George Washington and Thomas Jefferson. Can you imagine knowing such great men?"

"I can't." He pauses for a second, waiting for Walt to start working. "Ready, Mr. Whitman."

"My brothers, George and Jeff, are named after them."

"Mr. Whitman!"

"Oh yes." He shakes off the past. "Can you read?"

"The nuns worked with me some," Azariah says. "Can't read words but I know the letters."

"That's exactly what I need."

Once Walt begins, his hands move almost automatically, shooting from one tray to the next, finding the right letter, then sliding it into place, the metal crashing into the wood tray like tiny explosions. Azariah edits as Whitman works, and is surprisingly good at it. He catches several errors in the first column alone, catches that will save a lot of time with the printing.

In the article, with the headline SHERIFF HARRIS MURDERED, Walt begins with the suggestion that Lena Stowe might not have killed her husband and that Abraham's death might instead have had something to do with the underground body-snatching business and not the sensationalized and slanderous accusations of the Mary Rogers botched abortion. Walt figures that the tension created between the headline and the Stowe lead will jar the reader in a way that benefits his argument. Then he goes on to describe the illegal cadaver business itself — the demand for bodies, the point of view of the colleges — and finally transitions into what happened that night: his personal account of Sheriff Harris's murder and his own abduction.

This last part is where Whitman will grab the reader by the throat. He shifts into the first person, adopting a narrative style much like that in the stories he's been publishing. He wants the reader to feel what he felt, to be called to action as it were. He reads the passage to Azariah about being in the wagon with the corpse:

Upon waking under the tarp, I saw her. The girl's eyes, stretched wide open, glared as at some monstrous spectacle of horror and death. The sweat started in great globules seemingly from every pore of my face; my skinny lips contracted, and I showed my teeth; and when I at length stretched forth my arm, and with the end of one of my fingers touched her cheek, each limb quivered like the tongue of a snake; and my strength seemed as though it would momentarily fail me —

Azariah interrupts him. "No offense, Mr. Whitman, but that sounds a titch melodramatic."

"A titch?"

Azariah says, "You sound like you ain't never seen a body before."

"Fair enough," Walt says. "We'll delete that paragraph, then."

"And while we're on it. Didn't I tell you to stay away from James Warren?"

"You did."

Azariah shakes his head. "And you nearly got yourself killed."

Whitman smiles. "Nearly but not quite."

"I let you teach me how to build a fire," Azariah says, "now you got to let me teach you how to stay alive."

With the blocks of type set in the tray, it is time to run the proof.

When Walt finishes the print run at eight in the morning, he takes a rest and stares out the front window. The sun stretches over the buildings on Nassau Street and through the glass, but the air is cold. Icicles form in the crevice where the wall is joined to the window.

Walt approaches the sleeping Azariah and gently rocks his shoulders. "Mr. Smith? It's time."

The boy stretches, looks around, and when he sees Walt, he grins. "I dreamed I was taking a bath with those women doctors."

"My," Whitman says. "Perhaps, then, you'll return to the college for a spell after we're done here? See if dreams come true?"

Azariah plays along. "How can I say no to that?"

They load the newspapers into the *Aurora*'s wagon. They will pull it street to street, searching out the boys Mr. Ropes has hired to sell it, an exhausting task Walt himself has performed only once before. He appreciates having Azariah along for this — he's already helping by steadying the cart, which is always near tipping over on the cobblestones and sidewalks. They maneuver their way through the morning traffic, following the voice of their first newsboy. "Extra! Extra! Sheriff Harris murdered!"

Walt is astonished. Someone still beat him to the story. *No matter,* he thinks. *They certainly won't have the angle I do.*

The first newsboy, a burly sixteen-year-old with a missing front tooth, comes into view. He's standing on an upturned milk crate, holding the *Tribune* in each hand, calling out the headline. "Sheriff Harris murdered!"

Azariah and the newsboy size each other up.

"Who is this?" the newsboy says to Whitman.

"Who am I?" Azariah says. "Who the hell are you?"

Walt steps in between the two boys. "Now, gentlemen," he says, "don't we have business to perform?"

The newsboy agrees, and so steps down, takes the bundle of *Aurora* editions. He reads the headline. "A bit late to the party, no?"

"Ours is a better story," Walt says.

"It always is," the newsboy says.

"Just sell it," Azariah says.

As they leave, the newsboy's high voice hacks through the morning air: "Sheriff Harris murdered! Get the story here! Two cents!"

"What was that all about?" Walt says. "Do you know him?"

"It was nothing," Azariah says. "His sort thinks they're better than folks like me."

Whitman studies the boy but doesn't

grasp his meaning. Both Azariah and the newsboys are shabbily dressed, their speech equally rough.

Azariah is not smiling now. He's retreated deep within himself. The boy is a strange contradiction, Walt thinks. He operates with a maturity beyond his years, which Walt now believes is eleven or twelve.

"Let's finish delivering these newspapers. We both could use some sleep."

It is not until ten in the morning that Walt and Azariah return to the women's college. Walt's legs are heavy as tree stumps, his eyes dry and itchy. Mud cakes his boots and streaks his overcoat.

Azariah collapses in one of the classroom chairs.

"Let's get you upstairs," Walt says.

Azariah shakes his head. "I'll never make it."

"I'll carry you."

Azariah nods, and so Walt cradles him, the boy's warm body pressed up against his own. He thinks of his own brothers and sisters, and he longs to be with them, but he's grateful for this moment with his new friend. Azariah leans his head on Walt's shoulder.

In the large dormitory room, the students

116

are up and about. Most of them are reading. They smile and nod at Whitman as he carries Azariah around the curtain and lays him in bed. He's already fast asleep.

On the other side of the curtain, Elizabeth Blackwell waits for Walt. "What happened?" she whispers.

Whitman puts his fingers to his lips. "I'll tell you later."

She nods.

Walt acknowledges Miss Zacky, Miss Onderdonk, Miss Perschon, and Miss Emsbury. They are an impressive group, he thinks, as he goes down the stairs and into his room.

With the door shut, he drops into the chair next to the bed, unbuttons his coat, and slips into a trancelike state where he wonders about his ten-year-old brother, Jeff. Up already, no doubt, the cows milked and morning chores finished. He is probably sitting at the kitchen table, the sun's rays warming his arm through the window, the sound of Mother, Louisa, humming to herself behind him. On the table, a stack of flapjacks drips with hot maple syrup and a swirl of butter. The kitchen smells best in the morning, scented with coffee and pancakes, the mixture of bitter and sweet he will forever connect to growing up in that house.

The bed is too much to resist now, so he rolls onto the straw mattress, which crackles as he comes to rest. He closes his eyes and feels sleep take him over, his body weightless and spinning into darkness and silence.

CHAPTER 12

The protestors wake him. Their chants, rhythmic and agitating, shake him into consciousness. Idiots, he thinks. Surely they have better things to do than torture these poor women. Folks like these should be otherwise engaged. Walt stumbles out of bed, drowsy to the point of being uncoordinated, and into the classroom with every intent of going outside to confront them, but that's when he hears the students in the dissection room, and he follows their voices instead.

He finds them standing around Lena Stowe's half-dissected corpse, their cutting instruments to bear, their instructor monitoring their every move. "Careful as you cut," Elizabeth Blackwell says. "The muscle tissue needs tension as you peel it back. Then make a buttonhole in the muscle, yes, right there." Around them, jars and buckets line the counters and shelves, mixed with stacks of paper and publications: *Outlines of Anatomy and Physiology,* issues of *The People's Medical Journal and Home Doctor,* and William MaKenzie's *An Appeal to the Public and to the Legislature on the Necessity of Affording Dead Bodies to the Schools of Anatomy.* "Put your finger in the button-hole," Miss Blackwell continues, "and it will help you keep the muscle taut as you separate it from the chest cavity with your scalpel."

Miss Zacky taps Elizabeth's shoulder.

She turns around, and when she sees Walt, she smiles. "Mr. Whitman, good afternoon." All the students stop and stare at him now, and he looks down at his own sleeping gown, disheveled, the chest open —

"Pardon me," Walt says, taking a step toward Miss Blackwell, pulling his gown closed, and this is when Lena Stowe's body comes into full view: on her back, rib cage visible, skin peeled back like fabric — tendons, cartilage, muscles, and nerve endings sprouting out of her body. Walt has always imagined the inside of the human body as bright red, like the blood from a cut, but instead, he sees shades of gray and faded yellow.

Miss Blackwell anticipates his reaction.

"It's a bit of a shock your first time, isn't it?"

Whitman feels a bit light-headed. He grasps the table to steady himself, looking at the floor and then the body again. He is speechless. There's something so awful about what is happening in this room, and yet so beautiful.

Miss Blackwell says, "More than anything else, Lena wanted us to keep this college going. She wanted her body to be used in the manner that we have used the bodies of others. If she had to die, she did not want to die in vain." She pauses. "She told you so herself."

A sliver of black pupil shines through the slit of Lena's left eyelid, and her chapped lips are colorless. It is her hair that stands out to him most, long and flowing, just as it was before the trapdoor dropped out from under her. He reaches out and touches her cheek, which is ice-cold.

He runs his fingers across the front of her face and down her arm until he reaches her fingers, which slip between his own. Dirt lines her fingernails. Red welts around her wrists. On her left ring finger a tiny strip of skin is lighter than the rest.

"What about the baby?"

Elizabeth points to a tiny bundle of cloth

on the counter. "The Hathaways will bury her with Lena."

"Her?"

"The Stowes were going to have a daughter."

Whitman holds on to this revelation in reverence, giving himself a chance to reflect on its significance. "Had she quickened?"

"The fetus measured almost six inches. There is no doubt."

The room quiets down at this, acknowledging the second victim, and in the solitude, the protestors' chants come through.

Whitman breaks the moment. "They're still out there."

"They never go away," Miss Blackwell says.

"They should be otherwise engaged," he repeats to himself.

"What happened to you, Mr. Whitman? Your face is swollen and bruising, and you have turned pale."

Miss Zacky approaches from around the table, touches his forehead. "He's warm too."

"I'm overtired is all," Walt says. "I had just fallen asleep when they woke me."

Miss Zacky pulls him by the arm to a chair back against the wall. "You sit down," she says. "Rest."

"We'll be finished here in a few minutes," Elizabeth says, "and the Hathaways, Lena's mother and brothers, will arrive soon after. I could use some help in the meantime — but only if you're well enough."

"I'd be happy to," Whitman says.

From where he sits, Walt watches the students work. He's impressed with Miss Blackwell's leadership — she has stepped forward without trepidation, and the students have responded. This is good news. He wipes his forehead, exhausted. He has the sensation that if he stands, he might faint. Walt checks the clock on the counter next to him. Almost one already, which means his article on the sheriff's murder will have made its way around the city. He wonders what the reaction will be, what folks will make of his suggestion that the Stowe murder was a setup by body snatchers. Whatever the reaction, he will have stirred the pot, which is exactly what he needed to do.

The students are finished now, and Miss Blackwell directs them in the cleanup. Miss Emsbury sweeps the floor. Miss Onderdonk takes out the trash. Miss Perschon wipes the counters. When Whitman says he's feeling better, she even gives him a job. "Straighten up those books, won't you?" He does, and when they've all finished their assignments, Miss Blackwell gives them more. Miss Zacky will check on Azariah Smith while the other students clean the classroom. Walt and Elizabeth must prepare the body for burial.

"After you put on some proper clothing, of course," Elizabeth says.

Walt again looks down at his sleeping gown. He had forgotten.

Walt and Elizabeth fold the skin on Lena's legs and arms, then sew the skin flaps together. To Walt, the dark thread looks like a jagged body tattoo. The chest is next, where the students have diligently investigated her insides. They removed her organs one by one, storing them in pots of water until only an hour ago, when they began readying the college for the Hathaways' visit. While Walt and Elizabeth prepare the body, the students are in the large furnace room that doubles as a crematorium. Walt can smell the organs burning, a smell difficult to describe, but not at all as unpleasant as he would have thought.

Miss Blackwell reattaches the rib cage and while Whitman holds it in place, she stitches the skin together.

"They'll be here soon," she says.

Next, they have to fight Lena's dead weight to get her dress on. Miss Blackwell works the arms into the sleeves and eases the dress up over the chest, turning the body on its side to fasten the back buttons.

After combing Lena's hair, Elizabeth applies perfume to her neck and wrists, and Walt puts stockings on her feet, which cover up the sliced tendons. The body looks *almost* normal, he thinks. A few unnatural bunches remain in the chest, but it is the best they can do.

A banging at the front door jolts them, and they assume it is the protestors.

"I've never understood the opposition to dissection," Miss Blackwell says. "I understand that it makes folks uncomfortable, of course, but it's the only way to improve upon our knowledge of the human body. If dissection prevents resurrection, what about decomposition?"

Whitman is formulating an answer he hopes will give voice to people like him, who are not necessarily opposed to anatomical dissection but who seem to innately resist it. Before he can get the words out, however, she has moved on.

"In practical terms, what that opposition means is that families cannot bury their loved ones in church graveyards — this, of course, is the church's fault, but it comes with a real cost to the families of the deceased. If I could speak to the public, without the influence of the church, I know I could convince New Yorkers of both the necessity and benefits of anatomical dissection — and you know me, Mr. Whitman. My faith is central to everything I do."

She is devout if a tad idiosyncratic, he thinks.

"We learn so much by looking inside the human body. I know that an omnipotent God, the God I believe in, has no objections to dissection. He wants us to understand his creation, and that understanding brings me closer to him."

Walt interrupts her. "But the theological problem of resurrection is not the only stumbling block," he says. "And I have to be honest: What you've done to Lena's body has had a great effect on me, and not a positive one."

"Believe me," Elizabeth says, "I understand. My first dissection filled me with dread. I can remember being sleepless with worry the night before, and then when Abraham made the first cut, the whole process was remarkably scientific. And beautiful."

Whitman ponders this, then says: "What

about all the accounts of medical students desecrating the bodies?"

"Ah, of course." Miss Blackwell nods. "Lena herself told me of the time she witnessed a medical student prank. One evening, shortly after they first met, Abraham asked her to meet him in the dissection lab at New York University Medical College. The room was dark, and so she lit a candle. A half dozen half-dissected cadavers came into view, but no Abraham. She shined her light on a corpse dressed like a doctor, his head propped up with a wooden rod. A sign around his neck read *Happy Birthday.* The Stowes decided that night never to condone the mistreatment of the human body, and made that vow part of the Women's Medical College of Manhattan's mission. We will make medical progress through anatomical dissection while respecting the human body."

"That's a start," Walt admits, even while thinking that the war of public opinion might be too lopsided to overcome.

"We must keep at it," Elizabeth says. "Will you accompany me to a meeting tomorrow with a possible cadaver supplier?"

He's about to say yes, of course, when a knock at the back door startles them.

Lena's family has arrived.

■ ■ ■ ■

Darlene Hathaway is a thin, delicate woman
about the same size as Lena. In her early
sixties, her dark hair has grayed and her
posture stooped. Her skin has that worn
quality that comes with years, but she is fit
and strong, as her daughter was. She says
nothing as she steps past Walt and Elizabeth. Lena's two brothers, in their forties,
follow their mother into the room, with a
pine casket on their shoulders. Both wear
black pantaloons, white shirts, and dark
wool coats, and Walt knows from his conversation with Lena that both her brothers are
married, that they each have four or five
children, and that they live near Mrs.
Hathaway to help her maintain the family
farm. Lena's father died of cholera a decade
earlier.

When they see Lena's body, they let out a
groan.

"Mrs. Hathaway." He holds out his hand.
"My name is Walt Whitman. Lena asked me
to help run the college in her absence."

But the woman ignores him.

The brothers set the casket down next to
the table and join their mother in front of
the body.

128

"Let us pray." Darlene Hathaway bows her head and waits for the others to do likewise. Her voice is strong, confident. "To thee, Lord, we commend the soul of your handmaid Lena, and her daughter, that being dead to this world they may live to thee; and whatever sins they have committed in this life through human frailty, do thou in thy most merciful goodness forgive. Through Christ our Lord. Amen."

"Amen," Walt says.

Mrs. Hathaway looks at him as if he has just done something horrible. "Jeb, Nathaniel," she says. "Be careful with your sister." Jeb, the taller of the two brothers, takes hold of Lena's feet.

He's thick and muscular, his hands big and powerful. Nathaniel is short and stocky, his hands pudgy, and he bears little resemblance to Lena, her mother, or Jeb. Must look like his father, Walt thinks. Nathaniel slides his arms underneath Lena's shoulders, and as they lift the body off the table, it bends at the hips. The pressure pops off the two top buttons in the back, and the dress opens enough to expose the black thread holding the chest together.

Her mother rushes to cover her daughter's skin. "How could you?" She helps her sons lower the body into the casket, then tucks the loose fabric underneath.

"Her body is material now," Miss Blackwell says. "Her soul is with God."

"I wouldn't talk about God in this room," Mrs. Hathaway says. "Not if I were you."

"We *loved* your daughter, Mrs. Hathaway," Whitman says. "We wouldn't do anything to harm her."

"No church will take her body now." Mrs. Hathaway lifts her veil. "That's what you've done to her." She takes a step closer to Walt. In this light, Mrs. Hathaway looks so much like an older Lena, with the same full lips and china-doll face, and Walt knows he shouldn't, but he can't help himself: He reaches out and touches her cheek. Mrs. Hathaway slaps him so hard he sees tiny flashes of light. "Stay away from *me.*"

Mrs. Hathaway leans over Lena, rubs her forehead. "My daughter." Her fingers trace the outline of her nose, eyebrows, and cheeks. Her fingers stop just short of the stitches in her head.

Jeb puts his arm around his mother. "Let's take her home."

Nathaniel prepares to lift the casket. "Jeb's right, Mother. It's time."

Jeb slides his hands under the pine box. The brothers nod at one another and lift.

Walt steps in front of them. "I'm going to

prove that Lena didn't kill Abraham."

"*That* man." Mrs. Hathaway hesitates, then covers her face again with the veil.

The brothers carry the coffin around Whitman, then Miss Blackwell, and out of the college. Mrs. Hathaway gently takes the bundled fetus into her arms and follows.

Walt calls out, "It wasn't easy for us, either."

The Hathaways don't turn around.

"We have to press on," he continues. "Lena understood that."

The footsteps trail off and the door shuts. From the window, Walt watches them load the body, then drive away. The wagon disappears around the corner, and they are alone again.

An emotional Miss Blackwell excuses herself to her room upstairs, which leaves Walt in the dissection room alone. When he closes his eyes, all he hears are the chants outside. *Dissection stops the resurrection. Dissection stops the resurrection.*

He has had enough.

CHAPTER 13

Walt Whitman steps out onto the porch, his eyes blinded by the sun's reflection off the snow piled high on the sidewalk. The Hathaway visit has left him feeling empty and angry, and he wants a confrontation. The protestors' chants grow louder at the sight of him. *Dissection stops the resurrection!* Still blinded by the sunlight, Walt feels for the railing beside him, steadies himself, and raises his voice. "For God's sake, leave them alone!"

The protestors recede, and Father Allen steps forward in the company of a strong bald man. Across the street, a gaggle of men with empty eyes and long, cold faces skulk in the shadows of the grog house, as they do every day, watching.

"My son," Father Allen says, "you don't understand what you do." His coat is too small for his long, muscular arms.

"What I do understand is that you've

turned the city against this college," Whitman says. "Any hope we had of saving Mrs. Stowe was crushed by your movement."

"Whoever sheds the blood of man, by man shall his blood be shed; for in the image of God has God made man."

"But she didn't kill anyone."

Father Allen says, "God works in mysterious ways."

Walt descends the staircase to the sidewalk, his boot pressing into the snow.

The priest steps closer to meet him. "God commanded me to gather his people here to call you to repentance."

"What these students do here," Walt says, "is important to the future of all people."

"Important enough to desecrate the human body?" the bald man says.

Whitman takes a deep breath. "Without anatomical dissection, medical knowledge will never progress." He's trying to remember Elizabeth's argument. He hopes the students cannot overhear. "They might have stopped the cholera breakout a few years ago."

"Progression at the expense of the human soul," the bald man says, "is not progress at all."

"God gives us what we need," the priest says. "The cholera outbreak was a means to

133

an end."

Walt steps so close he can smell the priest's tobacco breath. "Are you saying that thousands of people dying is God's will?"

"I am saying that I don't need to understand God's plan," the priest says. "Only that it is *his* plan."

"Abraham and Lena Stowe's deaths were not part of God's plan." Whitman is shaking now.

The priest puts his hand on Walt's shoulder. "I am not the enemy here," he says. "God loves you. He loves those medical students, misguided as they are." The priest smiles now, a warm and welcoming smile. "God wants them to stop. That's why we're here. To get them to stop."

For a moment, Walt almost believes him. He feels love and concern emanating from the priest, not hate and intolerance. These folks believe in their cause. That's what makes them so dangerous.

Whitman pulls back from Father Allen.

The priest says, "You know what I'm saying is true, don't you?"

"No," Walt starts, and then something's wrong. He closes his eyes. He's sweating. Maybe it's the lack of sleep or the stress or the grief, but he stumbles backward, his vision blurs, and he loses consciousness —

— until he hears familiar voices, not those of the priest or protestors but those from beyond, and when he opens his eyes, Abraham and Lena Stowe are floating in a bright light, dressed in white robes, their chest cavities gone, their hearts nothing but pulsating light, singing:

O living always, always dying!
O the burials of me past and present,
O me while I stride ahead, material, visible,
    imperious as ever;
O me, what I was for years, now dead, (I
    lament not, I am content;)
O to disengage myself from those corpses
    of me, which I turn and look at where I
    cast them,
To pass on, (O living! always living!) and
    leave the corpses behind.

Walt closes his eyes, then opens them again.

"Are you okay, sir?" Father Allen leans over him.

"How did you do that?"

"Let's get you inside," Father Allen says.

The protestors place their hands on Whitman, lift him high above their heads, and carry him through the front door of the women's college and into the classroom, where they lay him on the floor. The priest bends down, places his hand on Walt's forehead. "You're not well," he says. "You need rest."

"I'm fine," Walt says even though he is not. His body feels hollow, his head hurts, and he can't stop shivering. He tries to stand, but the priest stops him.

"Rest," Father Allen says.

The protestors encircle him, and Whitman can sense their anxiety, and with their numbers in the small classroom space, it hits him all at once that this is exactly what they've wanted all along. They're here to cleanse the earth, and he's the only one who can stop it.

Behind the priest, Walt hears the bald man say, "Father, the Lord has delivered this place into our hands."

A growl ripples through the protestors, and then they thump their feet on the wood floor. Whitman sits up, calls for them to stop, but his own protests are drowned out by the rumbles.

Above him, upstairs, he hears a commotion. The students know something is happening. Their footsteps scramble as they move toward the back of the college.

"No, Jedediah," Father Allen says to the man. "Not this way."

"But God has told me as much in my heart." Jedediah Matthews is several inches taller than the priest, and the other protestors recognize him as a leader too. He pulls them closer and he raises his voice. "The Lord has commanded me to destroy this place so that they may do no more evil unto the children of men."

"But the students live here," Walt says. "Have you thought about them?"

Matthews ignores Whitman. "Father, this is what we've been praying for."

"Out," Father Allen says, his voice betraying panic. "All of you."

The two men glare at each other, and then Matthews exhorts the protestors. "What will you do? Will you let this opportunity pass? Will you turn your backs on God?"

The group stills.

Father Allen stands on a chair. "Brothers and sisters. God has said through his servant Paul: 'Therefore thou art inexcusable, O man, whosoever thou art that judgest: for wherein thou judgest another, thou condemnest thyself; for thou that judgest doest the same things.' We protest with our hearts and words, not with violence and destruction."

Whitman pushes himself to his feet and tries to step in between the two leaders and their followers, but Matthews blocks his way. He's stronger than Walt first thought, and he knows how to fight.

"You have lost your way, Father Allen," Matthews says. "You must have the courage of the Lord to do as he commands. He has not brought us to this moment today to retreat."

Matthews knocks the priest to the floor.

That leaves Whitman. He steps in front of Matthews. "I won't let you do this."

The man lunges at him. Walt ducks, then hits him in the mouth.

Matthews kicks Whitman in the ribs and shoves him to the ground next to the priest.

And then they come. From under the dissection sign march the students arm in arm. Elizabeth Blackwell, Marie Zakrzewska, Karina Emsbury, Olive Perschon, and Patricia Onderdonk. Their faces are haggard but fierce. The protestors might take the college, but they'll have to go through these women first.

Walt pushes himself to his feet, and Matthews gets ready for more. The whole room is about to explode, when comes a swirl of voices:

Elizabeth Blackwell: "We've done nothing to deserve this —"

Father Allen: "My brothers and sisters,

please —"

Jedediah Matthews: "The Lord has delivered this place into our hands —"

A beautiful woman, pale and thin, with shiny blue eyes, steps forward from the crowd: "They dissected my husband," she cries. "They damned his soul!"

The protestors heave. They shove tight, and become one body —

— and the mob attacks the college with full force. They overturn tables, empty jars, and shred books. Walt fights them as they come, deterring them as he can, but he and the students are simply outnumbered, and so he focuses on protecting them, helping Miss Blackwell move them to safety while the mob smashes the instruments of medical education. They are ripping textbooks to bits, tearing the anatomical drawings from the wall. They make a pile in the center of the room, stuff the crumpled-up book pages in the cracks, and douse them with whiskey. The young widow tosses a lit match into the center, and all they can do is watch as the fire leaps to the ceiling.

And then it happens —

Azariah Smith bursts through the entryway, calling for them to stop. Surprised, everyone turns around, and in lumbers a man with a flushed face and straggled auburn hair. Isaiah Rynders. A long scar starts between his eyebrows and runs up over his forehead. He limps inside and goes straight to Matthews, who instantly stops.

"Mr. Rynders."

"Put the fire out."

Rynders directs the protestors to the well behind the college, and together they pass buckets of water from the back, in through the kitchen, and into the dissection room and classroom, tossing water on the fire until it is out.

When it is, Rynders turns on Matthews, face red and yelling. "What the hell are you on about? I got the whole city of New York to worry about and now you're making more trouble."

"But, Mr. Rynders, this college —"

"Shut your gapper, you hear me? These poor young women, after everything they've been through, and here you are making things worse." He stands on his tiptoes, makes eye contact with Elizabeth Blackwell. "Miss, my apologies for the overexuberance of these fellows. They, and those who follow them, are obviously idiots, and I'm grateful to young Azariah here for alerting me to the seriousness of the situation so I might put an end to it. It goes without saying that I will cover the costs of damages."

Whitman can't believe Azariah is with Isaiah Rynders. All the events of the past couple of days come back to him with a new understanding: Rynders planted Azariah in the jail after Walt tried to save Lena Stowe, which means Rynders knows everything Whitman has done since. He turns to Azariah, but the boy looks away.

"But, sir," Matthews tries again.

Rynders need only make eye contact to shut him down.

"Where's the priest?"

Father Allen calls out from the back corner.

Rynders goes to him, helps him to his feet. "Why don't you take these folks home, Father? I think you've done enough here for one day."

The priest can only nod in shock. He gestures to the protestors to follow him, and they all do, maneuvering around the smoldering fire, save Jedediah Matthews, who remains standing in the same spot opposite Whitman. It takes several minutes for the protestors to clear out, and when they have all gone, Rynders approaches the bald man, shaking his head. "What am I going to do with you?"

"Mr. Rynders, I was only following orders."

"That's the one thing you clearly were not doing. I want to see you in my office in one hour. Understand?"

The man nods.

"Now leave."

Matthews hesitates only a moment before he exits through the front door.

All who remain in the room are the students, Whitman, Rynders, and Azariah.

Mr. Rynders approaches Elizabeth Blackwell. "Let me personally apologize for the events of today, and may I also offer my condolences for the deaths of Lena and Abraham Stowe. It is a real tragedy, and I admire the strength and fortitude you've displayed since their deaths. May God be with you, and should anything threaten your well-being, please contact me personally. No such calamity shall reoccur. Now please excuse me."

Rynders nearly runs into Walt. "Ah, Mr. Whitman. How nice to see you again."

"Surely, you're not surprised?"

"Your ego surpasses your reputation. Not every New Yorker believes you're the next Charles Dickens."

"Your nose appears to have healed."

Rynders looks as if he might jump out of his skin but, after taking a deep breath, says, "Time heals most wounds." And then he disappears out the front door.

Miss Blackwell approaches Azariah. "We're all very grateful to you," she says, clearly not understanding the depth of his deception. She senses that Walt wants to speak to Azariah in private, so she corrals the students upstairs. "We've got work to do," she says.

Whitman nods Elizabeth's way, lets her know with his eyes that he appreciates her gesture.

Azariah's ever-present smile is long gone, replaced by a blank stare.

"Mr. Smith, I know you risked your standing with Rynders in order to save the college."

His eyes light up at this.

"And I know what kind of man Rynders is," Walt says. "I'm not angry."

"Really?"

Walt needs to find out what Azariah knows. What are Rynders's plans for the college? What does Rynders want Azariah to learn? And what does Azariah know, if anything, about the Stowes?

"Let's sit down," Whitman is light-headed again, and the chills return. Yet he will not be deterred.

The boy does not sit.

Walt says, "You can trust me."

Azariah paces restlessly, muttering to himself.

"Azariah?"

Nothing.

Walt tries again. "Azariah?"

All at once the boy stops. "Aw, hell, Mr. Whitman. I'm sorry but I gotta go." And before Walt can protest, Azariah is gone.

CHAPTER 14

On his way to the *Aurora* to meet with Henry, Walt runs into the boy shouting the *Herald* headline "Suspect in Harris Murder Captured!" He flips four half-cent coins to the scruffy boy and leans up against the lamppost. It takes only one sentence for him to realize that Snuffy's prediction has come true.

The article goes on to suggest that the City of New York wants to make an example of the suspect, that sheriff killers will not be tolerated. Mr. Warren will be tried and, if guilty, put to death within the week. As if that is not provocative enough, the last paragraph of the article exonerates Samuel Clement of any guilt, saying that Mr. Clement regrets the loss of life caused by the man who *used* to work for him. The writer of the article, James Gordon Bennett, cites Whitman's own article in the *Aurora* as erroneous and scurrilous.

It appears as if Mr. Whitman has been caught up in the emotion of the moment, and given his attachment to the Stowe family, who can blame him? We must, nevertheless, move forward, brandishing the truth, as readers of the *Herald* have come to expect.

Walt slams the newspaper against the lamppost. *How could Bennett be yet another mouthpiece for corruption?* He checks his watch. If he keeps his appointment with Henry, he'll miss out on his chance to visit James Warren before the jail closes to visitors for the day. He needs to act quickly, to see if Warren can help him find Clement again, and he owes it to Warren to make this right.

Inside the prison, Whitman finds a guard at the front desk, drinking coffee and eating a piece of bread with strawberry jam. "Good evening, sir."

The guard continues eating. He's a skinny older man with ruddy cheeks and knotty fingers.

"I'm Walt Whitman, reporter for the *Aurora,* doing a story on the recent grave robberies, and I understand you have Mr. James Warren in your custody."

The guard takes another bite.

"I wonder if I might have a short conversation with the man."

The guard says nothing.

Whitman sets a half-eagle coin on the desk.

The guard turns around to where a ring of keys hangs on a hook and motions for Whitman to follow. Inside, the corridor smells wet and moldy and is not much warmer than the air outside. He hears people he can't see. Groans, coughs, and laughs.

They stop halfway down the hall, where through the bars he can see Snuffy sitting on his bed with his back against the wall of his cell. His face shows no expression when he sees Walt, who is not sure Snuffy recognizes him at all until the prisoner says: "How's your head?"

"You two know each other?" the guard says.

"No," Whitman says. "Not at all."

The guard unlocks the door.

Snuffy watches Walt but says nothing. In the light, he looks considerably younger than Whitman's own twenty-three, his face smooth except for a mustache that drips down his face like spilled ink.

"You have twenty minutes," the guard says.

Walt waits for him to leave.

"You?" Snuffy says.

"I am as surprised as you are, *James.*" Walt hands him the *Herald* and points to the last paragraph, about Clement's exoneration. "But I need your help."

Snuffy glances at the paper, looks up. "Why should I help you? You're the reason I'm here in the first place."

Whitman says, "Read the article."

Snuffy regards the newspaper in such a way that Walt knows he can't read.

"Here." Whitman takes back the newspaper and reads the last paragraph, emphasizing the words *exonerate* and *Clement.* "What do you think of that? Getting off scot-free while you await trial for murder."

Snuffy stands up, paces nervously. "I told you this would happen, didn't I?"

What can Walt say to that?

"Jesus!" Snuffy bangs his fist against the wall. "And what can I do anyway? I *am* guilty."

"I was there, and you didn't pull the trigger," Whitman says. "You shouldn't hang for the one who did."

"And you ain't no good as an eyewitness if they already let Clement off the hook."

Snuffy's eyes meet his own. "So why did you come?"

"I want to help you," Walt says. "But to do that, I need information."

"Information?"

"About Clement. Tell me anything that will help me get him, and this will, in turn, help you."

Snuffy shakes his head. "For starters, you can't *get* Clement without provoking some very important folks."

"I already know about Rynders."

"Then you'll know that to get Rynders, you'll have to go all the way up the line." Snuffy stands up and raps the bars with the tin cup he holds in his right hand. "He's done, guard," he yells. "Come and get him."

"Wait." Whitman stands up. "Isn't there anything I can do for you in exchange for some information?"

Snuffy stops banging the cup. "What the hell can you do for me?"

"I can get you out of here."

Snuffy bangs the cup again.

"I don't know." Walt looks at his notebook. "You have family, don't you? I can take a letter to them."

The expression on Warren's face changes. "They'll let you do that?"

"Sure. Tell me what you know and I'll

write a letter and deliver it myself."

The door at the end of the hall opens. "What's the racket?" The guard sounds annoyed.

Walt looks at Snuffy.

"Nothing, sir."

"You okay, reporter?"

"Fine."

The guard approaches the cell, looks around to make sure, and when he is satisfied, turns to leave. "Ten minutes," he says. This time he leaves the hall door open.

Mr. Warren waits for the footsteps to stop. "Samuel Clement and Isaiah Rynders have worked together for years, and they protect each other. That's how I knew this would happen. Rynders doesn't need me like he needs Samuel."

"Why shoot Harris?"

Warren says, "How the fuck should I know?"

"Harris and Clement were discussing the Mary Rogers murder?"

"Samuel is obsessed with death. It's all he talks about. That's why he likes digging up bodies, I guess. He says death is beautiful, and he means it."

"Did he kill Mary Rogers?"

"I don't know what he does in his free time. Would I be surprised? No."

"Were you surprised when Clement shot Harris?"

Snuffy shrugs. "He'd run into the sheriff before while he was working the cemetery. They had an understanding."

Whitman says, "Is that a yes?"

"I guess it is."

"That's it?"

"What else is there? Samuel is valuable to Mr. Rynders and until that changes, there's nothing to be done. They're hungry to make an example of me, and soon. I'll be dead within the week."

"That's not good enough," Walt says. "Start again, and tell me everything you know about Clement."

Snuffy mulls over the question before speaking. "We had a room over on Ann Street, where they found me, but I doubt he'll ever go back there." He pauses. "You can sometimes find him at the Empire Club, Rynders's place."

"That's common knowledge."

"I told you I don't know anything else."

"Do you want to die?" Whitman grabs him by the shoulders. "They *will* let you hang unless you give me something useful."

Snuffy thinks for a moment.

"I'm not as ignorant as you think I am," Snuffy says. "Despite the fact I can't read."

Walt says, "I don't think you're ignorant."

"You know I wanted to be a priest growing up? I liked going to school, but I had to stop long ago and forgot more than I learned. I helped my mother sew at home, and I was good at it. I only come to body snatching recently when the work dried up. I had to do something. We didn't have any food. We didn't have anything."

Whitman waits for him to continue.

"Who will care for my mother when I'm gone?"

"You will," Walt says. "If you give me something useful."

Snuffy is thinking about what Whitman has said. "His sister is a prostitute named Frankie," he says. "You can find her at John McCleester's tavern."

Walt wrote this down. "Anything else?"

"I don't know, mister. If I knew how to get Clement, I wouldn't be in here waiting for the hangman to get me out."

"They haven't even tried you yet."

"You know better than that," Warren says. "In court tomorrow, dead by Saturday. Got the jury together already. Rumor is, they're going to make it real public, this one. Build a gallows right there in Washington Square. No damn sheriff killers." Snuffy stops. "Anyway, that's where you'll find my mother, at the hanging. She'll be the one in the front row, I guess, dressed in black and carrying her Bible. She's short like me." He pauses. "You ready to write the letter now, mister?"

Walt flips the page to a clean sheet. "Ready."

Snuffy closes his eyes and chews his bottom lip. "Dear Mother —" He stops. "Will you write that the letter is from the jail here and the date too, seeing as how this is the last letter she'll ever get from me?"

Whitman nods.

"I didn't kill no one. That's important to you, I know, the Ten Commandments and all. Did my share of grave robbing, but far as I know, that ain't much of a crime. Tell the girls I love them. Pray for me. James."

As he speaks, Walt adds words here and there so that the letter reads:

Dear Mother,
    I wanted to tell you before my unfortunate death that I killed no one. I know that this will be important to you, a devout believer in the Ten Commandments. I did do a fair amount of stealing bodies, that's true, but I was contributing to medical progress. Please tell my sisters I love them and I only wanted to

153

do my fair share. You'll be getting this letter from a Mr. Whitman. I'm praying for you, Mother, and I'm doing my best to believe that there's a heaven out there where I'll go. Pray for me?

Your son, James.

Walt looks up from his notebook. "Anything else?"

Mr. Warren is emotional. "Did I forget something?"

Whitman shakes his head. "It's a beautiful letter. Your job now is to pray we don't have to deliver it." He stands, makes ready to leave, when the thought occurs to him. "You wouldn't happen to know Azariah Smith, would you?"

"Azariah?" Warren's face drops. "Where did you hear that name?"

"I've spent the past few days with him." Walt sits down, crosses his leg, and says, "What do you know about him?"

Snuffy scoots forward on the mattress. "Azariah is Rynders's son."

"His son?"

"More like an indentured servant," Warren says. "Rynders purchased the boy from his destitute mother to work for him."

Walt thinks about the bruises. "How does Rynders treat Azariah?"

154

"You don't want to know, mister," Snuffy says. "But you want to stay away from the boy. Wherever Rynders sends that boy, death follows. I've seen it happen over and over."

At this, Snuffy stops cold.

"What is it?" Walt says.

Snuffy puts his head down.

"What? Tell me."

"It's a miracle you're still alive, mister, given the fact that you've been hanging around him."

Whitman sits back on the bunk, his head shaking, and he knows that for once in the past several days, he was just told the truth.

CHAPTER 15

Walt is close now, and as he rounds the corner, he fervently hopes to have Henry all to himself. Through the office window, he can see a middle-aged woman pleading her case to Henry, arms flailing.

Henry is handsome, the way he sits up straight, his shoulders back, his smooth skin and attentive eyes. Walt catches himself grinning.

The bell rings when he opens the door, and the woman turns around. Her long dress is ripped in several places and her face is rough and wrinkled, which makes her appear older than she probably is. She stands up straight and shakes his hand, exuding a strength that reminds Whitman of his mother.

Behind her, Henry smiles. "Glad you made it, Mr. Whitman." He emphasizes *Whitman* just as he did the night before, and relief washes over Walt. Then he sees the slightly younger man, scrawny and pale, sitting next to the woman — he's hunched over in the chair, and one of his hands is curled up in a ball.

"We're Ned and Harriet Runkel," the woman says. "Maggie's parents."

Whitman takes off his coat. "Maggie?"

Mrs. Runkel pokes her husband's shoulder. "See, he doesn't even know who she is." She turns to Walt. "It was Maggie's body they stole the night of the sheriff's murder."

Images of the young corpse's blue lips and cold, white face flash through his mind — he feels himself thrust back into the wagon, the smell of urine and feces and death, the way her face, punctured by the hook, rolled into his when the wagon turned. "Oh," Walt says. "I'm sorry for your loss." He looks over at Henry. "Shall I set the tea on?"

Saunders nods, then sneezes.

"Bless you," Mrs. Runkel says.

Whitman approaches the wood-burning stove, kneels down, and opens the door. The fire turns his thoughts to Azariah. Where is he now? The hot air brushes Walt's face. "A cold one today." He lifts the kettle. It is full. "Tea will be ready in a minute."

"I could use a cup of tea," Mrs. Runkel says. "Sounds grand."

"Me too," Saunders says. "Do you need

157

any help, Mr. Whitman?"

Walt turns, ready to say no, that he has the tea in hand, but Henry is already coming toward him. Their eyes meet, and Walt waits.

Henry lowers his voice. "Is everything okay? I was worried when you didn't arrive."

Walt, still crouching, reaches for Henry's hand, squeezes, then lets go, careful that the Runkels don't see. "I had a few setbacks today. I'll tell you about them once they've gone."

Henry nods. "I'm glad to see you."

Walt stands and looks at Henry. He didn't notice until now, but Henry's face is damp with sweat. And pale. "You don't look well," Walt says.

"How nice of you to say." Henry smiles. "That's what spending all night in the graveyard will do."

Walt shakes his head. "I think I have a cold too. The price of justice. Shall we?" He motions to the Runkels.

Saunders nods, goes first, and takes his place across from the couple. "Tea will be ready shortly."

Whitman sits on the bench next to Mr. Runkel, and the man's demeanor changes — he straightens up and appears stronger.

"Nobody has even looked for her," he says.

"Pardon?" Walt says.

"For Maggie's body," Mr. Runkel says.

Saunders shakes his head. "That must be difficult."

"We are grateful that they found the man who took her body," Mrs. Runkel says, meaning James Warren, "but we want *her* back."

The kettle rattles and clanks now. Walt stands. "Excuse me." Over at the stove, Whitman dumps the tea leaves into the strainer. He empties the steaming water into the teapot, retrieves four cups and saucers from the shelf above the stove. The tea steeps for a few minutes before Walt pours, then distributes the cups, careful not to slosh it over the sides. His own tea burns his tongue. "Still very hot," he says.

Harriet sets her mug down beside her on the bench. "An article on Maggie could help us find her body." She breaks down, recovers, and blows her nose with a handkerchief she keeps bunched up in her left fist. "She deserves to rest."

"It was *your* article today," Ned says, "that led them to the medical students who bought Sheriff Harris's body."

He is right. Harris's body was discovered in the NYU Medical College morgue. Walt learned of this in the same Bennett article that inspired his visit to Snuffy in the prison. Did the Runkels read it too? They must have if they know all this. Still, if they believed the *Herald* article, they probably would not have come here seeking their help.

He's thinking ahead now. Another article on body snatching would keep the Stowe story in the public's mind, and if it helps recover the Runkels' daughter's body, then even better. However, a search would not be an easy one — the body could be anywhere by now. Sheriff Harris's body was easily recognizable because of who he was; Maggie's is not.

For just a moment, he wonders if the Runkels' story is another diversion from his mandate to keep the college going, but he just as quickly realizes that keeping the college open long-term still depends, in large part, on exonerating Lena.

So Walt turns around and makes eye contact with Henry. "Exactly right." He takes out his green notebook. "A brilliant idea. Yes, an article on your missing daughter, the implications of body snatching from another perspective. Now, what can you tell me about your daughter?"

Ned starts. Maggie, the eldest of their two

daughters, started vomiting at night, just after dinner, the cause of which they had hoped was bad food. But during the night, she didn't get better, and around four A.M., her vomiting turned to diarrhea. Ned and Harriet Runkel had tried to make their daughter comfortable, but by morning, Maggie had died of cholera.

"Bad drinking water," says Ned.

Henry stops him. "The new water system — hasn't it helped stop cholera?"

Harriet looks him straight in the eye. "Not everyone in New York gets *that* water."

"We know about the resurrection men," Ned says. "People die around us all the time and folks stumble over each other to get to the body. That's why we paid the priest to bury Maggie in the graveyard far away from our neighborhood." Mr. Runkel drops his head. "All that did was raise the price of her body."

"We haven't always lived in Five Points," Harriet says. "Things happen. Circumstances beyond your control." She pauses. "*You* could end up living there, and then you'd see how everything changes."

"I can't imagine," says Whitman.

"You should come see for yourself," Ned says, "how bad it is."

"I don't know if that's possible," Saunders

161

says. "This isn't the only story we have to write."

Walt turns to Henry. "Whatever do you mean?" He sees Henry's eyes get bigger, but he can't stop himself. "Of course we'll visit. How about tomorrow?" Then he remembers the meeting with Miss Blackwell and the cadaver supplier. "I'm sorry. How about the day after tomorrow? I have a prior commitment."

Ned and Harriet both smile. "Thank you, Mr. Whitman. You have no idea how much this means to us."

They make arrangements to stop by the Runkels' flat, and Ned tells them that there are more body-snatching victims living in the same area. You can interview them too for the article, Ned says. It's important for the reader to understand how many folks are affected by this problem. Whitman agrees, and after he thanks the Runkels again for stopping by, they say their good-byes.

When the door closes behind the Runkels, Henry pounces. "What are you doing? You made a promise to people we have no business trying to help. We're journalists. We don't have time for this."

"If we don't help the Runkels, who will?"

Henry sits at his desk, twirls a pencil in

his hand. "Am I missing something?"

Walt scratches his head. "There might be something I haven't told you."

"Besides the fact you ran this morning's edition without me?"

"Well, that *and* —"

"Bennett's eviscerating response that could put the *Aurora* out of business?"

"What I was going to say is —"

"You realize that Mr. Ropes will want me to fire you for what you did this morning, and I'll have to beg him for your job." Henry takes a breath. "You don't know this, but he wanted me to fire you as my first order of business as editor."

Walt had no idea it had gone this far. "He did?"

Henry nods. "He said you are the laziest fellow who ever undertook to edit a city paper. I refused because you're a great writer."

Whitman clears his throat. "Oh. Thank you."

The two men stand in silence for several moments.

"Was there something else?" Henry says.

Walt knows what he has to say next will not go over well, so he takes his time. He goes to his desk, slides out the chair, and sits. He picks up a pencil, rolls it on the table, and finally he looks up at Henry and speaks. "I went to see James Warren today —"

At nine o'clock, Walt Whitman turns down the composition room's oil lamps and watches the flames sputter and disappear, the only light now coming from the office. Henry had responded to his solo visit with Warren much as Walt thought he would. Irritation first. Then curiosity. Now Henry is looking forward to their visit to see Clement's sister as much as Walt is. The day after tomorrow, they'll visit the Runkels first and then Frankie.

"Henry?" he calls.

No response.

In the office, he finds Henry, his head on the desk.

Walt says, "Are you ready to go?"

But Henry is asleep.

He puts his hand on Henry's shoulder, which is warm, and touches his forehead, which is even warmer. At this, Henry looks up, and his pallid face startles Walt.

"I'll get a cab," Whitman says. "You can't walk home like this."

Across the street from the *Aurora,* omnibuses and cabs have lined up outside the string of restaurants and bars already packed with people — most of them men who stopped on their way home from their Wall Street offices.

Walt crosses the street and speaks with the first cabbie he sees — a youngish man with molasses skin and greasy black hair. He asks him to pull up in front of the *Aurora*. "Too much to drink," he tells the cabbie, not wanting to say the word *fever*.

With Henry's arm around his neck, Walt helps him into the cab, and after the ten-minute journey to the Centre Street boardinghouse where Henry lives, Walt escorts him up the stairs. The tiny room holds a bed, a desk, a wood-burning stove, and a series of small shelves. The window is open, and the temperature is frigid.

He helps Henry into bed and covers him with a blanket.

He shuts the window. He starts a fire. Should he stay here and keep a watch on Henry or should he return to his room at the college? It is after ten now, and he still isn't feeling well himself.

He stokes the fire, then looks around Henry's room. On the desk, he sees a stack of letters from August and Edie Saunders. He sees a letter Henry started writing earlier that day, in which he mentions his excitement for his new job. He searches the prose for any mention of himself and when he reads, *I've met an old friend, a remarkable man, Walt Whitman,* his spirits soar.

He searches the room for another blanket, which he finds folded up underneath the bed. He situates himself near the stove and folds up his coat as a pillow. The blanket and the warmth from the fire soon warm him through, save his toes and fingers, and it doesn't take long for him to fall asleep.

The next morning, Walt wakes with a start. He's not sure where he is, but as Henry's room comes into view, he remembers everything. He shivers. Not from illness, but because the fire has gone out.

Henry is still sleeping, a good thing, no doubt. It is eight o'clock, and Walt is supposed to meet Miss Blackwell at nine for their visit to the coroner. He nearly forgot.

Whitman uses the embers to restart the fire and adds enough wood to ensure that it will burn for at least a few hours. He searches the room for food. There is not much. A bread end, some coffee, a few spoiled eggs. He prepares coffee and leaves it on the desk with the bread and a note: *Will look in on you later. Yours, Walt.*

Henry does not stir despite Walt's moving about. His forehead is still warm, and he looks worse than the day before. Perhaps Walt can talk Elizabeth into examining him. "You rest up," he says to the sleeping Henry, and then lets himself out.

CHAPTER 16

During the cab ride to the coroner's, Elizabeth tells Walt about yesterday's impromptu student meeting during which Karina Emsbury, Olive Perschon, and Patricia Onderdonk expressed a desire to return home with their families. "All but Miss Zacky," she says. "They remain shaken by the mob, and who can blame them? I pleaded with them to stay, and they responded with this question: Can you promise a future for us at the women's college? Of course the only thing I could guarantee was my diligence and devotion, and this isn't enough."

"What did you do?" Walt says.

"We have exhausted our resources. The students have studied the books. They have heard all the lectures. The only real way forward is anatomical dissection, and I have no bodies."

"But why the coroner?" Whitman says. "Why ask that man for anything?"

At this her face turns red, an odd reaction for Miss Blackwell, given her usual composure.

And then Walt knows. "You and the coroner?" he says.

"Only for a short time," she says, "but yes."

At this he smiles, and she turns defensive. "What is it, Mr. Whitman? Do you think me the sort of woman who is not allowed to have such feelings?"

The cab drops Walt and Elizabeth in front of the house at 104 Washington Street, and they step onto the stone walkway next to the lamp, which glows in the frosty haze.

Walt bangs on the door with his fist.

Kenneth Barclay takes his time answering, and when he sees Whitman standing on his porch, he smirks. "My, what a surprise. Have you come to inflict more pain?" Then he sees Miss Blackwell. "Lizzy? Why are you with this brute? Come in." He says this to Elizabeth, but then motions toward Walt. "If he's with you, I suppose he'll have to come in too."

"Your hospitality overwhelms me," Whitman says.

Barclay steps onto the porch. He shivers. "Why, it's perfectly frigid out."

"I'm surprised you noticed," Miss Blackwell says. "You always did like it cold."

"Makes my work easier, my dear."

Elizabeth steps in first, then Walt. Barclay closes the door, sets the latch in place.

"Not much warmer in here," she says.

Barclay shrugs. "Shall we go into the other room?" He leads them down the hall, to the right, and into the morgue, the site of Whitman's confrontation with Barclay. This time the examination tables are all occupied, each of the four corpses covered by sheets.

Without hesitation, Barclay approaches the table nearest them, flips back the sheet, and examines the corpse. It takes Whitman a moment to recognize Sheriff Harris. His body has been cleaned, and the gunshots, one in the chest, one in the forehead, are small dark holes in the skin.

"Can you hide the wounds?" Walt says.

Barclay nods. "A little makeup goes a long way for something like that. The family won't notice."

"They found him nearby, didn't they?" Walt says.

"That's right. Dr. Liston of NYU purchased this body, and when he read about Harris's murder in the newspaper, he sent a telegram to all his medical colleagues.

That's how they found the body so quickly."

Yes, I know, Whitman wants to say. *That was my article.*

"The wake is tomorrow, so I have a little work to do yet. I told Mrs. Harris I'd do it for free so she doesn't have to pay the mortician."

In spite of his loathing for the coroner, Walt admires his gesture. Harris's widow should not have to worry about the body after her husband's murder. But then it occurs to him: With the free access Barclay has to bodies as they pass through his morgue on the way to the cemetery, he controls the narrative of their deaths.

Walt looks at Harris's body again. There's a strangeness to it he can't articulate. He was with this man as he passed from life to death — a quick pull of the trigger and the bullet entered his forehead, exploding out the back.

He reaches for Harris's cheek. The skin is cold to the touch, his silver hair coarse and matted. He tilts the head to the side, so he can see the back of Harris's head —

The bullet blew out a grapefruit-size chunk of the sheriff's head, leaving behind a clumpy mix of flesh and hair and viscous fluid.

"That," Barclay says, "is more difficult to

fix, which is why the mourners will not be allowed to move the head as you have."

Miss Blackwell says, "And how do you prevent that from occurring?"

"We fasten the head to the coffin," Barclay says. "No one will be able to move the head by the time I'm finished with it."

"How nice," Walt says.

Barclay says, "So, Miss Blackwell. Mr. Whitman. To what do I owe the pleasure?"

"It's difficult for me to say this," Elizabeth says, "but I need your help."

"My help? How flattering."

"Can we sit down?" she says.

"Sure. Why not? I've nothing better to do."

"Kenneth, don't."

"Did Mr. Whitman tell you about his last visit? How he attacked me?"

Miss Blackwell looks at Whitman.

He shrugs. "Mr. Barclay deserved it."

"Mr. Whitman was upset with the way I characterized Abraham's idiosyncratic marital habits," Barclay says. "Weren't you?"

Walt holds his tongue for Elizabeth. She needs to do this, and so he will support her. "If I offended you in any way, then I apologize," he says. "It was not my best day, to be sure."

"But you think I'm wrong about Abraham, don't you?"

"What I think is irrelevant to this visit," Walt says. "I'm here as a support to Miss Blackwell."

"I saw Abraham with many women," Barclay says. "I think Lizzy knows I speak the truth."

Whitman doesn't take the bait. "Perhaps we can discuss this another time? We're here about another matter altogether."

Kenneth Barclay turns to Elizabeth Blackwell. "And you — this matter for which you seek help must be important to bring you here. If I remember correctly, your last words to me in this very room were to the opposite effect, no? *I'll never come back,* I seem to remember you saying. Is that right?"

"This was a mistake," Elizabeth says. "You were right, Mr. Whitman. We should not have come."

"No, no," Barclay says. "What is it that you need? What? Please sit." Barclay leads them to a small sitting area in front of the corner fireplace. The furnishings themselves are of the highest quality, but the presence of ample dust indicates that Barclay is an infrequent host. Barclay and Miss Blackwell sit on the sofa, and Whitman sits in the chair.

"I need bodies," she says. "I need to know where to buy bodies."

"Lizzy." Barclay sits back. "I'm not in the body trade."

"Of course not." She gathers herself. "But you can put us in touch with those who are."

"In my line of work," Barclay starts, "I encounter medical men every day, and they universally remark that women should not be doctors."

"They've always been against us," Miss Blackwell says. "You know that."

"That may be, but helping you *that way* is not a smart professional move for me."

"Why not?" Elizabeth counters. "If we can acquire cadavers, it shows the students that the school will survive." She stops. "You *want* the school to fail, don't you?"

"Why on earth would I want that?"

She is thinking now. "Of course. You've been trying to get back at Abraham since —"

"Elizabeth." Barclay rubs his chin. "Let me get you a drink." He stands, opens the cabinet door. He lifts one bottle, checks the label, and sets it down. He does the same with a second bottle. From the third bottle, he pours three small glasses of whiskey.

She raises her hand. "You know I don't drink liquor —"

"Lizzy." He hands her the glass anyway, another to Walt, raises his own, and takes a

174

sip. "I'm worried for you. You shouldn't have to agonize over running a medical school with no funds, not at your age."

She sets the glass on the cabinet ledge, sits down. "But Abraham and Lena —"

"You can't resurrect the dead, dear."

"What has happened to you, Kenneth?" she says. "You were close friends with the Stowes. *We* were close. What has changed?"

Barclay turns away.

"What is it?"

"I'm sorry, but I can't help you."

"Don't make this about us," she says.

Barclay doesn't say anything.

Miss Blackwell stands up. "I should have known better than to come here."

Barclay sounds desperate now. "You have no idea what this is all about."

"And you do?" Whitman rises to join Miss Blackwell.

"Sell the building," Barclay says, ignoring Walt, "and go home to your family."

"I'm surprised by you," she says. "Without Abraham, you'd be nothing."

"Nothing? I am what I am despite him!"

Elizabeth storms out of the room, finds her coat, and waits in the entryway while Whitman lingers.

"Abraham was *careless,*" Barclay says.

"What do you know about it?" Walt says.

"That you should encourage her to sell the building as I suggested."

"Lena was innocent, wasn't she?"

Barclay answers in a riddle. "You already know what I know."

"This isn't over between us," Whitman says. "I will find out what you know, and then all of New York will know too."

"Why not just leave it alone?"

"Because Abraham and Lena are *dead.*"

The crowded tables at Delmonico's, where South William Street meets Beaver Street, offer a public kind of privacy. It is an hour past noon. At the back of the room, carvers and cooks work to prepare a ceaseless round of lunchtime orders.

"I should have known better, Mr. Whitman. I'm sorry for wasting your time."

"Not at all, Miss Blackwell."

She appears disjointed. Strands of hair hang over her face, and her eyes bulge with fatigue.

"I know you probably have a few questions after what happened back there."

"That sounds about right," Walt says.

"The first thing you need to know is that Kenneth Barclay was Abraham Stowe's protégé long before Lena Hathaway. Indeed, it was her arrival that changed everything."

"So he didn't like her."

She shakes her head. "In fact, Barclay is the one who discovered Lena's secret." Elizabeth pauses here.

"Secret?"

"Lena pretended to be a man so she could attend medical school." She proceeds to tell the story of how Lena Hathaway took on the name of Anson Dunbar. Dressed as a man, she was a medical student for several months before Kenneth Barclay exposed her. "Yes, before Lena came along, Kenneth was the genius upstart surgeon," Miss Blackwell says. "When Kenneth earned his MD, Abraham deferred to him on everything. Kenneth led dissections, taught surgical techniques, and even took lead in surgery.

"Then this new student, Anson, arrives, and he is simply better than Kenneth at everything. Kenneth was devastated. When he later discovered Anson's secret, he thought he would retake his place as Abraham's right-hand man. But the opposite happened. Abraham and the newly discovered Lena became closer, and you know the rest."

"Ah," Walt says. "So this is why he is so interested in Abraham's indiscretion."

She nods. "But it's even slightly more

complicated than that."

The waiter brings their food: Whitman has potatoes and beef, and Miss Blackwell, the chicken and sweet potato.

"Before I was a medical student at the women's college, Kenneth and I were engaged to be married," she says.

"Married?"

Elizabeth blushes. "He was different then. He was generous and supportive. He rooted for those around him to succeed. We loved each other very much."

"What changed?"

"Kenneth introduced me to Abraham about a month after Anson arrived, and for a short time, the situation was perfect. We felt like anything was possible, like the medical world was about to explode." She pauses here, reflective. "But when Anson surpassed Kenneth, he came undone. He turned on Abraham, and he forced me to take sides." She pauses. "I chose the Stowes, and this is why he is so cold toward me. Soon after, he quit NYU and moved on to work alongside Dr. Quigley."

"Eli Quigley? The former coroner?"

She nods. "And Quigley is, well, it's hard to explain."

"On the fringes, isn't he?"

"That's a generous way of putting it," Elizabeth says.

"I read about the body-parts scandal. I know how he operates, and —"

"He's reckless and unethical." She shakes her head. "He's known for not throwing anything away. He encourages his students to discover new ways of exploring what the human body can do, but his methods are nothing short of horrible. The body-parts scandal is nothing compared to what he's doing now. He's a real Victor Frankenstein."

Whitman gives her a moment to gather her thoughts. "So Barclay studied with Quigley —"

"Oh yes, and they deserve each other. Some of my colleagues tell me that Quigley even started performing abortions and then keeping the fetuses for his students to dissect." She shakes her head. "Some doctors have claimed to see a room full of aborted fetuses kept in jars."

"Abortions?" Walt is thinking about the Mary Rogers case now.

Elizabeth says, "I know it from a few reliable sources that he does, in fact, give abortions. But what does this have to do with anything?"

"What if Quigley performed the abortion that killed Mary Rogers?"

"Let's suppose he did," she says. "Then what?"

At this, Whitman smiles. "Abraham had an affair with Mary Rogers. She ends up dead by botched abortion. When law enforcement fails to find the killer, a rumor emerges that Abraham performed said abortion to keep their relationship secret. Abraham is scapegoated for the Rogers murder, which also happens to protect the body-snatching business. Lena is held responsible for Abraham's death, and her execution closes the loop."

"That's pretty elaborate."

"Yes, but it seems to have worked," Walt says. "Will you accompany me to Dr. Quigley's place?"

"What about everything that's happened? The students are terrified. They want to go home. Can't we focus on keeping the college open, keeping the students here?"

"You have to trust me," Whitman says again. "Keeping the college open is my main goal."

She stares out the window for a moment before she says, "You'll have to go to Quigley's without me."

"Will you at least look in on Henry?"

"Henry?"

"Mr. Saunders," Walt says. "My new boss.

He's very ill and in bed."

Elizabeth smiles. "Now, that I can do."

CHAPTER 17

In the New York Hospital basement, Walt walks in on three medical students in wrinkled suits and bowler hats, posing stiffly behind a dissecting table. On their dark, stained aprons, they've painted their names in white script: *MCCRAY, GREY, & SMELHOVEN.* A partially dissected corpse is propped up, cross-legged, arms folded in its lap as if it's waiting for a train. On his head is a bowler hat; on the table, the students have painted *We have shuffled off his mortal coil.*

A daguerreotypist holds up his finger. "Steady . . . steady now, boys . . ."

"Wait!" Grey, a beefy, athletic sort, comes around from behind, takes a half-smoked cigar out of his mouth, and jams it between the jaws of the cadaver. The others laugh as he puts his arm around the cadaver, and the daguerreotypist reminds them to stay still if they want the image to work.

Whitman waits until the daguerreotypist signals that he's finished to approach the very average-looking man in charge, watching from across the room. Average height, average weight, neat brown hair, well-groomed beard, and gentle eyes. If you were to see this fellow on the street, Walt muses, you would look straight past him, everything about him suggesting safety and comfort, everything but his bloody apron around which hangs a makeshift holster for variously sized scalpels.

"Dr. Quigley?"

The man nods. "At your service."

"Walt Whitman. I'm here from the *Aurora* newspaper, doing a story on grave robbing, body snatching, what comes after, that type of thing." He breathes deeply. "I understand that some of the bodies end up here."

"It's not illegal to *have* these bodies, Mr. Whitman." Dr. Quigley opens his arms as if to include the entire hospital. "It is only illegal for us to acquire them."

"I'm not interested in the legality," Walt says. "I want to know —"

"I know what you want to know, Mr. Whitman. I've read your *Aurora* article. I've read Bennett's response. I knew the Stowes."

"You did?"

Quigley's face changes. "Of course I knew Abe. He and I worked together on early drafts of the Bone Bill legislation."

Walt doesn't know what to say.

Quigley continues: "I'm the one who proposed it to Abe. I want to be able to do my work legally and without the nuisance of dealing with the resurrectionists. Think about the irony, Mr. Whitman. Medical doctors rely on criminals so they can learn how to care for the same folks who want to lock the criminals up for doing the very thing that allows them to live longer and healthier lives than the criminals."

"So have you dealt with Samuel Clement?"

"Everyone has," Quigley says. "He's good at what he does. If you need a body, he will get it for you within a day or two. If all body snatchers were like him, then this would all be a lot easier."

Suddenly, a clanging noise sounds from across the room — the rod holding up the corpse's head has fallen to the floor, and Quigley's students are laughing. Quigley sighs. "You'll have to forgive them. They're just blowing off steam."

"I would have thought they'd have had enough of that at Yale."

McCray and Smelhoven are holding the

body upright while Grey reinstalls the rod beneath its chin. "Don't forget the cigar!" Smelhoven stuffs it back into place.

"Excuse me," Quigley says, drifting toward his students. "Smelhoven!"

"Sir?"

"I thought I put you in charge."

"You did, sir."

Quigley angrily yanks the cigar out of the stiff's mouth.

"This is a disgrace."

The three students exchange looks. Smelhoven looks at Walt.

"Oh, I see," Smelhoven says, winking. "This most certainly is a disgrace. We are, all of us, ashamed. Forgive us as we may never forgive ourselves."

McCray and Grey nudge each other.

Dr. Quigley turns his attention back to Whitman. "You're welcome to stay and watch. We have a newborn today, a very unusual thing. Maybe you'll learn something about yourself."

"A newborn," Walt says. "What do you mean, a newborn?"

"When the soul leaves the body, all that's left behind is the material," Quigley says. "From that material, we can learn more than you can imagine. Aren't you the least bit curious to look inside the body of a hu-

185

man so young? Perhaps its organs are not yet fully developed. Perhaps we can determine how and why it died. Perhaps we can save such a baby in the future because we look inside." Quigley pauses. "And what right do we have to waste God's gift?"

Walt follows Quigley to another table, on top of which lies a draped object so small one might mistake it for a loaf of bread, and he can't help but think of the Stowes' unborn daughter.

Quigley rubs his fingers along the canvas sheet before removing it. The baby, a boy, appears like a doll, its eyes closed, its mouth open, and its skin waxy. There's a familiar quality to the body, one remove away from a living and breathing baby, the difference striking enough to make it seem re-created, like a sculpture. Whitman reaches out but pulls back.

Quigley notices. "Go ahead."

Walt touches the chest, stomach, and forehead. He tugs gently at the short black hair. He runs his finger down the front of the face, tracing the nose and the lips, and over the chin and down to the scrunched-up neck. The body is cramped together and tiny, and though it is dead, it is real, its layers of skin and muscle, bone and sinew, its heart, liver, lungs, veins.

"Isn't it beautiful?" Quigley says.

It is.

The body — parsed from its life, its mother and father, its siblings, its house — is art. Its new context is a series of images: the dissection table, the white sheet, the doctor and his averageness, the knife, the students face by face, the brick wall, and the window letting in only a peephole's worth of daylight.

Whitman can't say this to a quack doctor, and so instead he asks, "How did you acquire this corpse?"

"That is none of your business."

Walt asks, "Through an abortion?"

"Now, where did you hear something so ghastly as that?"

"I've heard that you perform abortions here, then keep the fetuses for your experiments."

Quigley shakes his head. "I'm a medical doctor, and I take my patients' well-being very seriously. I also respect their privacy."

"Did you give Mary Rogers an abortion?"

"The cigar girl?"

Walt nods.

Quigley shakes his head. "I understand that what we do might seem repugnant to the uninitiated, but we are" — he gestures to his students — "engaged in a mission to understand the workings of the human body for the improvement of us all. We understand that you would prefer to benefit from what we do while pretending not to know how we do it.

"But when you come in here and toss out reckless accusations about our connection to unsolved murder cases — that, sir, is unethical. You want to know where we get our corpses? You want to hear me say it? There is not a legal way for us to procure the very thing we need to do our jobs. So we rely on the dregs of society to provide us with what our own government should." He touches the baby's head. "But this corpse was donated to us by a heartbroken mother who wants to understand why her son died only moments after his birth."

"What about Kenneth Barclay?"

Quigley's face darkens. "What about him?"

"He was your student."

"Was."

"And you helped him get the coroner job."

Quigley nods. "Much to my regret."

"Why is that?"

"Again, none of your business."

"Has he ever brought you women who need abortions?"

"I thought we'd moved past this," he says.

"This is not an abortion factory, Mr. Whitman. I have helped a handful of women who had nowhere else to turn. I have used the remains to learn about the development of the human fetus, something I don't expect you to understand." He takes a deep breath. "I'm trying to be helpful here."

"Is it true that you keep a room full of fetuses?"

Quigley shakes his head. "Everything I do, and all anybody knows about is that?"

Walt says, "It's true, isn't it?"

"It's insulting that my life and career are reduced to that one thing. I'm not Dr. Frankenstein."

Walt looks up.

"I'm not an idiot," Quigley says. "I know what people say."

"But why would you?"

"You want to see it? You want to be titillated by the scandal of it? Well, then, sir, follow me."

Whitman is aware of the medical students watching them as the two men leave the dissection lab for a smaller room next to it. But Walt doesn't care about them — he's like Leontius in Plato's *Republic,* who cannot look away from the heap of executed corpses. But for Walt, it's even more than compulsion and curiosity; it's as if he needs to see the human artifacts to confront that thing deep within his soul, the myth of heaven, of peace and night, of beauty.

And so he follows.

The room is dark and dank. Whitman can't see a thing until Quigley lights the lamp, and they come into view. Shelves and shelves of jars containing various body parts and organs. Hearts and lungs and livers, hands, feet, eyeballs, and a jawbone, its teeth still intact. A man's head, cross-sectioned in two beakers displayed side by side, pickled in yellow fluid, the brain, esophagus, nostrils, and eye sockets arranged like a painting; an intestine coiled neatly in a jar like a thick worm; and a fetus, whole, pressed up against the glass like an odd-colored flower before it blooms. There's a hanging skeleton, its flesh not so neatly removed, scads of flesh and blood, shiny and gristled, still attached, and a bleached fetal skeleton, with two club feet, sitting in the corner, its eye sockets disproportionately large in its fist-size skull.

"Indulge yourself, Mr. Whitman. Tell the world about my ill-gotten collection. Sensationalize my commitment to medical progress. Give your readers something they not only cannot understand but refuse to consider. These are my specimens. These are my teachers. And from every one of them I have learned something that may keep you alive."

The sheer enormity of the collection overwhelms Walt. He looks away, but there is no *away* in this room, and he has to confront these objects, and so he regards them as they are, their colors and shapes, their escarpments and edges, their flesh and fluid, grimy and gelatinous, rigid, flaky, sharp, and he feels pulled at by their odd beauty, their untranslatable state, and he is overcome with the sense of his own decomposition, his flung likeness, coaxed to vapor and dusk, and he gives himself to the image of his impending death, to the dirt where he will grow among the grass he loves, to this odd pulchritude.

"I know you see it," Quigley says.

"But it's unnatural."

"No, you're wrong." Quigley swings his arm. "They are the most natural things here. This building, the clothes we're wearing, our pretense — these hold us back. These are unnatural. We are moving away from what we are. We should all become more natural, as Mr. Emerson has written."

"You read Emerson?"

"Contain your shock," Quigley says. "You

and I are more alike than you want to admit."

Whitman is thinking about what the doctor said, and then he's thinking about the doctor, and he's looking at this very average man in front of him, and he's wondering how the hell he ended up in this room with these things, and how it is that the doctor has begun to sound rational. Walt shakes his head, and reminds himself why he's here. The rest of it, natural or unnatural, is not relevant.

Walt gathers himself, restarts. "What do you think happened to Mary Rogers?"

"I don't know."

"Do you think Abraham botched an abortion that led to her death?"

He shakes his head. "He was a good man."

"Are there other abortionists out there who might have?"

"There are more than you think," Quigley says. "Do you realize how difficult life is if you're a woman? Men take advantage of you repeatedly and then when you become pregnant as a result — *That's your problem, life is sacred, train up a child in the way he must go.* There are those among us who understand this, and we will do what we can to help these women retain even a modicum of control over their own lives in a world that barely recognizes them as anything other than property."

"So someone may have botched an abortion, panicked, and dumped Rogers's body in the river?"

"Of course."

"And what about Abraham Stowe? Why was he murdered?"

"Sounds like his wife got wind of his deep and abiding friendships with other women."

"What do you know about that?" Walt says.

"It's no secret," Quigley says. "He was a good man but not a perfect one. Like us all."

Whitman closes his eyes. He's been clinging to a particular version of Abraham for so long that he has failed to be objective. He thought the infidelity was in the past despite all the evidence to the contrary. A good but imperfect man indeed.

Quigley says, "You really didn't know, did you?"

Walt looks up, his eyes watering. "Do you think she killed him?"

"I'm too old to be surprised by much of anything anymore." Quigley puts his hand on Walt's shoulder. "Take heart. If it matters at all, I don't believe Lena killed

Abraham. They were fine people. Both of them."

Walt reminds himself, *I'm a reporter, not a copper. I should be otherwise engaged.*

"Now if you'll excuse me, Mr. Whitman, we have work to do." Quigley pats him on the shoulder again. "You're welcome to stay. Watch for a while. See what it is that we do in this dark place. I think you will discover, like we have, that the same beauty that belongs in life also resides in death."

Whitman follows Quigley back into the dissection lab, where the students are waiting with the tiny body. They are trying to read Walt to see what his response was to the specimen collection, no doubt, and he is careful not to betray any emotion in his face. He tries so hard to appear unaffected, however, that he feels exposed anyway. They don't seem to notice. He's committed now. He can't leave, if only to show that he can handle what he's seen.

The students make room for him around the dissection table, and they listen to Dr. Quigley, who explains the incision he's about to make in the tiny corpse. Quigley lowers the scalpel into the baby's belly button, pulls the blade up through the center of its chest, through the top layer of skin and fat, and stops just short of the heart.

He puts his hands on either side of the incision and peels back the skin, a few inches at a time, while the students and Walt stand on their toes to see what is inside.

CHAPTER 18

With the images of the specimen collection still scrolling in his head, Whitman plods along the sidewalk toward Mrs. Chipman's boardinghouse. The short March day has already lost its light, flickered away, hurtled toward darkness.

Now, that is a titch melodramatic, he thinks.

He hopes Henry is feeling better for having spent the day in bed. He wants to tell him all about his visit to the coroner with Miss Blackwell, his trip to the Museum de Quigley, and the ensuing dissection. Walt had ended up staying through the entire process. The tiny corpse revealed much to the students, but nothing so prescient as the poor thing's underdeveloped lungs. Dr. Quigley removed the lungs and laid them on the table. With his scalpel, he traced the approximate size of a developed fetal lung in contrast with what these were, and though the difference was slight, it was vital,

Quigley explained, and deadly. Whitman was struck by the precision of what had seemed to him before to be a strictly theoretical act — the body is a machine that can be understood by taking it apart — and he wants to tell this not only to Henry but to Abraham and Lena as well. *I understand it now,* he wants to tell them.

The first floor of the boardinghouse smells like piss and mold. The boarders have taken to relieving themselves in the recently installed shared sinks. The once ornate molding lining the ceiling and floor has begun to rot, and the wallpaper has bubbled, some of it falling away in complete pieces. Everything is falling apart, and he's overcome with the desire to preserve something that will not die. He can't explain it other than to say that he understands some of what Quigley is doing is preserving the stuff of humanity. He climbs the stairs to the third floor, knocks on Henry's door, and to his surprise, it is Elizabeth Blackwell herself who answers.

Her eyes betray her exhaustion, but she smiles to see him.

"You are still here," Walt says. "I'm so relieved. How is he?"

"I'm fine," Henry calls out before Miss Blackwell can answer.

She nods, shakes her head, shrugs. "Maybe a little better," she whispers.

"I heard that," Henry says, "and I'm doing *a lot* better."

Walt steps inside to see for himself. Henry is in bed trying to put on a good face, but it is clear that he is not yet well. Pale, feverish, fighting hard but losing.

"See?" Henry forces another smile. "Better."

"Let's ask the expert," Walt says.

"The bad news is he still has the flu," Miss Blackwell says. "The good news is he will recover." She wags her finger at Henry. "But you must stay in bed."

"Today, yes," Henry says, "but what about tomorrow? Surely I'll be able to go to the Runkels with Walt."

"Tomorrow," she interrupts, "you will remain in bed."

"But —"

"And the day after," Miss Blackwell says. "No *buts,* Mr. Saunders. Doctor's orders."

Henry says, "But women cannot officially become doctors, can they? Which means —"

Miss Blackwell's face reddens at this, but catches the grin on Henry's face and relaxes. "It's true I have no medical license, but what that means to me is that I can experiment on you, try all the things that medicine

198

forbids, all the procedures I've been dreaming of." She pauses, grins herself. "Something to keep in mind anyway."

Henry lies down. "I'll remain in bed."

Walt is struck by the realization that Henry is now firmly a part of his world, and he worries for Henry's health as he would for a family member. How strange to become so close in such a short time, and how grateful he is Henry decided to return.

"Thank you, Miss Blackwell, for looking after him."

"When will you call me Elizabeth as I've asked?"

"*Elizabeth,* then," Walt says.

She smiles. "I'll see you back at the college?"

"Certainly," Walt says, "but right now I need to be here with Mr. Saunders."

"I understand, and perhaps you'll fill me in on the details of your visit with Eli Quigley when I next see you."

Walt turns. "You were right about him."

"I was?"

"An entire room full of specimens."

"My God."

Whitman nods. "But it was more complicated."

"Complicated? Whatever do you mean?"

Whitman shifts his stance, forming a

triangle between the three of them so that Henry is a part of the conversation too, and then he tells them about the room — he's careful to inflect his description with words that complicate Quigley as a physician rather than reduce him to a quack. Henry shows little emotion as he speaks, but Miss Blackwell's mouth tenses, and her natural expression of indifference turns into rage. She's not persuaded.

She's shaking her head now, and Walt decides that this is quite enough, so he leaves out the fetal dissection altogether. He waits for her to speak, but she says nothing. "Am I to infer from your gestures that you are not convinced?"

"You are right to infer such an idea," she says.

"Might I ask why?"

"How are we ever going to make real medical progress with such an ethos as Eli Quigley's? I don't disagree with his notion of beauty and materiality, as you've put it, but we are in the minority. It is our job to convince a skeptical majority that anatomical dissection, and its accompanying issues, is a worthy price to pay for medical progress, and keeping a museum of body parts is not the way to do this. The inside of the body is beautiful — it's the most beautiful thing

I've ever seen — but we must be mindful how all this appears to the uninitiated."

Walt cannot disagree with Elizabeth's point of view, but he also remains convinced by Quigley's, and he's wondering then about beauty and its long tentacles, good and bad, and how they reach out into the world. He yearns for a way to articulate beauty's expansiveness, its cathartic pricking of the soul and its gross fecundity of decay. It strikes him that this might be why Henry prefers his poetry to his prose. Poetry has the capability, like a painting, to capture an object without the constraints of linearity. Walt feels as if something inside him is opening up, and he's able to see the complexity of beauty through Elizabeth Blackwell's careful and political respect for the human body *and* through Eli Quigley's reckless admiration for its beauty in all phases of life and death, the way the body demands attention of all our senses.

"Mr. Whitman?" Elizabeth says. "Did Dr. Quigley have any useful information about Abraham and Lena?"

"Oh, right." Walt relates what he learned about the many abortionists, about Quigley's work with Abraham on the Bone Bill, and his belief in the Stowes' innocence. But Walt doesn't reveal his own naïveté regarding Abraham's infidelities.

"That's good to hear," Miss Blackwell says. "I'm not so foolish as to turn away allies."

Whitman helps her with her coat, holds the front door open for her as she leaves. "Good night, Elizabeth."

"Good night, Walt," she says, then starts down the stairs.

Walt shuts the door, sits on the chair next to Henry's bed.

"She's a dear woman," Henry says. "She's been here for several hours taking care of me. I'm glad we are helping her."

Walt likes hearing this, and he likes hearing Henry use the word *we* almost as much. "She is fond of you too."

Henry coughs, and his entire body shakes.

Walt places his hand on Henry's shoulder. "Take your time," he says.

When Henry finally stops, he looks exhausted.

Walt tells him not to worry about speaking now, to instead focus on recovery.

And so while Henry rests, Walt brews tea and recounts the news of the last two days. He pays particular attention to the revelations about Azariah's servitude to Rynders, and he watches as Henry's eyes widen with astonishment.

With tea in hand, Walt puts his arm around Henry, holds the cup up to his lips — Henry's hands are shaking — and helps him drink. When Henry has had enough of the tea, Walt dumps the remaining kettle water, which is still warm, into a washbasin. He finds a cloth, which he drops into the water, and then he washes his friend's neck and face and arms just as Henry did for him a couple of nights before, all the while reminding Henry to relax, to do what it takes to get better, and saying that when he has, the two of them will finish what they've started.

While Henry sleeps, Walt straightens up the room, washing and putting dishes away, folding up stray clothing, careful to sort out those that need laundering. It's difficult to explain, but he feels at home here. He feels a part of something, and the best part is he knows Henry feels the same way.

Walt turns up the lamp next to the bed. Henry's color is better. His forehead is dry. He appears to be cycling out of the illness. Whitman allows his mind to spool out of the moment, to a time when the two of them might go to the opera together, ride the Brooklyn ferry, or just walk the Bowery. His happiness is so great he simply cannot sit still. He goes to the window, but there's nothing to see except the gas lamps a block away, burning in the haze, and he's reminded of Emerson's transparent eyeball. Walt wishes that he too could see all, be part and parcel with God. Emerson writes that in such a state "the name of the nearest friend sounds then foreign and accidental," but there is only one name on Walt's mind. Emerson wants expansive truth, wants to find God, wants the currents of the Universal Being coursing through him —

— but all Walt wants is Henry.

From the window, the earth recedes from Walt into the night, and he sees that it is beautiful, and he sees that what is not the earth is beautiful.

He turns from the window, from the vastness of the city to the particularity of his friend. Henry's chest rises and falls. Inside, he will resemble the corpses of Lena and the baby, but his insides also contain that thing which animates them all. Emerson misses this, Walt thinks. He is looking for God outside of himself, looking for God in nature, looking for God instead of looking for light within, and this is what the Quaker Elias Hicks understood: The light is inside all of us, living or dead.

Walt tosses a blanket onto the floor next

to the wood-burning stove. He stokes the fire, tosses in another piece of wood, leaving the door open long enough to make sure it will burn. Then he lies on the floor, his coat folded up as a pillow again, and he dreams in his dream all the dreams of the other dreamers.

CHAPTER 19

The next day, the air is mild as it often is before a good snowstorm, and ten thousand vehicles careen through the streets of the affluent. Inside one omnibus is Walt Whitman, en route to the Runkels. Both he and Henry Saunders slept late this morning, and for the first time in several days, Walt actually is feeling like himself. He wishes he could say the same thing for Henry. Though he has improved, Henry still has a fever and body aches. He has recovered some of his appetite, and so before he left the room this morning, Walt made a breakfast of eggs, toast, and ham. Henry ate as he hasn't in several days, and he was eager to change into fresh clothing. Walt helped him with that too. Last of all, he made sure the fire would continue to burn for a few hours, and then he left for the *Aurora,* where he produced the day's edition in record time. If Henry felt better tonight, they planned to eat supper at the Pewter Mug, where Walt has promised to fill him in on what he learns today.

Broadway Ike swings the omnibus around the corner, the dividing line between rich and poor, and sputters to a stop, waits for Whitman to hop out before swerving back into traffic and disappearing around the bend. Walt stretches his legs and buttons up his coat. His beard itches under the wool scarf, and his chapped lips sting.

The streets and buildings breathe people. Heads stick out of windows, men and women move in and out of open front doors, and children bounce through it all. The noises travel in and out of each other with no beginning and no end — dogs chase pigs in gutters clogged with sewage, chickens squawk and flap their wings as if they can fly. And the pungent odors created by the marshlands nearby hover oppressively, as if the entire neighborhood has spoiled.

In the long row of tenements before him, each building appears more dilapidated than the last. Most are two stories high; some are three; a few single-story buildings remain. Many of the windows have been broken or removed. Those that remain intact have gaping holes between the frames and the walls around them so that residents have to battle the cold air that rushes in on every floor and in every room.

The wooden staircase to his left is barely functional. Each of the remaining steps, nothing more than slabs of wood, bow in the middle, and the space between them is dangerously large.

He bends down to see three barefoot children sleeping huddled together. A girl with sunken eyes and cheeks, the oldest, leans into the corner, and uses her hat as a pillow against the brick wall. A smaller boy next to her wraps his arms around her torso and presses himself into her while another even younger boy lies in their laps. Their tiny bodies expand and contract together in one mass.

He wonders where their parents are, if they have any at all. When Walt was growing up, the Whitmans never had much money, and his father squandered most of what did come in, but it was never this severe. Every New Yorker knows about the thousands of orphans around the city, but to see them like this is different, worse. Whitman often spends his nights at one of the beer halls one street over, oblivious to their suffering.

They are only children — what chance do they have? He kneels. "Excuse me," he calls out to the sleeping children.

They don't stir. So he finds a few coins in his pocket and tosses them down. They land on the ground in front of the children, nearly roll into a grate he hadn't noticed. Now he understands. They sleep there for the heat that comes from tunnels below, their bare feet strewn across the metal bars.

Walt backs out of the alleyway and from where he stands, he has a view of the Old Brewery, once the famous Coulthard's Brewery built in 1792 and now a ramshackle dwelling for several hundred people. The five-story building was painted yellow long ago, but that paint has peeled away, taking down many of the clapboards with it. When he looks closer, the faces of at least fifty people loom in the broken windows. Like the others in the alleyway, they only stare at him, their eyes lit up like funeral candles.

That is where he has to go.

As if the living spaces are part of some elaborate, multifloored theater, humans fill the space in every imaginable way, in rooms without doors — one woman in a frayed orange shawl stirs a pot of what looks like potatoes on a stove while in the room next door a couple copulates, he with his pants pulled down and she with her dress pushed up. A barefoot baby in a blue nightgown sits on the ground next to them and plays with an iron key, thick and rusted. They pay Walt no attention as he makes his way up the stairway to where the Runkels live.

On the second floor, at least in this wing, conditions improve. Fewer people lie in the halls. Some of the rooms have walls and doors, but no numbers. So he counts from left to right, from one to eight, and on that door he knocks.

The door opens. "You found us." Harriet wipes her hands on her apron and shakes his hand. "Where's Mr. Saunders?"

"He came down with a fever," Walt says. "He sends his regrets."

"Sorry to hear it," she says. "Come in, and I'll get Ned."

The front door opens to the kitchen, a tiny room no larger than five feet by five feet with a wood-burning stove that nearly fills the space. Opposite the stove, potato peels are piled on the floor, which slants toward the back wall, and a dog lounges against the wall, his tongue flapping out of his mouth.

A small girl tugs on Whitman's jacket.

"*Who* did that?" He laughs to let her know he's not serious.

Her long brown hair is parted on the left side and hangs down over her eyes. Her cheeks are rounded in baby fat. The dress she wears is at least two sizes too big, her tiny frame almost invisible inside it.

"Call me Abby."

Harriet Runkel returns with her husband, Ned, who walks with his right hand under her arm. Half of Mr. Runkel's body is crippled — his left hand curls up in a ball and when he walks, he drags his left leg.

"In here." They lead Whitman through the doorway to the other room, which is only three times as big as the kitchen. Two beds line the walls, a clothesline droops down the middle as a barrier between the beds, and a shabby brown dresser has been installed under the window even though it doesn't fit the space. On one wall hangs a small cabinet displaying the family's china even though there is no table to set it on. Next to the cabinet is a tattered wardrobe, the doors of which won't shut, exposing the two coats and three dresses hanging inside.

Ned and Harriet sit on one bed while Walt and Abby sit on the other.

Abby takes his hand and rubs it as she speaks. "I prayed to God, and he told me he'd send someone to help us. That must be you." Her fingers feel brittle in his hand.

"You remind me of my sister Mary," Whitman says. "The way you speak, so much like a grown-up."

And then Abby cries. "The minister said

if we don't find Maggie, she won't get resurrected."

"Abby." Mr. Runkel sits up straight when he speaks.

"Well, that's what he said."

Walt places his hand on her shoulder. "I don't think God would allow that, now, do you?"

Harriet touches Abby's other shoulder. "Why don't you finish peeling those potatoes for dinner?"

Abby wipes her eyes on her sleeve. "You said that when the priest speaks, it's like the Lord himself."

"Abigail Helen Runkel."

"Yes, ma'am." Before Abby leaves the room, she curtsies.

"She doesn't understand death," Ned says. "She pretends that Maggie will come home, that finding her body will somehow resurrect her. Poor thing. Difficult being an only child now."

"Maggie took Abby everywhere," Mrs. Runkel says. "They shared a bed, and they shared clothes. Abby didn't mind that they didn't always fit her."

Ned continues. "Now she wants to be a doctor too."

"Maggie was unique," Harriet says. "She understood people. She had a gift with them. Could get along with anyone in any situation. If she were here now, she would already know everything about you."

Ned turns to Harriet. "Get the sketches, love, will you?"

She steps over to a small stack of books and notebooks in the corner past the wardrobe, picks one, and hands it to Walt. Inside, Maggie has drawn page after page of human anatomy, and like the drawings in the college, they are precise. The leg size matches the arm size and the head matches the torso.

"Impressive," Walt says. "How did she learn?"

Harriet reaches down and produces a book entitled *The Anatomy of Human Bodies* by William Cowper. "Neighbor gave it to Maggie for her eighth birthday. She's been doing these sketches ever since."

Walt turns the pages, and as he progresses through the notebook, the sketches become more and more about what is inside the body than what is on the outside.

"I need to ask the obvious question," Whitman says. "Why not leave her? It seems like the perfect place for her body, given her interests." He's thinking about Lena's donation to the women's college, Quigley's museum of specimens, the dissected baby.

Harriet asks, "Would you leave your sister?"

The image of Mary or Hannah on a dissection table turns his stomach.

"Of course not," Harriet answers for him.

Walt says, "I only meant that Maggie seems to have understood the importance of her own material body. Dissection allows us to learn more about the human body than ever before." He pauses. "I know doctors who believe they are close to a cure for cholera. Can you imagine how the world would change if that comes to pass?"

Ned says, "Do you believe in the resurrection, Mr. Whitman?"

He's not sure, but he says he does.

"What do you suppose happens to the soul that tries to return to the dissected body?"

The same thing that happens to a nondissected body, Whitman thinks, but remains silent.

"Nothing," Ned says. "Nothing happens."

"This is about more than Maggie's body," Mrs. Runkel says. "This is about her salvation."

Harriet helps Ned stand. "Come, Mr. Whitman. We want to introduce you around." They go out the front door and knock on the door to room number seven.

An older woman answers the door and smiles. She has no teeth. "Oh, good," the older woman says. "You're here."

"Good afternoon," Ned says. "Mrs. Swinburne, this is Mr. Walt Whitman, the man who is writing the article about Maggie."

"Oh," Mrs. Swinburne says. "How do you do?"

Walt takes her hand.

"Mrs. Swinburne, did they ever find your husband's body?" Mr. Runkel asks.

She shakes her head. "Sadly, no. And I can't bear to think about poor Mikey, wherever it is that he ended up. Those horrible medical folks think they can play God. Well, I hope one day they realize what they've done —" At this, she stops and wipes her eyes on her sleeve.

Ned touches her shoulder. "We're all in this together. That's why Mr. Whitman is here. To help us all."

Mrs. Swinburne nods, but keeps her head down.

"And what about your son's body, Mrs. Traubel?" Harriet asks.

Mrs. Traubel pokes her head into the room, "Nobody looked, dear. You know that."

Whitman touches her shoulder. "I'm sorry."

"They think we don't understand," Mrs. Traubel says, her blue eyes fierce. "They think we don't know anything."

"Of course you do," says Walt.

Ned turns to him. "At least half the people in this building have had a family member snatched from their graves, and none of them are ever found."

A man hidden in the shadows leans up onto his knees and grabs Whitman's arm, startling him. "Find our Maggie, won't you?" His wrinkled face radiates a calm confidence when he speaks. "I'd wring every one of their necks if I could."

"Was it your wife, sir, who went missing?" Walt says to the man gripping his arm.

"My son." The man dips his head. "My poor Jacob, God rest his soul."

Whitman follows Ned and Harriet back into the Runkels' rooms.

"That was Mr. Lankton," Harriet says. "His son was hanged for robbery and murder, then dissected as part of his sentence."

"That's terrible."

Ned glances about him. "It's all terrible here."

Walt says, "The article will be published in the next few days. But I have to be honest — the chances that they will find your

216

daughter's body in one piece —"

Ned stops him. "We *know,* Mr. Whitman. But we want to *try.*"

"One more thing," Walt says. "Can I borrow Maggie's drawings?"

Harriet hands him the notebook. "Remember what Mrs. Traubel said: We're not stupid, Mr. Whitman. Remember that when you write your article."

As he prepares to leave, Abby calls to him from the other side of the room. "Wait." She runs to him, holding out a single piece of paper. "I don't draw so good, so I wrote you a poem." She smiles. "You can read it when you get home."

"I can't wait." Whitman folds up the piece of paper and slips it into his pocket. "We'll help them find your sister," he says. "I promise."

CHAPTER 20

Walt pushes on until he reaches John Mc-Cleester's three-story drinking and gaming establishment. Built shortly after the Great Fire of 1835 on Elizabeth Street, the red brick is bright in the snow, its white sign McCLEESTER'S marked in black letters. Inside, business is slow. Card games at two tables, the rest empty. A dozen or so bar girls, in tight dresses and heavy makeup, devote their attention to the players, pretending to hang on their every word.

The bar is tended by McCleester himself, a thick man with his shirtsleeves rolled up over his elbows, known around the city for his 101-round bout with prizefighter Tom Hyer in 1841. He's speaking to a young woman with black hair. She is beautiful, but there is a hardness to her beauty — maybe it's the way the edges of her mouth tilt downward or her sunken cheeks or her dark eyes, or the combination of all those things, but she appears fierce.

She sees Walt come in and approaches.

"What is your pleasure, sir?"

"I'm looking for Frankie."

"And what do you need her for?" Her voice bears the same toughness as her face.

He feels self-conscious playing this role, and he worries she'll see right through it. He takes a deep breath, delivers his line: "A short meeting," he says, his voice shaky.

"Well, sir, your night just got better," she says. "Because that's me. I only need a moment — you wait here."

She didn't hesitate, and he's relieved. But the performance is only going to get more difficult, he knows. What is he going to do in the room? How far will he have to let this play out? She's not unattractive. He supposes he can go as far as he needs to get the information.

Over at the bar, she folds her apron and whispers something to McCleester. Then she returns to Walt. "I'm ready."

He nods.

"Aren't you forgetting something?" She's holding her hand open.

Of course, the money. He reaches into his pocket for two five-dollar coins, drops them in her hand.

"Thank you." She turns and tosses one of

the coins to McCleester. He catches it easily, nods, and returns to wiping glasses.

Whitman looks self-consciously at the card players, but they are so caught up in what they are doing, they don't even notice Walt and Frankie leaving together. He's been to such places before. He's not inexperienced.

But this was all before Henry.

If they had come to the tavern together, if Henry was not ill, then one of them would still have had to play this role, Whitman knows. But everything is different now. He suddenly yearns to be home with Henry again, like the night before, and he considers backing out.

Keep the college going. Lena's voice is still fresh in his mind, and so he redoubles his efforts, gives over to the performance.

Frankie leads Whitman by the hand up two flights of stairs to the third floor, past the sounds of music and dancing on the second.

He thinks of Elizabeth and her students. He can do it.

The third floor is a quiet hallway containing three, maybe four doors. Frankie's hand is warm, and her lilac perfume trails behind her. "This is it." They stop at the second door on the left, which she opens with a key from around her neck.

"You can set your clothes on the chair," she says. "I'll return shortly." Frankie exits through a door on the other side of the room.

The small room contains a bed, a mirror, a chair, and a washbasin. Nothing else. He sits on the bed, stands up, sits down again. He knows she expects him to undress, but that is, of course, unnecessary.

Over at the washbasin, he splashes water on his face and arms. He rubs his face and neck dry with a towel, and when he turns around, she is there, watching him, in nothing but a red negligee.

"Are you shy?" She smiles. "Let me help you."

He starts to protest, but the words don't come.

She unbuttons his shirt, presses her lips against his neck. The familiar sensations return swiftly, and he wonders if it would be okay to see this one through. She removes his shirt, washes his back, and the feeling is so similar to what Henry did to him a few days before that he shrugs away from her.

"That's enough," he says.

"You're so nervous," Frankie says. "Is this your first time?"

"Can't we just talk?"

"We can do whatever you want to." She kisses his neck again. *"Relax."*

She drags her fingernails along his shoulder blade, then weaves them across his back. Her hands wrap around his chest, slide down to his stomach and rest where his legs meet his torso. They stay like this for what seems like minutes before she begins to remove his trousers. He stands up so she can slide them down to his knees, and then she turns him around so she can reach him. He closes his eyes, and in his mind, it is Henry and not her at all, but that image troubles him, and the guilt returns. He knows he should tell her to stop, but he can't —

Henry's face flashes in his mind and suddenly he can see past the moment —

Abraham.

Lena.

The women's college.

Walt opens his eyes. "I can't."

She looks up at him. "Doesn't it feel good?"

"Oh, it feels amazing," he says. "But this is not why I'm here."

She smiles. "We'll get there. Be patient." She resumes her work, and he lets her. But he's too aware of himself trying to let it hap-

pen, and then it doesn't, and he's too worried to enjoy it. He stares at the washbasin,
trying to recall his time with Henry, the
washing, the kissing, and on the bed, but he
just can't.

Walt says, "I can pay you double."

"Double? For what?"

"If you tell me what you know about Samuel Clement."

She stands. "I don't know anybody by that
name."

"So he's not your brother?"

"Oh, honey, I wish he weren't." Her swift-
ness surprises him. She presses the side of a
blade against his neck. "For your sake." Her
hand is shaking, and the blade pinches his
skin. "Why did you come here?" she says.
"How do you know who I am?"

"Your brother murdered Sheriff Harris."

He feels her hand relax. "But the newspapers said he had nothing to do with it."

"I *saw* him pull the trigger," Whitman
says, taking a deep breath. "And now he's
letting the man who works for him, James
Warren, take the fall."

She lowers the knife, steps back.

"A sister should never have to make this
terrible choice," Walt says, "but an innocent
man will hang if we don't act."

She reaches down to the floor, looking for

something. He assumes she's gathering her things, but then she bangs her boot against the floor three times.

"Now, why did you have to go and do that?"

"I'm not turning in my brother," she says.

Footsteps on the stairs.

Walt says, "Where is Samuel?"

"Ask the new sheriff."

"Petty? What does he know?"

"He —"

"Frankie!" McCleester's voice behind the other door calls. "What is it?"

And with that, she disappears through the other door and into the hallway, which leaves Walt to deal with the fighter alone. McCleester is suddenly inside, swinging his fists in the air, and Whitman ducks, slips past him, and out into the hallway. As Walt runs, carrying his jacket, he slides his suspenders into place and tucks his unbuttoned shirt into his pantaloons. Ahead of him, Frankie Clement is going down the back stairway, which probably leads outside.

Whitman beats McCleester to the stairwell, takes two stairs at a time down the two flights, and exits the building in time to see Frankie disappear around the corner at the end of the alleyway and onto the main thoroughfare. Walt glances over his shoulder.

The fighter, athletic and agile, is still in pursuit. But Whitman is athletic and agile too. He sprints to the end of the alley, and explodes into the street, where the snow has become a blizzard. Hundreds of pedestrians, taxis, and horses struggle to make way by gas lamp. He won't be able to find Frankie, but McCleester won't be able to find him, either.

He runs until he is safely on Canal Street, the straightest route to Mrs. Chipman's boardinghouse.

Walt turns the corner, and he stops in front of Henry's building. It is quiet here. Leading up to the entrance, the snow is completely undisturbed but for two sets of footprints leading out from the building. His own feet mark his progress toward the front door, where he stamps the snow from his feet.

He trudges up the stairs, and when he reaches Henry's floor, he sees that the door is open.

"Henry?"

The flurries swirl about through the open window.

"Henry."

And then he's scrambling about inside, searching for any sign of him. Walt lights a candle that he finds lying on the floor, and as it burns brighter, the disarray comes into view: dishes, pots, books, and papers strewn about the room; overturned chairs and broken bureau drawers and an empty bed.

He kicks the chair against the wall. *How could I have left Henry to Clement's men?* He kneels down next to the drawer, the edges of which had come apart from the bottom, and reaches for Henry's banyan — the blue silk slips through his fingers.

No, no, no.

He sits on the bed and closes his eyes. In his mind, he wipes the day clean, puts time in reverse: Dishes return to their shelves, table and chairs flip up into place; he closes the window, lights the lamp, and sets the tea on.

He closes his eyes tighter until he can see *him.*

Henry would stretch and sit up in bed. "Tell me what you learned at McCleester's." His voice fills Walt's head. "I'm feeling much better now; my fever broke a few hours ago."

I should never have left you here alone.

"I thought it was you, at the door."

Keep talking, Henry.

"Tell my parents I love them."

Don't leave me yet.

But the voice stops.

226

Frankie gave me a name. Sheriff Petty. I don't know how it all fits together yet. Henry. Oh, Jesus.

"Say something." His own voice startles him. He clears his mind, hoping to hear Henry's voice once more, but the only voices he hears are those from the bar down the street. He opens his eyes. The cold air rushes through the gaping window, the blinds bang against the frame, and all he has left is reality —

Henry Saunders is gone.

CHAPTER 21

Walt is running as fast as he can. His chest hurts. He is sweating. The watch house is several city blocks away from Henry's room, and the accumulating snow makes the going difficult. His feet stick in the fresh drift, scraunch, then slip. He catches himself with his arm before he hits the ground, then keeps running. He's counting on the sheriff to help him.

Whitman is frantic. He and Henry were supposed to go to dinner together. They should be there right now: Henry in the Pewter Mug, a glass of sherry on the table in front of him, smartly dressed, a dark coat over a white shirt, black tie, silk vest, and he's smiling at Walt, telling him how much better he feels now. Henry takes his hand, squeezes —

What if he can't find Henry?

The snow falls harder now. Whitman slogs through the blizzard and re-creates Henry in his head. What would he say to Walt if he were here?

"Keep your head up."

No.

"I wanted to come with you."

Too obvious.

And then it hits him. He can't imagine Henry into being. His thoughts have to be more precise in their conception, more deliberate if he has a chance of putting them into action. That's what Henry would say to him. Quit being sentimental. Be productive. Find a solution.

That's when he sees it up ahead, the light from the watch house window, a spotlight slicing through the snow. He stops at the front door, takes a deep breath, and goes inside.

The lobby swelters. A uniformed man rests his feet on the desk near the entrance, his hands behind his head. Whitman doesn't recognize him. The man's breaths are slow and deep as if asleep, but his wide-open eyes follow Walt across the room. "Can I help you?"

"My friend has gone missing. I think he's been kidnapped" — he pauses — "or killed." To say the words is different from thinking them, and Walt staggers as if fending off a physical blow.

"Hold on a minute." The man swings his legs down off the table, and he sits up in his chair. The skin on his face looks double layered, and his nose is riddled with tiny holes that resemble buckshot. "What's this here about a missing friend? You got to give me more information than that. I'm not a magician."

Whitman takes a deep breath. "When I arrived to check on him this evening — he's been sick with a fever — the door was wide-open, the furniture overturned, dishes broken, everything scattered everywhere, and he was gone."

"With all due respect, mister. An empty room does not mean someone is missing."

"But someone clearly ransacked his room."

"Last time you saw him?"

"As I said, when I left him this morning, he had a fever," Walt says. "If you're suggesting that he's out on the town or that he's decided to move elsewhere, you are mistaken."

"Easy there, sir. I'm only gathering information," the man says. "Please sit down. I can see you are very upset, and I'm going to do my best to help you find your friend. There's a process we have to follow — that's all I'm doing." He waits for Walt to sit, and when he does, the officer continues. "Let me ask you a few questions."

Whitman nods. "Thank you, sir." The last time Walt was here was a few nights before with Henry, what now feels like weeks ago.

The man stands up. He stretches his long body and moseys to the other side of the room, where several shelves lean against the wall. There, he searches through a stack of papers, finds the one he's looking for, and returns to his desk. "Like I said, this is procedure. Now, let's see." The man drags his finger across the form and then down. He picks up a pencil. "This will only take a few minutes. What is your friend's name?"

"Henry Saunders."

The man sets down the pencil and folds his arms. "*The* Henry Saunders?"

Walt says, "What's that supposed to mean?"

"And you're the other one, aren't you? Walt Whitland."

"*Whitman.*"

"Excuse me," the officer says. "This one is above me."

"What are you talking about?" Walt says, as the man disappears into the staging room. "What about procedure?"

Soon, Sheriff Petty appears in the doorway, staring Walt down. "Mr. Whitman, what brings you out on this snowy evening?"

"Mr. Saunders has gone missing."

The sheriff sits down and stretches his arms out in front of him. With his right hand, he fiddles with a rifle bullet — he pushes one end against the desk, slides his fingers to the other end, flips the bullet, then does it again. "Missing?"

Walt nods. "I was telling the officer how I arrived to an empty room —"

"Officer Robertson said it was ransacked."

Walt nods.

"And what time was this?"

"An hour ago."

"So you really can't be sure he's missing."

"No, I *am* sure."

"Maybe he had someone over? Things got out of control. They might still be out somewhere causing mischief. We see it all the time."

Walt shakes his head. "Are you going to help me or not?"

"Am I going to help you?"

Whitman can only look at the new sheriff. He's tall and strong where Harris was not, and his face is marked with sharp features — nose, cheekbones, jaw, mouth — his mustache is perfectly groomed, not a whisker out of place. "That's your job," Walt says. "To help —"

The sheriff interrupts. "Your article, the one that accused us of hanging the wrong person, has created quite a stir around here."

"Is that what this is about?"

"Why is it that an individual like yourself, who criticizes the way we do our job, should now demand our assistance?" Petty stops. "That's what I mean by the word *stir.*"

"Enough of a stir for you to exonerate Samuel Clement?"

Petty says, "You do keep at it."

Whitman is desperate now. "Why did Clement's sister give me your name when I asked where to find her brother?"

"What sister?" Petty says. "What are you talking about?"

Walt presses on. "Yes, Frankie Clement. I went to see her this evening at McCleester's place, and she didn't hesitate when I asked her how to find her brother. She said to ask you." Walt pauses. "So I'm asking: Where can I find Samuel Clement? If I find Clement, I'll find Henry."

"You're taking your cues from a prostitute?"

"When the law doesn't do its job, the citizenry has to do the best they can."

"We *do* our jobs, Mr. Whitman."

"You didn't go after Clement, and now

he's taken Mr. Saunders."

"You've done irreparable damage to our reputation with your sensationalist reporting." Sheriff Petty tosses the bullet to himself. "Sounds to me as if your article hurt both of us. You'd know better than me, but isn't that *poetic justice*?"

"Are you saying you won't look for him?"

"Those are your words," Petty says. "We'll look for him in the morning if he's still missing."

"What if Clement kills him?"

"Have you checked the bars? The theaters?"

"I saw Clement murder your former boss," Whitman says. "Should I take that information to Tammany Hall?"

"You're either the smartest or the stupidest person to walk through that door today." When Sheriff Petty stands up, his knees creak. "I wouldn't put my money on the smartest." He pulls his arms back and up over his shoulders in a giant stretch. "Time for bed," he says as he starts to march back the way he came.

Whitman cuts off the sheriff before he reaches the staging room door.

"I guess I shouldn't be surprised," Walt says, "that you would allow another innocent person to die. Will you blame James

Warren for that too?"

Sheriff Petty thrusts his forearm under Whitman's chin and slams him against the wall, where he studies Walt with a half smile. Walt Whitman is a big man, but Silas Petty has him beat in pounds and inches. "Be careful, Mr. Whitman," he says. "If they knew who Mr. Saunders is, then they know who you are too." He presses his forearm into Walt's throat until it is difficult to breathe.

Whitman forces out the words. "I'm not intimidated by you."

Petty lets go. "You should be."

Walt drops to his knees, gasping.

"Now, you can sit here all night as far as I'm concerned, but I'm leaving."

Walt coughs. "I'll find Mr. Saunders myself." He is still trying to catch his breath. "Then I'm going to prove that Samuel Clement framed Lena Stowe for her husband's murder."

"You've been reading too many books." The sheriff shakes his head before he disappears into the staging room.

Whitman waits another minute or so before he pulls himself up using the chair next to him. The other officer returns and retakes his place at the desk as if Walt were no longer in the room.

Outside, the snow has stopped, and the moon shines brightly. Walt's flesh quivers with the bitter coldness of the air. His breath appears like steam, and through it he sees the figure materialize up ahead.

For one ecstatic moment, the figure floating toward Walt Whitman in the night *is* Henry Saunders, and that moment expands temporally and spatially, exploding outward in every direction until all that exists is Walt and Henry meeting on a cold winter night outside the watch house.

The figure runs toward him, a fleck in the snow that grows bigger with each step until the boy stands in front of Walt, smiling. "Mr. Whitman, I need to speak with you."

CHAPTER 22

Walt Whitman is so overjoyed to see Azariah Smith that he lifts the boy's scrawny frame off the ground and hugs him tight. It is only when Azariah coughs that Walt remembers the bruising, and he quickly sets the boy down. "I forgot, Mr. Smith. My apologies."

Azariah musters a pained smile. "I've come with news of your friend."

Whitman's insides turn. "Do you know where Henry is? Is he okay?"

"I don't know where he is, but I know who has him."

"Clement?"

Azariah nods. "When Mr. Rynders found out Clement took your friend, he was furious. I've never seen him so angry and so he sends for Clement, and when he arrives, the two of them go at it, and I'm worried Mr. Rynders is going to shoot Clement right there." The boy shakes his head. "If it were anyone else, he would have, but Clement gets away with more."

"Why?"

"It's simple. Clement also works for the mayor."

"Morris?"

Azariah nods. "So they're arguing about your friend — Mr. Rynders wants to know why in God's name Mr. Clement abducted him, and Clement says it's none of his goddamn business and Rynders says that everything Clement does is his goddamn business and then Mr. Rynders demands to know where Mr. Clement is keeping Mr. Saunders, but Clement won't tell him. Rynders says *You're making this personal* and Clement says *No, I'm fixing it,* and Rynders says *I can't keep protecting you like this.* So Clement gets real close to Rynders, and he tells him to piss off. I couldn't believe it. Before Rynders could say another word, Clement was gone."

"And you don't know where Clement works or lives or spends his time?"

Azariah shakes his head, and his eyes water. "I'm sorry."

Walt puts his hand on the boy's shoulder. "Where might Clement keep him?"

"Clement moves around a lot. Mr. Rynders is always complaining about not

238

being able to reach him."

"Hmm." Whitman is thinking about their next move, perhaps another *Aurora* article, and then he notices Azariah grimace in pain.

"How are you feeling?"

The boy shrugs.

"I can help you get away from him."

Azariah smiles, but the edges of the smile turn down as quickly as they form. "You have been kind to me, and that is why I'm here now, but no one can help me when it comes to Mr. Rynders."

"I can," Walt says, determination in his voice. "Give me a chance. Stay with me now." He's improvising. "I'm on my way to the *Aurora* as before. We'll write another article together, stir things up."

Azariah considers the offer, but Whitman can feel his hesitation.

"You can teach me to build a fire," Walt says.

Azariah looks up. "I do know what the hell I'm doing." He smiles. "And I suppose I have time to teach you a thing or two."

The *Aurora* office is cold and dark and silent. Walt watches as Azariah builds a fire in the composition room's large woodstove. The boy leaves its iron door open to let the air in. Walt can't help but smile that Azariah has learned well.

He allows himself a moment to wonder on Henry's location, if his fever lingers, if he's alive — this last thought catches him unaware, and a feeling of profound sadness washes over him. Walt cannot imagine a life without Henry now.

"You're thinking about your friend, aren't you?" Azariah has joined him at the composition table.

Whitman nods.

"Mr. Clement said he is still alive. Let's find him."

Walt gathers himself, and then explains what they are going to do. "I'll be writing the article as we typeset it, and —"

"You want me to follow the letters again."

"I would be grateful," Whitman says.

Azariah climbs onto the table, kneels over the tray that will hold the article type. "Ready."

They begin. Walt drops the block letter *g* into the tray to complete the word *missing*. The headline stretches all the way from the left side to the right, each block letter in the largest typeface available, three inches high. Nobody who sees the newspaper can miss it.

Last night, Henry Saunders, editor of the *Aurora* newspaper, was abducted from his room on Centre Street. Saunders, known for his incisive article on the underworld of body snatching, made enemies with the New York law enforcement when he suggested in this newspaper only yesterday that city officials and law enforcement may have hanged the wrong person in Lena Stowe. Now, instead of using Saunders's disappearance as an opportunity to prove the article wrong, to show the citizens of New York just how committed to justice it is, New York City Law Enforcement has refused to acknowledge Saunders's disappearance, turning its back on one of its own citizens. Not only is this act dangerous and cavalier, but it speaks to the safety of all New Yorkers. If your loved one goes missing or finds trouble, will the law help you? Tell your family and friends about this injustice. Pressure your local law enforcement to do the right thing, and if you have any information at all about Henry Saunders's disappearance, please contact this newspaper, your local newspaper, or your alderman.

The article goes on to retell Whitman's account of Clement's responsibility for the

Stowe fiasco and Sheriff Harris's murder, for which he uses much of the same wording from the day previous, and he even makes the provocative suggestion that Clement is, as Sheriff Harris suggested, Mary Rogers's murderer.

When Walt is finished, he sits on the table next to his handiwork, and for one moment he appreciates the aesthetic accomplishment of six columns of blocked text. Azariah points out three errors — Whitman misspelled *Saunders* in two places, and in place of Lena Stowe's name, he had put Elizabeth Blackwell's. Walt fixes the errors in under a minute, and he is ready to run the press, when he hears the front door.

"Who is that?" Azariah says.

"No idea." Walt checks his pocket watch. Ten a.m.

Mr. Ropes pokes his head into the composition room. "Mr. Walt Whitman. Good morning. Is Mr. Saunders around? I'd like to discuss yesterday's edition with both of you."

Mr. Ropes notices Azariah, nods his way. "And who is this?"

The boy slides to the floor, shakes Mr. Ropes's hand. "Azariah Smith, sir. I'm Mr. Whitman's apprentice."

"Apprentice? You continue to surprise,

Mr. Whitman." Mr. Ropes pauses. "And Mr. Saunders? Is he here?"

"I'm afraid he's not feeling well." Walt moves a few feet to the right to block Mr. Ropes's view of the typeset edition. "He's spending the day in bed."

"I'll speak with him later, then," Ropes says. "As for you, Mr. Whitman. Perhaps we should speak alone."

Azariah understands. "I'll wait in the office."

Mr. Ropes waits until the door closes. "As I was saying: The article you wrote and Mr. Saunders published yesterday has caused me a considerable amount of trouble with the mayor's office."

"And it has the unfortunate problem of being true," Walt says. "Every word of it."

"We are not the *Herald*, Mr. Whitman."

"Meaning?"

"Meaning that sometimes we don't have the luxury of printing the truth."

Walt says, "What do we have the luxury of printing, then?"

"Your poems are innocuous enough." A few months earlier, Mr. Ropes had encouraged him to print his poem "Time to Come" in the *Aurora*.

"Hmm," Walt says. "Is it not a reporter's job to uncover the truth?"

"One more article with that kind of truth will put Mr. Herrick and me out of business."

Whitman has not yet met Mr. Herrick, but if he's anything like Mr. Ropes, then —

"The problem with journalists," Ropes says, "is they live in a world where their words mean more than even they think they do. What I'm suggesting to you, Mr. Whitman, is that journalists, as difficult as it is to believe, undervalue their own work. The written word is powerful, and reporters often don't care about anyone but themselves. They think about what their words *might* do, not what they *will* do."

"What are you saying, then?"

"What I'm saying, Mr. Whitman, is that you're fired."

"Excuse me?"

Ropes nods. "Mr. Saunders will also be dismissed when I next see him."

"But, sir —"

"Mr. Nichols will begin tomorrow."

"The former editor?"

Mr. Ropes says, "It's a temporary appointment until I can find a permanent replacement."

"What about today's issue?"

Mr. Ropes steps into the composition room. "It's simple, really. There won't be

244

one."

Outside, dirt, slush, and puddles cover the streets and walkways, and the wind has stopped. People scamper about in droves trying to finish their errands during the abbreviated daylight of winter. Walt Whitman and Azariah Smith cross the street from the *Aurora* and sit on the park bench, where they watch children frolic in the sun. One little girl chases a dog with a red ball in his mouth. Freckles cover her cheeks, and her lips are bright red from the wind.

What can they do now? That article was their best chance at finding Henry.

The girl waves at them as they stand and cross the street. Azariah waves back.

Walt tries to empty his mind as he does when he writes stories. Next to him, Azariah walks quietly, sensing Walt's trouble. His eyes are bright and anxious, his taut body ready to be called into action.

They walk northeast until they reach Chatham Square where auctioneers are mounted upon tables, or barrels, crying the goods and the prices. Customers pore over hills of furniture of every description and quality, mulling potential purchases. Walt stands awhile and looks vacantly upon the market scene, thoughts of Henry churning in his mind.

"Any ideas?" Azariah says, unable to stay quiet any longer.

Whitman shakes his head, and the boy gets the hint. They walk on.

All around them is the deafening noise of people engaged in their thousand employments. Walt gazes curiously at the shops, which exhibit their merchandise in large, handsome windows, a few of their best articles hanging out front to entice the passerby. In the air ring the voices of newsboys announcing the day's headlines: *Boy killed in carriage accident. Alderman Sickles arrested for embezzlement. Madame Restell to fight charges of malpractice.*

And then the idea comes: Mr. Ropes does not know how to run a press. He will not have done anything at all with the ready-to-print MISSING article, and so the tray likely remains ready on the composition table. As long as Mr. Ropes has left the office, then Walt and Azariah can simply find a way back inside the *Aurora* and run the edition anyway. What more can Mr. Ropes do to him now that he's already been fired?

When Walt explains the idea, Azariah smiles.

CHAPTER 23

Walt Whitman and Azariah Smith are on their way to the women's college. They have been all over the city in only a few hours, distributing thousands of copies of the *Aurora*, its front page featuring the MISSING article, and much to Whitman's delight, they began to witness its impact immediately. The newsboys proclaimed the headline to the New Yorkers on the street as they whisked and brambled their way through the melting snow, and several hundred of the city's more than three hundred thousand residents have responded by paying the two cents for their own copy of the *Aurora*. Walt watched it happen several times as they read his article, their curiosity turning into disbelief, then contorting into rage, and he'd turned to Azariah, who watched it all along with him, and say: "We have something here."

But now that they're approaching the

women's college, Azariah's demeanor changes. It's true they're both tired. Walt's legs are sore, he's hungry, and his clothing is wet. He prods his young friend; "Come on in, then," he says. "They'll have some dinner for us. You can dry off next to the stove."

Azariah shakes his head.

"Don't be stubborn, Mr. Smith."

"Do they know?"

"Do they know what?"

"That I lied to them," Azariah says. "Miss Blackwell and the other women."

Whitman shakes his head. "All they know is that you saved the college from the mob."

Azariah thinks for a moment. "Why didn't you tell them?"

"Why would I?"

"I *am* sorry."

"We've been over this," Walt says. "Now let's go inside."

Azariah nods.

The students are in the dissection room again, Elizabeth in the lead. She does not see Walt and Azariah come in. A cadaver is laid out on the table.

"Before we begin," Miss Blackwell says, "let me say how grateful I am that you decided to remain at the college despite all we have been through in recent days. It is my prayer that this dissection demonstrates my commitment to this college, to your educations, to Abraham and Lena Stowe's legacy, and to medicine."

She takes the scalpel and makes an incision at the dead woman's sternum. As the blade slowly, steadily draws downward, the students' faces reveal fascination and revulsion. Miss Blackwell pauses at the chest cavity. She looks from one student to the next, lingering, forcing them to look away from the cadaver and make eye contact with her.

"Before we remove this woman's chest cavity, I want you to know who she was: Her name was Loretta Carver, the wife of a fishmonger." She continues to cut and, as she peels the skin back, says: "Recall how we created a buttonhole in Lena's skin the other day," she says. "I'm doing the same thing here, as you soon will. Once we get the muscle off, we'll remove the chest cavity as we discussed."

"With the bone cutter?" Miss Zacky says.

Elizabeth nods. "Ribs one through six all around." She traces the circular path around the chest cavity with her index finger. "The clavicle is next, and then you remove the rib cage in one piece." This is when she notices Whitman and the boy in the back. "Excuse me, ladies. Miss Zacky will take the lead.

Once you have the rib cage off, let's stop for today." She washes her hands in the basin behind the dissection table and wipes them on the apron, which she tosses in the corner bin.

Miss Blackwell smiles as she comes toward them. "Mr. Smith, how nice to see you again. We've missed you."

"Ma'am." Azariah bows, shakes her hand.

"Mr. Whitman, any news on Mr. Saunders's whereabouts?"

Walt sent a message through a courier earlier that morning to let Elizabeth know what had happened. "Mr. Smith and I just ran an article we think will agitate the situation, didn't we?" He wants to sound hopeful.

Azariah nods.

"The two of you look ragged. We'll be eating soon. Please join us. Both of you."

Whitman looks at the boy.

Azariah hesitates only a moment. "Thank you, ma'am."

"Good," Elizabeth says. "While we eat, we can discuss our next move with regard to finding Mr. Saunders. Now, you said his family lives nearby. Have you sent word to them?"

Walt shakes his head.

She comes closer. "I know how upset you

must be, but don't give up hope. We will do everything we can to find your friend."

Walt is overwhelmed by her compassion. Behind Elizabeth, her students have just removed much of the rib cage in one piece, and Miss Emsbury holds it up for her instructor to see. Miss Blackwell praises her students on a job well done. They are all doing their best in difficult circumstances.

And then it occurs to Walt. "May I inquire as to where you found the corpse?"

"Mrs. Carver came to us from Kenneth Barclay."

"Oh?"

"He sent it along with his apologies and best wishes." Elizabeth shrugs. "Why he really did it, I'm not sure, but we've been grateful to have it. It is incredibly meaningful to the students."

Whitman considers this new development. Miss Blackwell is not naïve. She knows Barclay has his own motives, so instead of probing further, he smiles. "This is good news, Elizabeth. I'm glad you didn't have to dig one up yourself."

Miss Zacky interrupts. "We've finished for the day," she says. "Shall I help Miss Perschon with dinner?" She makes eye contact with Walt. "I'm so sorry to hear about your friend."

Whitman nods. "Thank you."

Miss Blackwell says, "Yes, splendid. Miss Perschon can use the help and maybe Mr. Smith can assist as well?" She turns to Azariah as she says this.

"Helping pretty young women such as these," Azariah says, "is both an opportunity and a blessing."

Miss Zacky takes him by the hand, and they leave the room.

Elizabeth waits until they're out of hearing range. "How are you holding up?" She takes Walt's hand.

He shakes his head. Tears are threatening to spill over, but if he cries now, he'll never stop.

She can see. "It will be okay, Mr. Whitman. God is watching over us."

Walt says, "I hope you're right."

"I want you to pray with me."

"Pray? Me?" Walt looks at Elizabeth's face, earnest and brimming with faith.

She puts her other hand on his arm. " 'Is not prayer also a study of truth — a sally of the soul into the unfound infinite?' "

Walt smiles. "How can I disagree with you *and* Mr. Emerson?"

She smiles.

And now Walt is crying.

Elizabeth holds both his hands. "With all

that's happened these past weeks, I thought God was singling us out, and then I realized how backward my thinking was. God has taken Abraham and Lena back into his presence. They are well, and it is ours to carry on. I don't know why it has happened this way. I'm not supposed to know." She pauses. "What I do know is that he is watching over us," she says, "and Henry too."

Whitman wants to say he agrees with her, but he cannot. At this moment, God feels irrelevant. Would that God reach down from heaven and arrange events in their favor, but what evidence do they have of this? For it is by their own works that they have made any progress at all, and it is the actions of others that have left them in such a precarious spot. Where is God in that?

The best he can do while she prays is search for a safe image from his past — the soothing rustle of the waves, and the saline smell, the clam digging, barefoot, and with trousers rolled up; hauling down the creek; the perfume and the sedge meadows; the hay boat, and the chowder and fishing excursions —

Elizabeth finishes her prayer with an *Amen,* and she looks up at Walt. "Better?"

He nods. "Thank you."

Uncharacteristically, she takes him into

her arms, and he lays his head against her as he used to do with his mother, softly sobbing, and they stand like this for a very long time until broken up by a knock at the door.

Frankie Clement stands on the top step. Her dress is soaked, and her hair is disheveled. She's out of breath. She's trembling. She clambers to the stoop, stumbles inside, on the verge of hysterics. "We have to talk, now. We have to talk."

Walt and Elizabeth step aside to let her pass, and she's muttering all the while. "What did you do to him? What did you do to Samuel?"

"What did we do to *him*?" Whitman says. "What has he done to us?"

"I've never seen him like this," Frankie says. "He's out of his head. What have you done?" She drops into one of the students' desks, forming a triangle with Walt and Elizabeth.

Yesterday she was so smooth, so in control, Whitman thinks, looking to Elizabeth for guidance.

"Can I get you something to drink?" Miss Blackwell says.

Frankie ignores her, grabbing on to Whitman instead. "What did you do?"

"I didn't do anything." He rips his arm

away from her. "Your brother abducted my friend. He's a murderer and a criminal."

Frankie is shaking her head now. "No, no, no, no. That's not possible. Not my Samuel. After our father died, he took care of mum and me. He worked all hours of the day to make sure we had food to eat, to keep us in that room."

"And where are you now?" Walt says.

Elizabeth looks sharply at Walt. *Not now,* she is saying with her eyes.

"Samuel does have your friend," Frankie says. "That's why I'm here."

Whitman rushes toward her, and if Miss Blackwell hadn't blocked his way, he would have taken hold and shaken her.

"Mr. Whitman, no," Elizabeth says. "Let us hear what she has to say."

"Mr. Saunders is safe for now," Frankie says.

Walt says, "Have you seen him?"

Frankie shakes her head. "I don't know where he is. Samuel doesn't trust me with that information, but he did send me here."

"Tell me," Walt says.

"You are to meet Samuel tonight at eight in St. Peter's Church."

"Meet him? But why?"

"He says you have it all wrong," Miss Clement says. "What happened between my brother and Jack Harris isn't exactly what it seems."

"What is it, then?"

"How should I know?" Frankie says. "He said he wants to clear it up."

"By kidnapping Henry?"

"I told Samuel this was a waste of time." She stands. "I told him he ought to just get rid of your friend."

"Get rid of him?" Walt's standing over her now. "We're not finished here. Now *please* take your chair, miss." The two stare at each other until she sits again. She's trying to appear tough, he knows, but she's weak. She's also afraid of her brother.

Elizabeth cuts in. "Can I get you something warm to drink? You look cold."

Frankie twists her head. "I look cold? Who are you to tell me I look cold?"

"I only meant —"

"You only meant? You don't know me. You don't know what I've been through."

"Maybe not, but I see the sore on your face," Miss Blackwell says.

Whitman hasn't noticed it until now, but there is a red penny-size sore on Frankie's left cheek. The edges crumble and crust; its center shines red like a bad scrape.

"It's a spider bite," Miss Clement says.

"I also know that you're going through

withdrawals," Elizabeth continues. "The shaking and sweating. Your bad color. Laudanum probably. It's unpleasant, yes, but it's also dangerous. You need medical attention. You're very ill."

Frankie is taken aback by this. Her eyes turn dark, and she fidgets in her seat. "This is none of your goddamn business."

"Lucky for you, you came to the right place," Miss Blackwell says. "We'll help you."

Frankie closes her eyes, drops her head.

"We can help you off the laudanum while we treat the infection. You're welcome here."

Much to Walt's surprise, Frankie appears open to Elizabeth's offer. She glances around the room, then at Whitman and Miss Blackwell again. She stares out the window. "We never had a chance, you know? We grew up in Five Points, right in the center of it all. We were always poor. That's just the way it was. My pap worked hard, harder than most, but it didn't add up. Everything is stacked against folks like us." She stops, lost in her thoughts.

"We'll help you," Elizabeth says again. "There is hope."

From the other room, they hear voices. Sounds to Walt like Miss Zacky and Azariah in the kitchen.

"Who is that?" Miss Clement says.

"Those are my students," Elizabeth says. "They live and work here."

"Women doctors?" Frankie says.

"They're not doctors yet." Miss Blackwell smiles. "But they are studying to become doctors. It will happen."

"Hmm." Frankie is mulling something over.

Elizabeth picks up on it. "Are you interested in medicine, Miss Clement?"

Frankie shrugs.

"Because once you're well, you can study here too."

"Me? Really?"

Elizabeth says, "Why not you?"

"My occupation, for one," Frankie says. "Add to that the fact that I have no money, and my current employer might come for me if I quit."

Elizabeth has set up the perfect scenario for getting more information about Henry. Frankie is really considering Miss Blackwell's offer, and her face has transformed from a dreary mess to an expression of promise. She's sitting up straight, alert, glancing about as if picturing herself among the students. Walt waits and hopes. He believes Elizabeth wants to help Frankie.

Does Frankie believe it too?

Miss Zacky appears first, a broom in hand, and Azariah Smith follows with the dustpan. They're singing a song Walt doesn't recognize, and they're laughing — until they catch sight of Frankie Clement.

Azariah's smile disappears.

Frankie stands. "You?"

"It's not what you think," Azariah says.

But she's already out the door.

Outside, Walt catches up to Frankie just as she enters a waiting cab that speeds away. He follows the cab on foot as long as he can, keeping an eye out for a cab of his own, but there simply aren't any around in this neighborhood at this hour, and so in the end, all he can do is watch as the white cab becomes smaller and smaller, and along with it too his hope of Frankie leading them to where Clement is keeping Henry.

Back in the college, Elizabeth Blackwell and Miss Zacky are still in the classroom. Azariah is not.

"Where is Mr. Smith?" Whitman says.

"He slipped out right after you left," Miss Zacky says. "I tried to stop him."

"We both tried," Elizabeth says. "He kept saying how sorry he was. What does he mean?"

"Well," Whitman starts, "that's an interesting story." He sits again, and stares at the anatomical drawings on the wall. He looks at them long enough to forget what they are, and instead focuses on patterns and colors. It's when he's looking at a drawing of the circulatory system, full of purples and reds, that he remembers the sore on Frankie Clement's cheek. "So what is the matter with her?"

"Syphilis."

"And what will happen to her?"

"She'll continue to pass the disease on to others, possibly go sterile herself, and the infection might kill her. All this will be made worse if she goes through unaided withdrawals from laudanum."

"So you offer her a position as student?"

"Call me an optimist. It is treatable." She sighs. "I think I can treat it, anyway."

"Maybe she'll come back, then," Walt says. "I thought we had her."

Elizabeth takes his hand. "You can't go tonight. You know that, don't you?"

"Go?" Miss Zacky says. "Go where?"

Walt takes Elizabeth's other hand. "I think you know I have to go."

"So much death already," Miss Blackwell says. "We can't absorb any more. I need you. The students need you. You can't go."

"Go *where*?" Miss Zacky repeats.

"But Henry needs me too," Walt says. "I have to go."

CHAPTER 24

James "Snuffy" Warren is sleeping when the guard opens the cell door. He sits up and wipes his eyes. "You came back," he says.

On this day for Walt Whitman, seeing one of the men who tried to kill him is like seeing an old friend. If anyone can tell him how to approach his meeting with Samuel Clement, it is he.

Snuffy continues. "Frankie told you something?"

Walt nods, puts his finger to his lips.

Whitman sits down. "I'm afraid the situation has gotten much worse," he says, once the guard has left them. Walt recounts recent events, the news article, Henry Saunders's abduction, and Frankie Clement's strange visit to the college.

"He'll kill you." Warren runs his fingers through his hair.

"If I don't go, he'll kill Mr. Saunders." Whitman pauses.

Snuffy shakes his head. "With all due respect, sir, if you show up, you and your friend will both be dead."

Walt says, "If I don't go, you'll be dead too."

At this, Snuffy falls silent.

"That's why I'm here," Whitman says. "You know the workings of his mind better than anyone. You can help me surprise him."

Snuffy swings his legs onto the stone floor. The skin on his face and hands is splotchy from the cold.

"The way someone like Samuel stays alive is to do what normal folks won't," Snuffy says. "He knows you'll show up because you still imagine a world in which good people find justice and bad people get what they deserve. You want to catch him off guard? Shoot him in the head before he says a word, and then use his sister to find your friend. You'll get one chance."

"Shoot him?"

"Samuel Clement's strategy is based on the notion that you don't have the stomach to pull the trigger."

"But I don't even own a gun."

"Then buy one."

"Where?"

"Jesus Christ." Snuffy shakes his head. "It's a wonder you're still alive."

Whitman shrugs.

"Find the little shop on Catherine Street that sells tobacco, newspapers, that sort of thing. Use my name, and the man there will sell you a gun."

"Thank you." Whitman writes down *Catherine Street,* then looks up. The cell is freezing, and apart from the small blanket wrapped around Snuffy's waist, he has nothing. "How are they treating you here?"

"How do you think?" Snuffy says. "They pay me little attention except to throw a piece of bread my way now and then, or to tell me how the gallows are coming along in Washington Square." He stops, gathers himself. "Do you still have the letter to my mother?"

Walt pats his coat pocket. "She'll get it."

"Remember, one shot is all you'll get. If you don't kill him, he will kill you."

The thought of killing someone seems abstract even as Snuffy explains how. The thought of Henry, conversely, is concrete, and a rage Walt has never known before has taken root deep in his gut, and it is spreading —

Can he kill Samuel Clement to save Henry Saunders?

Yes, Whitman thinks. He can do anything.

■ ■ ■ ■

Catherine Street is only a few blocks away, but to get there, Walt has to pass through three different neighborhoods, the residents of which all speak different languages. German, Italian, and another he doesn't recognize. Even in winter, laundry hangs on lines strung from one side of the building to the other. Carts and wagons and carriages speed in both directions, and Walt darts in and out of them. He has almost crossed the street when he gets stuck between a carriage and a cart.

"Out of the way," someone yells.

He turns and faces an oncoming freight wagon, and it barrels down on him until someone grabs him by the coat and pulls him out of the way. He tumbles to the ground. A watchman reaches down for him. "Jesus, son, watch where you're going."

Whitman gathers himself. "Thank you."

The man hesitates. "Aren't you that reporter?"

"No, no, no, but thank you!" Walt skips away.

Two blocks down, he finds it. A small, one-story building sandwiched between two three-story tenements. The door squeaks as it opens, releasing a musty tobacco smell. Inside, stacks of newspapers lie against one wall, and opposite that stands a short man with rail-thin arms and a black mustache. "Can I help you, mister?"

"I want to buy a gun."

"Well, then, I'm sorry to tell you that I don't sell 'em here."

"That's not what I've heard."

"You heard incorrectly."

Whitman pauses before he says, "James Warren said to use his name, and you would sell me one."

He hears the click of a gun from behind the counter. "Put your hands where I can see them."

Walt does.

"Move." The man comes around the counter and pushes him. "Into the back."

They go through the back door past stacks of newspapers and books to another, smaller room. "Stand against that wall and start talking. What the hell do you have to do with James Warren?"

"He's in prison."

"I know he's locked up," he says, "but you haven't answered the question. How do you know my son?"

"I'm sorry," Whitman says. "Your son?"

"Are you deaf, mister?"

"I met with him today and that's when he said you'd sell me a gun."

The man's face changes. The hard edges turn soft and his eyes wide. "Is he okay? How does he look?"

"He's doing fine, given all that's happened to him."

"You know I haven't seen him for three years? Had a big fight." The man pauses. "I don't know, mister. I tried to be a good father. I work hard; that's what he don't get, how hard I worked for him and the rest of 'em. Then I hear about his name in the newspaper for murder and I figure I'll probably never see him again. Next thing I know, he sends you along looking for a gun. Don't know what to make of it. No, sir, don't make a lick of sense. What's happened to my boy?"

Walt steps closer.

"Not so fast, mister. Stay right there."

"Look, your son didn't kill anyone, and I'm trying to prove it. But first I need a gun."

"The newspapers say he'll hang for sure."

Whitman remains still.

"Goddammit, say something."

"The man your son worked for, the man who turned on James, also kidnapped my friend. If I'm going to help either of them, I need a gun."

The man considers what he's said. He sets his gun down, then pulls a suitcase from behind the counter. He struggles to get the latches open, but when he does, he slides the case toward Walt. Inside, Whitman sees at least ten pistols of various makes and sizes.

"What's your pleasure?"

Walt scans the guns, but one looks just as good as another. "I have five dollars. What do you recommend?"

"Hmmm." The man turns over the pistols and pulls out a smaller model. "This is a Colt pocket pistol. Here, see how it feels."

"Is it loaded?"

The man shakes his head.

Whitman holds the gun out in front of him by its handle. "How do you load it?"

The man takes the gun from him, folds the barrel back, and shows Walt the empty chambers. "Slide 'em in here," he says. "Lock it into place. Nothing to it."

When Walt puts the gun in his pocket, his fingers brush the letter he has written for Warren's mother. It would be nice for his father to read it. He thinks of how his own parents would feel if he were in jail awaiting execution.

Whitman holds the letter out for the man to see.

"What's this?" The man's face lights up when he understands. He holds it in his hands like a vase, or statue, as if it might break with the slightest bit of carelessness.

"It's from James."

"My boy wrote me a letter?" He unfolds it.

But like his son, the man can't read. So Walt takes it from him and reads it as if James Warren wrote it to his father. He reads it word for word, substituting father for mother until the end when he adds something:

I'm sorry we haven't been closer and I hope, God willing, that we should have the chance to put the past behind us.

"Oh, my son." Whitman gives the man the letter. "Do you have a father?" he asks, staring at the handwriting.

Walt nods. He pictures Walter Senior, his white hair sticking up, his eyes red from being out all night, and he can hear his straggly voice, hoarse from yelling —

"I hope you appreciate him." The man turns emotional but doesn't cry. "Help me get my boy back, mister. *Please.*"

CHAPTER 25

At St. Peter's Church, Walt Whitman disturbs a funeral in progress when the sound of his boots echoes through the spacious hall. In the center of the nave, a coffin rests before rows and rows of pews, where a congregation of thirty mourns. A priest, whom Walt recognizes as the antidissectionist Father Allen, stands next to the coffin, his head bowed in prayer, his face hidden from view.

More quietly now, Walt makes his way to the sacristy at the front of the cathedral where he finds himself alone. Standing where he can see the church entrance, he checks his pocket watch. 7:25.

While Walt waits, Father Allen continues with the funeral sermon: "And Mary said to Peter and John: 'They have taken away the Lord out of the sepulchre, and we know not where they have laid him.' " He raises his voice. "Mary had gone to treat the Lord's body with spices and found the stone rolled away from the tomb. She went inside and the body was not there."

Father Allen hesitates.

"She worries that they had taken the Lord's body to humiliate him. For as yet she knew not the scripture, that he must rise again from the dead. Imagine that: She assumed his body had been snatched from the grave. So what does Mary do? She seeks out Peter and John.

"So they ran both together: and John did outrun Peter, and came first to the sepulchre. And he, stooping down and looking in, saw the linen clothes lying; yet went not in. Peter and John didn't know what to do, so they went home and left Mary at the grave.

"And then the miracle happens. A man approaches Mary and asks why she is crying. 'Sir,' she says — she thinks this man knows something about the body — 'if thou hast borne him hence, tell me where thou hast laid him, and I will take him away.' Brothers and sisters, that man was Jesus! And Jesus called her by name, and she knew it was him. He was resurrected and so shall we all be resurrected if we believe in him we call Christ the Lord."

The door to the cathedral opens, and

Samuel Clement appears in his overcoat and leghorn hat. Alone. At least, Whitman can't see Henry Saunders or anyone else. Perhaps Henry is outside with one of Clement's men. Maybe he is hidden somewhere in the church. Or —

He grips the gun in his pocket.

Clement sits in the last pew and surveys the room.

Father Allen ends the funeral a few minutes before eight. As the parishioners exit, Whitman makes his move. He tiptoes to the side of the chapel, amidst the commotion, and ducks behind a pew. Clement hasn't seen Walt yet.

Now, as he walks, he pulls the pistol from his pocket and holds it pointed downward at his side. He feels like a character in an Ainsworth novel.

When Samuel Clement sees Walt Whitman, he stands to greet him. "You are the author of *Franklin Evans.* Imagine my surprise."

"Where's Mr. Saunders?"

"After I read your novel, I abstained from alcohol," Clement says. "Your portrayal of the evils of alcohol moved me to improve my own life."

"You said to meet you here. I did. Now what about Henry?"

"I'm trying to pay you a compliment, Mr. Whitman. Your story did what years of sermons could not: It changed me. And now, a few months later, business is thriving, my relationship with Frankie is on the mend — she's so good to help out and she refuses to give me up to persuadable folks such as yourself — and I am seeing matters more clearly than I can ever remember."

"Your sister is ill for the laudanum you give her."

"Nonsense." Clement pauses. "I've done all I can to get her off the stuff."

Walt clutches the pistol. His hands are sweaty.

Clement says, "You don't seem sufficiently impressed by your own work, Mr. Whitman."

Walt shifts his grip on the pistol. "Tell me where Henry is."

"Your work has incited the sheriff and his men."

"They hanged an innocent person."

"And city hall? I met with the mayor today, and your name surfaced more than once."

Whitman surveys the church.

"Oh, the watchmen aren't inside yet," he says. "But, clearly, you have no idea what you've done."

Walt raises his arm.

"Mr. Whitman." Clement shakes his head. "The way you hold that pistol — you've probably never shot a gun in your life."

He has. Once. And he missed. "Tell me where Henry Saunders is."

"Hand me the gun."

Walt's hand trembles as he aims it at Clement, who takes another step toward him.

Walt wraps his index finger around the trigger.

"Either you kill me." Clement takes another step. "Or I'll kill you."

Whitman aims his gun at Clement's head just as Snuffy told him to do, but he doesn't know if he can pull the trigger.

Clement is only a step away now.

Walt squeezes the trigger halfway before he lets go, and then, before he can react, Clement knocks him to the floor, takes the gun, and straddles Whitman, holding the gun to his head.

But instead of a gunshot, he hears the voice of the priest. "Get out." Father Allen points a rifle at Samuel Clement. "And I *have* shot a gun before. Many times."

Clement's green eyes bore into Walt. The look on his face suggests he would rather kill Whitman than save himself by obeying the priest.

Father Allen's voice rings out again. *"Out."*

Clement takes his time, the gun still pointed at Walt's head. "As you wish, Father," he says. Then he steps over Walt and lowers the gun.

Whitman breathes a sigh of relief.

But then Clement turns and kicks Walt in the gut, knocking the wind out of him. He rolls over, gasping —

"Out," repeats the priest.

Clement sets the gun down on the cathedral floor, looks at Walt again, then the priest, and backs away into the shadows.

The priest extends his hand to Whitman. "Come with me."

"No," Walt says as he is pulled off the floor by the priest. "I have to follow him. He has my friend."

Father Allen grabs him by the arm. "*Trust* me."

"If I don't go now, I'll lose him."

"You have no idea, do you?" Father Allen says. "You've been set up. A dozen men, including the sheriff, are waiting to arrest you."

"How do you know that?"

"I'm guessing it has something to do with this." The priest holds out today's copy of the *Herald* featuring a front-page story about Walt's break-in at the *Aurora* and his slanderous articles about New York City law enforcement. Samuel Clement was right.

Whitman stares at the article for a moment, then turns to the priest.

"Trust me," Father Allen says.

The priest leads him through a door at the back of the nave — a heavy door with three locks — that leads to his living quarters. Inside, the sitting room is warm, heated by a large fireplace. Several paintings hang on the walls, most of them of Catholic saints or popes, Walt guesses, but the one above the fireplace is of Christ himself, floating in the air above his disciples, back from the dead.

"I need to show you something." The priest holds out Walt's pistol. "Here," he says. "Take it."

The gun sits heavy in Whitman's hand. He strokes the barrel with his index finger, lets his hand grip the gun, slips his finger around the trigger. His mind is a whirl, flashes of Henry Saunders's face interspersed with Samuel Clement's. He aims the pistol at the fireplace.

Father Allen stands behind him, takes his arm, and holds it out straight. "Like this," he says. "Before you shoot, take a deep breath and let it out halfway to better hold your aim. And shoot for the head. Leave no room for error. You can be sure the other man won't."

"Where did you learn to shoot a gun?"

"I was not always the man you see before you."

Whitman wants to ask more, but he's silenced by Father Allen's suddenly stern countenance. Instead, he asks, "Is it a sin to kill a man who has killed someone close to you?"

Father Allen rubs the back of his neck. "It is not a sin to kill a man before he kills you, no. Not something to take lightly, however. Killing a man crosses a line and you might — well, you might end up like me."

"You just told me to shoot for the head."

"We all have *that* power, you know. To take another's life. God knows sometimes it has to be done, and I'm only telling you to be careful." Father Allen looks lost in himself.

"Father?"

He snaps out of his reverie. "I'll lead you out."

At the back door to the church, Father Allen says, "Allow me to survey the area before you leave." He opens the door. "I won't be long."

Minutes later, Father Allen returns. "One man stands on the corner closest to the front entrance, and another four or five across the street. I can't see the others, but they're probably there. You've become a popular man, Mr. Whitman." Father Allen removes his overcoat, whose sleeves were too short for his long arms. "Give me your coat and hat."

Whitman hesitates.

"They'll mistake me for you."

Walt goes through his pockets and finds the gun, bullets, the note from Abby Runkel, and his green notebook. "They'll know you're helping me if you wear my coat."

"The Lord will provide."

"You believe that?"

The priest nods. "Of course I do. Now, your coat?"

They switch coats. Father Allen's is tight around Walt Whitman's body, the arms even shorter on him than on the priest.

"I'll lead them away," Father Allen says. "You follow in a few minutes — take the long way, south a block, then east, and you should be clear. Watch for others — I'm not sure how many there are."

Father Allen steps through the door and walks in clear view of the man at the front entrance.

The officer doesn't move until Father Allen is twenty-five feet past him. Another man emerges out of the shadows, and together, the two men rush the priest and take him by the arms. A black carriage appears from the other direction, stops, and the three men get in.

Whitman resists the urge to go to the priest's aid.

On Barclay Street, the frigid night air stings Walt's neck. Flakes the size of silver Liberty dollars swirl above him. He looks into the sky and sees nothing but a fluttering whiteness. He pulls up the collar of the priest's coat and makes his way south, the cobblestones slippery under his feet.

He won't stop until he reaches Mc-Cleester's tavern.

CHAPTER 26

Frankie Clement is worse now than she was earlier today. Paler, sweatier, hair matted against her forehead, quilt pulled up to her chin, quivering, and she smells like feces. She doesn't even bother to pretend she's okay when McCleester lets Walt Whitman into the room. "I've never seen her this bad," he whispers to Walt before he leaves the room.

Whitman slides the stool from the corner to the bed. "Are you ready to ask for help now?"

She tries to speak but gets caught coughing. She finally says, "Not if I have to rat out my brother."

"You won't rat out the man who got you addicted to laudanum, who manipulates you into doing things that only help him — look at yourself. Where is he? Why isn't he helping you now?"

She drops her head. "You don't know us."

"I know he's not here, and I am," Walt says. "I know that we can help each other."

She says nothing.

Whitman shakes his head. What can he say to get her to help him? "You're right, Miss Clement. My meeting with your brother did not go well, and now I'm afraid he's going to kill my friend. I don't want you to rat out your brother, as you say, but I am asking you to tell me where he might be keeping Mr. Saunders." He pauses. "I can offer medical help in return, if you want it, but to be honest, Miss Blackwell will help you whether you help me or not. So I'll ask again. Please help me find my friend."

"My brother isn't as bad as you believe him to be."

"I don't doubt it, Miss Clement."

"He didn't give me laudanum," she says. "He told me I was stupid for doing it, and he wants me to quit. He doesn't even drink alcohol anymore because of some stupid book he wants me to read." She stops. "Samuel is a successful businessman with slippery ethics. That's all. And the only reason he's not here now is because I don't want him to see me like this."

Whitman knows he has to play this just right, and he knows he has to hurry. "Will you help me find my friend?" And then for good measure: "Please. I'm begging you."

Miss Clement starts to cry. This is difficult for her, Walt knows, and so he waits. He holds her hand, tells her everything is going to be okay. She shudders and shakes, her skin is hot, and she mumbles to herself.

And then, finally, she's ready. "I can't help you if it means hurting my brother. Now please leave so I can rest."

Walt feels numb. There's nothing left for him to do. He can't go door to door searching every corner of every building in New York, and he can't call the sheriff again.

Whitman doesn't say anything to Frankie as he exits the room, and when the barkeep asks him how it went, he only looks at the man, then drifts out the front door.

The night is chaotic in this neighborhood. Hordes of drunk men scamp about in packs, growling and cursing. They bump into Walt as he passes, and they shout at him to watch where he's going. He stumbles into a saloon he's never visited before, the Rusty Nail. He collapses in the chair and buries his face in his hands.

He bangs his boot on the floor.

"Mister?"

He looks up, expecting one of the drunks reclaiming his chair, but it is John Mc-

Cleester.

"I spoke with Frankie after you left," he says, "and I want her to get the help she needs even if she doesn't. You told her that woman doctor can help her if she tells you where her brother might be keeping your friend?"

Walt nods. "But she refused."

McCleester holds out a piece of paper. "I don't know where he's keeping your friend, but I know he has worked out of these three addresses in the past."

Whitman reaches for it, but McCleester pulls it away.

"I want to make sure Frankie gets help. Where do I bring her?"

"Here," Walt says, "I'll write it down for you." He pulls his green notebook out of his borrowed coat pocket and scribbles down the college's address. "Tell them Walt Whitman sent you."

McCleester nods, and they trade pieces of paper. "Much obliged."

Whitman knows the addresses — they aren't far from here — but he can cover ground more quickly if he can find Broadway Ike.

The streets and sidewalks are treacherous, and Ike has no choice but to drive much slower than either man would prefer. Each turn requires such a slow speed that they might as well stop. Whitman is frustrated by their lack of progress, but he appreciates what Ike is doing for him and so he holds his tongue.

He sees the marker for Chatham just down the way. Address number one. Finally. Ike takes the turn slow and then brings the omnibus to a stop. "It's faster for you to run the rest of the way," he calls out. "I'll wait here."

Walt jumps out of the omnibus and heads toward the first address, a butcher shop called Anderson's. He checks his pocket for the pistol. Aim for the head, the priest said.

The single-story building's front windows are dark. He knocks on the door. Nothing. He slinks around to the back, where he finds another entrance. He tries to open the door, but it is locked. So he bangs his large frame against the wood until it opens.

The inside smells like wet wood and oil and meat. The back room is an office — it contains nothing more than a desk, a filing drawer, a woodstove, and a coatrack. On the coatrack hang three bloody aprons. He finds a candle on the desk and a match in the top drawer. In his right hand, he holds the pistol and in the other, the candle.

Through the hallway, he tiptoes into the next room.

The candle highlights three hanging corpses. Walt jumps, takes a deep breath. But a closer look reveals exactly what one should expect to find in a butcher's shop: three dead cows ready for butchering.

Whitman takes a quick look around the lobby of the shop but finds nothing there either. Not only is Henry not here, but there is no trace at all of Samuel Clement's ever having been here. A sick feeling spreads over him. What if the barkeep gave him a list of bogus addresses to give Clement more time to get away?

The journey to the next address is not long, two blocks east and one block south. The omnibus comes to a stop in front of the building, a newer, two-story building constructed sometime after the Great Fire of 1835. A light is on in the front window, visible through the curtains. Whitman knocks, and a woman dressed in a housecoat answers.

She twists her face at Walt. "You're not my Robby."

"No, ma'am," he says. "I'm here looking for Samuel Clement."

"My husband kicked him out weeks ago," she says. "If you find him, let me know. He still owes us fifty dollars."

"Any idea where he's gone?"

She shakes her head. "That man is trouble."

"How do you know him?"

"I don't," she says. "My husband does and I don't ask about his business. What I do know is that when Samuel Clement is around, my husband turns into someone I don't like."

"Would your husband know where Mr. Clement is?"

She shrugs. "You're welcome to ask him when he returns."

"Do you expect him any time soon?"

"I thought you was him, didn't I?"

Walt nods.

"Truth is, mister, I don't know when he'll be back. Do what you want. Wait or don't wait. I wish I could be more help."

Mud and water soak Henry Saunders's boots and socks, and his body is one giant shiver. It is only a matter of time now, he knows. His one hope is that Walt miraculously finds him.

He smiles at the thought of Walt Whitman. His fit body and thick forearms. His sarcastic smile. The way his eyes dance back and forth at the men, women, and children he passes. He wears that grin, the one that says he knows a little bit more than everyone else around him, the grin that drives Henry mad. That is the thing about Walt. He is unflappable. So confident that it doesn't matter to him if you think he is a genius or not, and that is what Henry loves about him.

Henry focuses on happier times — hunting rabbits in the woods with his father behind their home or fishing for trout, the smell of fish cooking in butter. The way the flesh peeled off the stringy fish bones when his father cooked it just right, the way the meat dissolved on his tongue. He concentrates on his parents, but the reality of their lives without him is too much, so he returns to the rabbits and trout and butter crackling in the frying pan over the stove.

"Comfort me, Father," he prays. "I am done."

Henry Saunders closes his eyes and imagines going home one last time.

The air is thick and gray, and as he gets closer, the house materializes in front of him. The two-story house and barn are painted red. A long piece of black cloth is draped over the doorframe. Two large pine trees stand on either side of the house, and several maple trees grow between the house and barn.

His mother opens the door. Her brown hair is pulled up on the back of her head and the wrinkles on her cheeks have grown more prominent. She kisses his cheek. "It's time."

"But I'm not ready."

"Ours is not to decide when or how," she says. "We go when we are called."

Then he sees it across the room. The wooden casket is framed on either side by candles, and the emotions hit him all at once — fear, dread, yearning, regret, loss. He looks at his mother. "Are you sure?"

"Go on," she says gently. "It's all right."

"What will happen to me?"

She smiles. "I will watch over you."

He steps toward the fireplace and takes it all in — the rocking chair, the bench, the white cat sleeping in the corner. Standing next to the casket now, he lowers his body inside, the planks of wood warm from the fire, the smell of cut wood reminding him of his visits to the lumberyard with his father. He panics, and loneliness settles in. "Mother?" He checks to see if she is still there.

She sits in the rocking chair with her arms resting on her lap. "I'm not going any-where," she says. *"Ever."*

Henry lays his head down and closes his

eyes, his mother's voice floating in the air around him. *"I love you,"* she says over and over.

A banging at the door startles him from his trance. It's Samuel Clement.

"Don't go to sleep on me yet, Mr. Saunders. We've got an appointment to keep."

The adrenaline from acquiring the list of addresses has faded, but Walt pushes himself to visit the last location, the farthest of the three. Perhaps this is the one that will house Henry. His heart races at the thought, and he boards the omnibus yet again.

The omnibus slides around the turn from Mulberry Street toward Mott, and nearly clips a carriage going the other direction. The force of the turn sends Walt crashing into the sidewall. He rights himself and peers out the window. The driver of the carriage shouts something inaudible in the wind at Broadway Ike, who acts as if nothing has happened.

The journey slows to a stop as they encounter clusters of New Yorkers in the streets, and what should take a quarter of an hour ends up taking nearly the whole.

The omnibus finally stops, and Walt steps out into the snow and moves toward the third address. He makes it only a few feet before he notices fresh wagon tracks. He follows them into the alley, noticing that they stop where something large and bulky has been dragged and presumably placed in the wagon.

His heart beats faster.

At the door, he reaches for the latch and turns it. The door is locked, but one good kick is all it takes to open it. Walt steps inside, where all he finds is an overturned chair and a wilted boutonniere.

He is too late.

CHAPTER 27

As Walt is trying to formulate his next move, a thunderous explosion rips through the air. The sky lights up several blocks over in the direction of the Women's Medical College, and then a chorus of voices shouts its approval. Worried about the students, Walt hastens across Centre Street and up to Delancey, where a crowd has formed. Thousands stand shoulder to shoulder from one end of the street to the other, and when one person moves, they all move. Some hold torches, which illuminate the faces of those around them like demons.

A young watchman, who looks barely old enough to shave, struggles to keep control of his horse.

"What's going on?" Walt calls to the young man.

"It's that medical college for women. You know, the one where they done all that killin'."

"What's happened?" says Whitman.

"Don't know myself," the man says. "I was at home with my wife when the messenger arrived."

"Why aren't you doing anything?"

"Orders are to stay here," he says.

Whitman starts toward the commotion.

"Sorry," the watchman says. "Can't let anyone through. Gathering can't grow any bigger than it already is."

The man steers his horse to block Whitman from moving. Without hesitating, Walt grabs hold of the reins and directs the horse to the side of the road.

"You can't do that," the man calls after him. "Stop."

Walt ignores him, quickly wrapping the reins around the lamppost. He runs toward the mob, an overwhelming sense of dread filling him.

The clang of fire engines reverberates several blocks out.

Whitman advances until the crowd is at a standstill. To better see what is going on, he climbs a nearby streetlamp and hangs on to the pole, his feet resting on the metal ledge a few feet off the ground. The mass of people extends all the way up the street to the women's college, which has gone up in flames. A sick feeling takes hold. Did the students get out?

The crowd begins to dissipate, allowing him to navigate his way north toward the college. Several hundred feet away from the burning college, he runs into another crowd of people. Firemen are trying to get to the building, but they are blocked by what remains of the mob, which has formed a wall between the college and the firemen. The sheriff and his men scramble to organize a militia. In all the commotion, Whitman sees no sign of Elizabeth Blackwell and the other students. His heart races as he tries to figure out how to reach them.

Elizabeth Blackwell takes two steps at a time to get to the dormitory, and she bursts inside, yelling for the students, "Get up!"

The young women open their eyes. A few of them groan and one sits up.

"Now!"

The students rub their faces.

Elizabeth runs to the window, pulls the curtains, and steps back. Down below, the torches spread out in front of the building like fireflies as far as she can see.

"Are they here for *us*?" Miss Emsbury asks.

Before Elizabeth can answer, a rock crashes through the window. Through the broken window the mob is louder, their voices blending into one another until they stream one loud buzz.

The students follow Miss Blackwell down the stairwell only to find the mob already inside the college, surrounded by flames. One man, standing closest to the door, sees the students and charges. She slams the door and pushes the lock into place just as the man's body bangs into the other side.

Elizabeth attempts to exit out the back door to the alley, but the mob is there too. She latches that door and returns with the students upstairs. None of them speak. They sit on their beds and hope.

Knowing he cannot fight against the crowd, Walt weaves down several alleyways to reach the college's back door, only to find it locked.

A man at the end of the alleyway sees him. "Did you get the door open?"

Whitman turns to face the man. He is probably in his fifties, clean-cut except for a strip of thin facial hair that wraps around his chin.

"What's wrong?" the man says. "I asked if you got the door open."

Walt shakes his head and slinks away to the side, but the man follows. "You're with them, aren't you? You work with those women doctors."

Whitman darts the other way, away from the man, but straight into the mob, which has filled the alley.

The man calls out behind Walt: "Grab him; he's one of them."

Their hands are upon Whitman, from his feet to his arms, to his neck and back, and suddenly he is above them all, being passed from one end of the crowd to another.

"But I'm not one of them," he yells without thinking. "I'm just like you."

The farther they pass him, the more people he sees — they fill every open spot on the street in front of the college except a tiny bit of space where the alley meets the street, and it is this space that saves his life. They drop him, and he hits the ground hard.

He pushes himself to his feet and races to the front of the building, where the militia fires their bayonets into the air. The back end of the mob turns around and throws rocks. One rock strikes Sheriff Petty in the cheek, underneath his left eye. Blood appears on his face and drips into his mustache. This time, the militia fires on the mob and drops fifteen men and six women. People scream, scramble for cover.

Whitman rushes over to Sheriff Petty. "The students are trapped upstairs."

"You're sure?"

"That's where they sleep," Walt says. "There's nowhere else for them to go."

The sheriff and ten of his men follow Walt to the back alley where they break down the back door. The flames have spread from the dissection room to the stairway. "Up those stairs," Walt says. "We have to hurry."

Minutes later, the men reappear out of the smoke, dragging the students behind them.

All of them scurry away from the building, reaching a safe spot across the street just in time to watch the college crumple in on itself.

The people shout their approval and march toward their homes. As they march, they pray to God for the souls of the dissected. *May you find it in your heart, O Lord, to raise the dissected,* they chant. *May the dissected find some peace in your kingdom.*

Whitman shakes his head. These people should be ashamed of themselves. He watches them as they go, noticing some of them stopping a block away. They are forming a circle around something, and chanting, but Walt can't make out what they are saying above the commotion.

"Excuse me, please."

Walt pushes his way through the crowd. The farther into the chaos he goes, the clearer it is what they are saying. These people, who just burned down the women's college, and with it everything he and the students own, are praying. *Receive his soul, O Lord,* they chant. He breaks through the throng, and that's when he sees Henry Saunders's body on the sidewalk. His chest is sliced open down the middle, exposing his gray lungs.

Stricken, Walt drops to his knees —

— he can't breathe —

— and the world around him crashes down.

He puts his ear over Henry's mouth, brushes his cheek and his nose —

— his face is puffy and bruised; dried blood and sludge stick to his cheek, chin, and left ear.

This cannot be happening.

His skin, a ghastly hue, is cold to the touch.

Walt cleans Henry's face with his handkerchief. The sludge comes off with a little work, but the blood stays.

They are praying again, and all he can think is that Henry Saunders is not a goddamn Barnum exhibit. He is yelling at them now, but the din around him is so loud he can't hear himself. The people stand wide-eyed and wide-mouthed, leaning and swaying while a light snow begins to fall.

Behind Walt, a hand touches his shoulder. He whips around and shouts for the sheriff to leave him alone.

"I need you to come with me, Mr. Whitman," Petty says.

"You're here to arrest me for slander, aren't you?"

The crowd closes in, engulfing him, and a rage unlike any he's experienced worms its way inside.

Petty, aware of the onlookers, pleads with Walt. "Let's not make a scene."

"Too late for that." Walt feels like he's teetering between sanity and madness.

He lays Henry's head on the sidewalk, reaches for the large rock on the ground next to him —

"Please, Mr. Whitman." The sheriff tries one more time.

But Walt hurls the rock through the shop window behind him. The horde scatters and the glass shatters, crashes to the ground, but is not louder than Walt Whitman's own screams, which ricochet between the alleys and buildings as he leaps up and runs through the streets, the crowd sealing off the sheriff behind him.

Henry Saunders's apartment sounds dead. That's the best way Walt can describe it. The usual sounds swirl around him: men and women talking and yelling, animals snorting and grunting, the clomping of hooves on stone, but a dead pitch hangs over it all and inflects everything.

He hasn't been able to cry yet. All the emotion is deep in his chest — he feels it when he breathes — but it won't come out. He sits down on Henry's bed, wraps himself up in the blanket, and lies down.

Walt's mother used to make tea with honey whenever he felt sad. She would put her arms around him and rub his back, and somehow she made everything seem better. He pretends that his mother is there with him now. She wears her black housedress and has already let her hair down for the night. It has always surprised him how long her hair is — what is a tight bundle during the day almost touches the floor at night.

"You've had quite a day," she says.

Growing up, Walt experienced nightmares and would often wake up in the middle of the night, screaming. Louisa Whitman would rush into his room and, after making sure the other children were still sleeping,

299

would lie in bed with him until he fell asleep.

As she did then, she massages his back and his neck. She whistles "Rock of Ages" and tells her son all will be well again.

"Jesus," she says, "died that all may live again, and that includes Henry Saunders." She kisses his cheek. "Oh yes, Henry is in a better place now. A place without fear or hunger. Without violence or war, where people treat each other with dignity and respect. A place where there is no such thing as poverty. Henry has been greeted by family members who have died too. They have welcomed him home, Walt. That's what you should believe. Henry has gone home."

Walt pulls the blanket tight under his chin and closes his eyes. The other voice in his head tells him to get out of the apartment, that to stay here is dangerous. But he doesn't listen to that voice right now. He listens to his mother.

"You will see Henry Saunders again," she says. "When the Lord God claps his hands three times, the dead shall rise, and then you will dance together forever in the clouds while the angels sing hymns."

CHAPTER 28

When Walt wakes the next morning, it is the absolute stillness that surprises him. The stillness is more than the absence of sound; it comprises everything around him — the vacant apartment, Henry's clothing that he will never wear again, the frigid morning air, the absence of Walt's own belongings burned up in the college fire, the unperturbed snow rolling softly from the sky. He lies in bed, focusing on his breath. He holds it in and takes in the stillness of his chest. This is what he would look like dead. Images of Henry Saunders's body flash in his mind, and tears spring to his eyes.

Walt composes himself and glances about the room, which is still in shambles. He knows Henry would prefer it tidied up, and this is enough to get him out of bed. Shivering, he removes his pants and white shirt and searches through Henry's wardrobe for fresh clothing. He slips on a blue banyan, and the cold silk sends a chill through him.

Next, he builds a fire in the woodstove and sits on the floor next to it to warm himself. Watching the fire calls to mind the night before, the women's college up in flames, the students trapped upstairs. He thinks of all that he lost in the fire, but nothing compares to the loss of Henry.

He stares out the window, fighting to retain the image of Henry Saunders in better times, but it has already begun to fade. Around Walt are the objects of Henry's life: his walking cane, desk, and books, all physical proof that he was once here and is now gone.

Walt sniffs the banyan collar — Henry's smell lingers in these things, but that too will wane. And then comes the awful realization that philosophy and religion, despite their explanations and promises, will not bring Henry back to him.

What he knows with a surety is that Henry's body has been transported to Barclay's workroom and, once the autopsy has been completed, will be shipped to the Saunders's farm in northern Manhattan for burial, where Henry's corporeal self will spiral outward through the earth forever.

But what of the soul? The question unfurls the unknowable darkness before him. Deism suggests that Walt will have to reason out his own belief in an afterlife, and Elias Hicks taught that the afterlife is now — neither doctrine brings any relief to Walt Whitman in his moment of crisis. Henry Saunders is gone from this life, which means Walt will have to live today, and every day thereafter, without him.

He pushes himself to his feet, the cold air rushing up through the open end of the banyan. Books go back on shelves, pans return to cupboards. He lifts the desk from where it lays on its side, and he folds the clothing that has been scattered on the floor. He folds his own dirty clothing, and this is when he sees Father Allen's overcoat — a reminder of what the priest did for him, a reminder of his own status as a wanted man, the sole survivor of an elaborate cover-up.

He hangs the overcoat, and Abby Runkel's poem flutters to the ground. He picks it up, reads:

I need you, sir, to find my sister
Who left this earth too soon
God wants her to come home to him
But needs her body too
I cry to think of her in little pieces
all about the room

Please bring her home, Mr. Whitman,
Bring her to me soon.

Walt smiles and lays the poem on the windowsill. Quite something from someone so young. He wants to help her find her sister, but the sad truth is, it is probably too late for Maggie's body.

The knock at the door startles him. He tiptoes across the room, carefully removes the pistol from Father Allen's coat. He stares at it as if he's never seen it before. Another knock, louder, more determined.

Should he call out or just answer it? He steadies himself with deep breaths, and then a voice from the other side of the door calls out: "Walt? Mr. Whitman? Are you in there?"

The voice belongs not to Samuel Clement or Silas Petty but to a woman. Of course, either man might be with this woman, he reminds himself.

"Who is there?" he finally says.

"Miss Zacky, from the college."

He wipes his face with the banyan sleeve, the light blue silk absorbing his sweat. "Are you alone?"

"Yes. Elizabeth told me where I might find you," she says. "She's been charged with Mr. Saunders's death."

Walt opens the door, pistol at the ready.

Marie Zakrzewska is alone. Her red hair is a mess, and her face tinted with charcoal streaks. Her dress too is covered in soot. "She's in jail."

"But the last time I saw her, she was fine," Walt says. "I was with the sheriff when he rescued you from the burning college."

"Yes," she says, "and we are all grateful."

Whitman continues. "When I left, she was with the students outside, with you — you all were being cared for by Dr. Liston."

Miss Zacky nods. "After you found Mr. Saunders's body, the sheriff arrested her."

Walt shakes his head. "But —"

"Lizzy found your friend in the same position as Lena found Abraham. Whoever did it, cut him open with a bone saw to make it look as if *we* had dissected him. Ridiculous, of course."

"Samuel Clement."

Miss Zacky nods. "That's what Lizzy said."

Walt is suddenly aware of the flimsy banyan, and pulls it closed to cover his exposed chest. "Please come in." He steps aside to let her pass, then does a quick check of the hallway for any signs of someone following her. He sees none. "We aren't safe here," he says. "Where are the other students?"

The question makes her cry. "They've all gone home," she says. "They're terrified, and who can blame them?"

"But you stayed."

"I have to help Lizzy."

Whitman excuses himself so he can change clothing. With her back turned, he puts on a pair of Henry's dark trousers and a white shirt, a fresh pair of socks and his boots. Then he brews tea and cooks eggs. "So what do we know?"

Miss Zacky tosses him the morning's *Herald,* and while she eats, he reads:

REPORTER MURDERED!

The dissected body of Mr. Henry Saunders was discovered last night by a medical college mob at the Women's Medical College of Manhattan. Reports are that the body was being used under the guise of medical training to another purpose. Saunders, readers might recall, was the author of an article exposing the evils of these medical schools and their ungodly practice of human dissection. City officials surmise that the murder was the college's answer to that article and a warning to others who might have more traditional beliefs about the human body and its sanctity in the eyes of God.

Miss Elizabeth Blackwell, who was alone with Mr. Saunders when he died, was then interrogated, but denied all knowledge of the murder. She was watched, and later removed a vial of arsenic from her dress. Suspicion of foul play was then for the first time entertained, and the Coroner, Dr. Kenneth Barclay, determined upon a *post mortem* examination that the stomach of the deceased was found to contain a large quantity of arsenic. The powder taken from Miss Blackwell was also tested, with like result; and the whiskey bottle from which Mr. Saunders had drunk during the night was also found to contain a quantity of the same drug. Miss Blackwell was arrested, examined, and committed to prison, to await the action of the Grand Jury.

Local officials are concerned about the possibility of more mob violence. A crowd has gathered outside the Tombs, where Miss Blackwell is being held, demanding speedy justice. The demonstrations are peaceful as of this printing, but city officials and law enforcement are keenly aware that unless something is done with Miss Blackwell, the situation has the potential to worsen.

Whitman sets the paper on the table and watches Miss Zacky eat. She senses his eyes on her and looks up.

"It's happening all over again," he says.

She doesn't say anything.

"How is Miss Blackwell holding up?" he says. "Have you seen her?"

"She's strong," Miss Zacky says, "but she's terrified."

Walt shakes his head. "Of course she is."

"We have to stop this, Mr. Whitman. We can't let it happen again."

"The crowd . . . how big is it?"

"Maybe a thousand, and growing."

Walt says, "They want a lynching." He thinks for a moment. "We know who killed Henry. We have to present evidence that forces city leaders to acknowledge Clement's guilt. Everything else is irrelevant."

"We couldn't do it for Lena. What can we do that we didn't already try?"

What indeed? Walt thinks. He stares at the newspaper, traces the perforated top edge to its smooth sides to its black type to the name of its editor, James Gordon Bennett. "That's it." Whitman points to the name. "We need to put out a reward."

"What good will that do?"

"As they did for the Mary Rogers case."

"But they found the wrong person."

"That doesn't mean it won't work this time," Walt says.

"But we don't have any money."

"We can raise the money by forming a committee of safety like James Bennett did for the Rogers case. He knew the only way to deal with an ineffective law enforcement was to bait the public with a reward, and if conducted in a public forum, city officials have no choice but to follow through when someone comes forth with evidence."

Miss Zacky nods. "Whom do we ask for help?"

Walt thinks for a moment. "I'll have to ask Mr. Bennett. He'll probably say no, but I see no other option at the moment." He stands. "But first we need to find another place to stay. It's not safe here."

She rises to meet him.

Whitman sees that this is difficult for her. "Don't worry," he says, "I won't leave his office until Mr. Bennett agrees to help us."

She musters a smile.

"Do you have money?"

She nods.

"Good. Get a room at Sweeny's Hotel, and I'll meet you after my meeting with Bennett, bearing good news."

She doesn't move.

"We will succeed," Walt says, trying to

convince himself as the words come out of his mouth.

"I believe in you," she says as she leaves.

Walt watches at the window to make sure no one is following. He sits at Henry's desk to gather his thoughts. Bennett will be a tough sell for sure, but this is their best chance, given the exigency. He glances about the room. He might not return and so he wants to record it in his mind. Under the bed, he finds a leather attaché, which he stuffs with a couple of shirts, some socks, and an extra pair of trousers. That's all that will fit. He picks up Henry's walking cane, then scans the room one last time before he attempts to get a meeting with James Gordon Bennett.

CHAPTER 29

James Gordon Bennett, who founded the *New York Herald* in May 1835, is known for his sensationalist reporting style and refusal to back down from any lead. Walt's own battles with Bennett have played out in the papers, but he has never met with the man until today. In the large corner office, bookcases line the walls to Whitman's left and right. And at a mammoth-size desk sits the man himself. The editor of the *New York Herald* is a hunched-over, frail-looking man with an eyepiece in his left hand and a pencil in his right. His black coat matches his black shoes, and his white hair shines in the light from the window. Mr. Bennett turns his head, and Walt sees for the first time that he is cross-eyed. "Who are you, again?"

"Walt Whitman the reporter."

Bennett says, "I've never seen you before."

"You write about me with the disdain of

someone who knows me well."

"And yet you're still here?"

"I need your help."

"My help? I should have you arrested."

"Elizabeth Blackwell," Whitman says, "did not kill Henry Saunders."

"Of course she didn't," Bennett says. "I have yet to meet a guilty criminal. Next you'll tell me her husband was innocent too."

Walt does not point out that Bennett has confused Elizabeth Blackwell with Lena Stowe.

"I suppose you didn't break into the *Aurora* and print another one of your stories after you were fired either, did you?"

Whitman says, "Perhaps I made a mistake in coming here."

"Really? That's all it takes to get rid of you?" Bennett is shaking his head. "I must say I'm disappointed. I had you pegged for someone more like myself, someone who will fight even when he might be wrong."

"I'm nothing like you."

Bennett smiles at this. "Obviously."

"I'm trying to prove Miss Blackwell's innocence."

"So you say."

"I thought you might want the story when I do."

312

"If I want the story," Bennett says, "I'll get the story. Now, is there something you wanted to ask me?"

Walt pauses, then decides that he has nothing to lose. "I want you to organize a committee of safety as you did for the cigar-girl murder case."

Mr. Bennett sets the eyepiece on the desk and leans back in his chair. "That was a mistake."

"Mistake?"

Mr. Bennett glances out the window. "Mr. Whitman, I'm afraid I *can't* help you."

"Why?"

"The Mary Rogers case; it seemed simple. The committee of safety has always been a way for the powerless to fight the powerful, and this case was the perfect scenario for such a committee. But something happened — there were more things going on than any of us ever imagined."

"What types of things?"

"Threats against my family, friends, and business," Bennett says.

"I didn't know. I'm sorry."

"We can't afford to be naïve, Mr. Whitman."

"Elizabeth Blackwell has devoted her life to medicine. She administers to the sick and poor without any thought for herself. She's not a murderer, Mr. Bennett. You know it as well as I. Now, please, I beg you, help me."

Bennett considers the proposition, and it appears as if he'll do it. But then his face changes, and he says, "I'm sorry, but no."

"I know that the same folks on the committee of safety are some of the same folks we are fighting against. But we can create a new story with new rules, and the committee members will have to follow."

Bennett shakes his head.

Walt stands, puts on his hat and coat, and turns to leave. At the door, he tries one last time. "Is there nothing else I can say to change your mind?"

"I'm very busy, Mr. Whitman. Please understand."

Outside, the sun is bright and the air is mild. Walt has no idea what to do next; he can't bear facing Miss Zacky or Miss Blackwell. He can't bear to think about Henry's body in the care of Kenneth Barclay.

He passes a peddler hawking hot sweet potatoes, and the smell evokes in Walt a childhood memory: a rare moment when his father was sober enough for the family to share a meal. He is struck by how far away that life is now. He moved to Manhattan to escape, and now he finds himself in the midst of crisis his writerly self could not have imagined.

He closes his eyes and tries to return home, but all he can see is a woman's body hanging. He has to press on.

Walt realizes he's hungry, and buys two sweet potatoes. Candied and delicious, they buoy his spirits, and he's pondering his next move, when Bennett's secretary approaches. "Mr. Whitman," he says, out of breath. "I didn't think I'd find you." He presents a piece of paper. "Mr. Bennett asked me to give you this."

Walt takes the piece of paper and reads:

Dear Mr. Whitman:

I'll arrange for the meeting announcement to be run in the evening edition of Greeley's *Tribune,* but I won't lead it. I can't have my name attached to the committee this time. There are people in high places, higher than the sheriff even, who do not want this murder revisited, and I can't put my family in danger again. You should take care of yourself too, Mr. Whitman.

Sincerely,
James G. Bennett

Walt looks up to thank the secretary, but

he is gone. No matter, he thinks. This is good news indeed, and he walks toward Sweeny's Hotel with more energy in his movement. He can't wait to tell Miss Zacky about the meeting tonight.

Marie Zakrzewska appears rested — she's bought a new dress, and she's cleaned the soot from her face and hair.

"Well?" she says. "How did it go?"

"Meeting tonight at eight."

"That's wonderful news." She throws her arms around him, pulls him close. "I knew you would come through."

This catches Walt off guard, and he realizes it is not entirely unpleasant to be held by a beautiful young woman. They stand like this for a few seconds until he lets go. He goes to the sink, turns the water handle. The spigot gurgles, then spits water into the sink. He cups his hands until they are full, and splashes the water on his face. "I noticed a restaurant in the lobby where we can have our dinner."

Miss Zacky hands him a towel. He dries his face, and when he turns, she is near. She doesn't say a word. She leans in, kisses him softly on the lips. "Thank you," she says. "For everything."

Walt can only stand there. He knows what

she wants. He's been through it before, and he's not ashamed. But Henry —

— is gone, Walt thinks, and she comes closer.

She kisses his neck.

"Miss Zakrzewska."

She kisses his cheek.

"I was in love with Henry."

She kisses his mouth.

This time he does not say anything. Perhaps they can forget the events of the past weeks, the difficulties that lie ahead, and disappear into each other, even for a short time.

He removes her dress, then her corset, then chemise and pantalettes. She giggles. "I'm going to make you work for this."

He smiles, self-conscious of the act now, until she pulls him into her and he is again lost —

But then too quickly, he returns to himself and everything around him and he's thinking of Henry and he can't stop crying. "I can't," he says.

And she tells him not to worry over and over and over.

CHAPTER 30

Inside Horace Greeley's gilded mansion, it is bright and noisy and full of people, and while Walt Whitman knows most people by name, he has not personally met many of them. Mr. Bennett greets him at the door, per their agreement, and introduces him around. The men wear tailcoats and neckcloths, sipping drinks and smoking cigars, and they nod his way when Mr. Bennett calls out their names. Among others are Gerard Hallock, Henry Raymond, George Morris, and William Snowden, the very same who published Edgar Poe's "The Mystery of Marie Rogêt." Poe himself is hunched over in the corner, looking even worse than he did almost a week ago when Walt saw him in the Pewter Mug. Snowden sees Walt looking at his writer and pulls him by the elbow to Poe's corner.

"Mr. Poe," Snowden says, "meet Walter Whitman."

Edgar Poe looks up as if awakened out of a trance. "Pleased to meet you, sir." His voice is shaky, half-hoarse.

Whitman shakes his hand and says, "I admire your work very much."

"Oh? Oh?" The poor author attempts to sit up but simply can't. He's too feeble to do more than sit where he is, and so he thanks Walt for the kind words about his work, which he discounts himself by saying, "It's a surprise anyone takes me or my work seriously anymore."

Walt glances at Mr. Snowden, who shoots him a look signaling that this is typical behavior for Poe.

"Well," Snowden says to Mr. Poe, "I need to see Mr. Whitman off to his host."

At this, Mr. Poe stiffens. He grips Whitman's hand and pulls him close. "This is all a conspiracy." His voice is strong and clear now. He keeps the volume low so Mr. Snowden can't hear. "Abraham Stowe was innocent. His wife was innocent. You are correct about it all, and I will help you in any way I can, do you hear?"

Walt pulls back, awkwardly, and nods.

Mr. Snowden guides Walt to the back of the room, where he introduces him to a short man with wire-rimmed spectacles. He is bald on top, with long white hair in the back. "Mr. Horace Greeley."

Whitman shakes his hand. "Pleasure to see you again, sir." Greeley was a big supporter of the Stowes and held a fund-raiser in this very room for the women's college a few months back.

"We've met before?"

"I am a friend of Abraham and Lena — or was, anyway."

"Ah yes, I remember. You are the author of the temperance novel?"

"The very same, sir."

"My wife found it instructive, but I" — he holds up his glass — "remain unconvinced."

"Then we'll get along very well." Walt grabs a bourbon from the waiter's tray and takes a drink. "An author's life should never be confused with that of his character's." They clink their glasses together.

Mr. Greeley smiles. "Now, the meeting will proceed as follows: You will present your case and then we'll vote on whether or not the committee will move forward. A simple majority rules the day."

"Thank you for hosting this meeting," Walt says. "It is very kind of you."

"I'm lucky to be able to assist. It's a tragedy what happened, and if you're correct, perhaps we begin to set it right."

The bourbon relaxes Walt. The whole

evening has come together. None of this will bring Henry Saunders back, but he owes it to Henry to make sure Samuel Clement bears responsibility for his actions.

Walt follows Mr. Greeley to the front of the room and is just about to sit down when he sees him.

Isaiah Rynders.

Blood rushes to Walt's face, and his stomach flips.

Mr. Rynders nods his way. His auburn hair is neatly combed, the knife scar on his forehead barely visible. Walt wonders about Azariah, and whether he is well. He makes a decision to find him when all this is over, to try and get him to safety.

Mr. Greeley sees the two men make eye contact. "You know Mr. Rynders?"

"We've crossed paths a few times," Walt says.

"Let me tell you — a good man," Mr. Greeley says. "A lot of what he does for this city goes unheralded."

"Oh?"

"He creates jobs for the thousands of immigrants who arrive in the harbors every day. Indeed, no single man does more to maintain order in our city." Mr. Greeley waves to Mr. Rynders. "Yes, every New Yorker owes Isaiah Rynders an enormous debt of gratitude."

Whitman is speechless. Over Mr. Greeley's shoulder, Mr. Rynders smiles at him, and Walt knows the entire evening is in question. How can he persuade a room full of New York's most prominent men to go along with his premise with Rynders in the room?

"Are you feeling well, Mr. Whitman?"

"Yes," he stammers. "Will Mr. Rynders support this meeting?"

"Oh yes," Mr. Greeley says. "When he found out about it, he insisted on coming. Now let's begin, shall we?"

The meeting begins with a brief welcome by Mr. Greeley, and then all eyes turn to Mr. Walt Whitman. "Good evening, gentlemen," Whitman says. "Tonight, I ask for your help in averting another tragic event in what can already be called a disaster. As you know, my colleague, Mr. Henry Saunders, was murdered and his body found yesterday in the now destroyed Women's Medical College of Manhattan. The young woman who ran the college, Miss Elizabeth Blackwell, is set to stand trial for his murder.

"What I am about to propose will sound grandiose and far-fetched, but please keep an open mind. As this committee knows firsthand, New York City's legal system and

322

law enforcement have had their challenges. Many do their jobs well, but some are corrupt. Your committee's scathing report after the Mary Rogers murder was clear on that point and gave several compelling and accurate examples to support your conclusions. In that context, I suggest to you that Miss Blackwell's trial is part of a larger conspiracy to protect the lucrative business of body snatching."

Whitman glances at Mr. Rynders and takes a deep breath. He recounts the events leading up to Henry Saunders's abduction and murder, his meetings with Frankie Clement, his confrontation with Samuel Clement at the church. "Mr. Clement made no attempt to hide the fact that he abducted Mr. Saunders. He wanted me to know. That was the whole point."

Mr. Hallock raises his hand. "Mr. Whitman, we want to help, but what you haven't addressed is the history of that medical college. This is the second such murder in three weeks."

"Precisely," Walt says. "The city hanged Lena Stowe for the murder of her husband, Abraham Stowe, and then a short time later, after Lena's execution, Mr. Saunders is murdered in precisely the same manner as Mr. Stowe. One thing this demonstrates is

Lena Stowe's likely innocence." Walt doesn't want to oversell what to him is obvious, so he proceeds deliberately. "And the second thing this shows is that the same person likely committed both murders."

The men whisper among themselves.

Whitman continues, "So either Elizabeth Blackwell or Samuel Clement committed both murders."

"And all the evidence points to Mr. Clement," Mr. Poe says in a wobbly voice from the back.

"Both bodies were gutted like deer," Walt says, "not dissected. Clearly, the murderer wanted to cast blame on Lena Stowe first and Elizabeth Blackwell second by making the victims appear dissected."

"With all due respect, Mr. Whitman" — Mr. Rynders speaks now — "the autopsy results suggest otherwise."

"Then they are incorrect," Walt says. "Something we also saw with the Mary Rogers case."

Mr. Hallock stands up. "But why?"

"Well, sir. I don't have all the answers, but Abraham Stowe's involvement with the Bone Bill is well known, and if that legislation passes, the body snatchers are out of business."

Whitman pauses to give them a chance to

reflect on what he's said so far.

"As many of you probably know, I witnessed Sheriff Harris's murder — for which, despite his clear guilt, Mr. Clement was dismissed as a suspect. Yes, Mr. Warren was there, but he didn't pull the trigger. Nobody would be the wiser if I had not been there to do a story on body snatching." Walt gets emotional, stops. "And unfortunately, Mr. Saunders paid the price for what I saw."

Mr. Hallock, still standing, says: "And this committee of safety would raise funds for a reward, then?"

"Yes, for information about Henry Saunders's murder."

Mr. Rynders raises his hand. "Excuse me, Mr. Whitman. You haven't stated the obvious problem with your proposal: Should this committee go forward, we will, all of us, accuse the City of New York of hanging an innocent woman in Lena Stowe. A very serious charge."

"Yes, but we will save the city from doing it again."

"Surely this will work itself out in the courts," Mr. Hallock says. "Why the hurry? We don't want to show up the new sheriff with this committee."

Walt doesn't bring up how the courts let Lena down. Instead, he says, "The hurry is simple: A crowd of New Yorkers has gathered in front of the Tombs. They want justice, and unless we do something, they will take matters into their own hands. Thank you for your time and consideration."

The men then discuss the merits of the case. All of them seem to agree that Walt has made a convincing case, and that if there is no doubt of Miss Blackwell's innocence, they should act. Most of their concerns revolve around the committee's relationship with law enforcement. Sheriff Petty is new, and he is doing, by all accounts, good work. This committee has the potential to permanently damage the sheriff's reputation.

Mr. Hallock calls for the vote. The man nearest them, George Morris, is the first.

"Aye," he said.

"Mr. Snowden?"

"Aye."

"Mr. Rynders?"

Isaiah Rynders makes eye contact with Whitman before he speaks. "Nay."

Mr. Hallock writes the results in a notebook with a silver pencil. "That's one for no. Mr. Raymond?"

"Nay."

The rest of the vote is split right down the

middle, which leaves Mr. Greeley as the deciding vote. When it is his turn, the room goes silent, and all eyes are on him. He recounts the numbers on the paper, makes a few notes, then says: "Before I cast my vote, I have a few questions."

"Questions?" Whitman can't contain his surprise.

"You want us to humiliate New York law enforcement by essentially taking the law into our own hands," Greeley says. "I want to be sure of the facts before making my decision."

He continues. "This plot you're suggesting — it's so elaborate. Why would this Clement *dissect* his victims as you suggest?"

"A clumsy attempt to frame Mrs. Stowe and Miss Blackwell," Walt says.

"Yes, yes," Greeley says. "Fair enough, but what about the Mary Rogers case? Our committee did not lead to its resolution. Indeed, it may have done more harm than good with regard to public perception of law enforcement. You yourself are here tonight under the pretext that New York law enforcement cannot do its own job."

"With regard to the Mary Rogers case, most New Yorkers believe Abraham Stowe is responsible for her death." This is difficult for Walt to say. "In that sense, many would say the committee did work."

Mr. Poe groans from the back of the room.

"Mr. Whitman, what you are suggesting sounds so obvious that, if it's true, then the conspiracy is so broad and far-reaching that —" Greeley pauses.

"The mayor himself might be implicated? Make no mistake, Mr. Greeley, this fact is not lost on me," Walt says. "This is why the committee must act — it is only as a body that we can confront such corruption. We, as citizens, have to take the law back. So, please, I implore you. Vote yes."

Mr. Greeley strokes his chin, holds up his glass. "Congratulations. It appears as if you've convinced enough of us."

CHAPTER 31

After the vote, a hat is passed around the room, and the men pitch in amounts ranging from $25 to $75. Later, Walt, Mr. Hallock, and Mr. Greeley each count the money, and when they all sign off on the same amount, $1,040, Mr. Greeley stores the reward money in his personal safe.

Whitman is elated. The sadness is there too, but he forces it deep inside where it will have to stay for now. He has to focus on his next task, and that is proving Elizabeth Blackwell's innocence. As he crosses the street in the direction of Sweeny's Hotel, a black carriage pulls alongside him and stops. The door opens to reveal Isaiah Rynders. "Mr. Whitman, a word?"

Walt glances inside the carriage and sees no one else.

"I assure you, it's safe."

"I have nothing to say to you." Whitman turns to walk away but is stopped by what

Rynders says next.

"I know what you're thinking, but I had nothing to do with your friend's death. Sometimes the people who work for me do things that I myself do not approve of, and I'm left covering for them. Please. I want to explain how we might all move forward."

Walt opens his mouth to respond, but Rynders holds up his hand.

"If I'd wanted you dead, Mr. Whitman," Rynders says, "believe me, you'd be dead."

After Walt climbs into the carriage, neither man speaks for a moment.

Rynders clears his throat. "I'm glad you changed your mind." Mr. Rynders smiles. "That was quite a presentation tonight," he says. "You had much of the room convinced."

"Not you."

"You can hardly be surprised." Mr. Rynders draws in a deep breath. "Besides, I'm not the one you need to convince." He folds out a small panel in the seat next to him, causing Walt to jump up.

"Relax, Mr. Whitman. Just trying to be hospitable." From the space behind the seat, he pulls a bottle of scotch. "Drink?"

"No, thank you." Walt sits back down.

"Very well." He pours himself a drink in a small glass from the compartment and takes a sip. "Warms the insides."

"With all due respect, sir, why did you want to see me?"

"Yes, yes." He takes another sip, sits back, and crosses his legs. "Since our altercation at Mr. Emerson's speech, I've taken to learn all I can about you. I studied your Democratic rally speech in the *Evening Post;* I read your novel *Franklin Evans* and your stories 'Death in the School-Room' and 'Wild Frank's Return.' And I have followed your editorials in the *Aurora.* You have a promising career as a writer."

He pauses to give Whitman a chance to respond, but Walt doesn't.

"I also know about your father's poor business habits."

Panic grips Walt at the mention of his father.

"He has trouble hanging on to his money, doesn't he? And he might also benefit from reading your temperance novel."

"How dare you involve my family?!"

"I see now, how to get your attention." Mr. Rynders continues. "This committee you stirred into action tonight — well, to be frank, it won't work."

"You don't know that," Whitman says.

"You think you're after Mr. Clement. Or even me. But we're not the people that matter." He coughs. "The people you're after — they have already shut down your committee."

"What people?"

"What do you know about the French Revolution, Mr. Whitman?"

"You said the committee won't work. Why?"

Rynders ignores him. "The common misconception about the French Revolution is that when the lower class overthrew the ruling class, the ruling class went away."

"Who will shut it down?"

"That's what I'm trying to tell you," Rynders says, "if you'd only listen. The ruling class did not go away; they simply retreated from the public eye. Yes, they had setbacks. But they didn't stay down long in France, or here, for that matter. You won't see any of them — or rather, if you did, you wouldn't know it. They are the ones who run everything in the country, and they shut down your little committee as soon as it was formed." He snaps his fingers.

"So why tell me this now?"

"They want to offer you a way out."

"A way out?"

"Drop this nonsense. Leave the city for a while, and it will go away."

"What about Miss Blackwell?"

"You can't save everyone, Mr. Whitman. She'll die whether you agree to this or not."

"If you think I'm going to stand idly by while the city hangs another innocent woman —"

"But you have nothing to do with it. Do you realize how egotistical that sounds?" He strokes his chin. "The citizens of this city want blood, and they want *her.* You don't have to die too."

"No!"

"Think about it. No need to answer now. They'll be watching, and if they see you leave town, they'll know your decision."

"And if I don't?"

"They'll know that too."

"What about the members of the committee?"

"They're good men who do their best to represent their communities. They want to believe they can make a difference. When the committee doesn't work, they will feel good inside because at least they did *something.* As far as the reward money goes, it will be given to anyone who comes forward with evidence." He sips his drink. "But I can assure you, no one will come forward."

"How can you allow this to happen?"

"You wouldn't understand." Mr. Rynders takes another sip of his drink. "Nobody understands what I do, but *everybody* depends on the results." He shakes his head. "Do you know how many immigrants arrive each day?"

"What does this have to do with anything?"

"My point exactly. Hundreds, sometimes thousands, come to our city daily. They all want a chance at a better life but we simply cannot accommodate them all. In fact —" Rynders knocks his cane against the carriage ceiling. "I want you to see. Driver?"

The carriage slows to a stop. A man wearing a top hat opens the door. "Sir?"

"Take us to the wharves."

The driver bows and closes the door.

Rynders turns to Walt. "When you see what I'm up against, perhaps you'll begin to understand," he says. "You're an intelligent man."

"You are the center of corruption."

"What do you think happens to immigrants after they come off the ships? Do you suppose they become productive members of our society without assistance?" The carriage stops and the door opens. "Come, Mr. Whitman," he says. "It won't take long."

Walt follows the shorter Rynders outside, where the wind springs off the water and bites into his exposed skin.

Rynders sees him wince. "Colder out here by the water, isn't it? Just think how *they* feel."

Whitman's gaze follows Rynders's outstretched hand into the pockets of shadows and light that line the walls and streets and crates. He sees scores of men, women, and children, huddled up like animals. A few of them sleep, but most of them merely sit there, their eyes open and blank.

"Who are they?"

Mr. Rynders sighs. "They are what's left over from the ships today," he says. "There isn't enough room for them."

"I don't understand."

"That's what I'm trying to tell you, Mr. Whitman. There are too many foreigners for this city to handle, but they come anyway. Many of the children will be dead by morning. Some of the men will find work; some won't. The women have the best chance once they find the bars and brothels, but I'd hardly call that success. Tomorrow, the ships come in and this starts all over again."

They pass a family in a rickety one-horse wagon. A man sits on a low board in front, driving, and a gauntish woman perches by his side with a baby well bundled in her arms, its little red feet and lower legs sticking out directly toward them as they pass. In the wagon behind, they see three crouching little children. It is a queer, taking, sad picture.

"What will happen to them?" Walt says.

"The children in the wagon are not well, and unless one of the parents can find employment, it is only a matter of time. Add to that the risk of disease, or crime, or the weather, and you see what these folks are up against."

Whitman considers his words carefully. "Why doesn't anyone do anything about this?"

"That's what I've been trying to tell you." Mr. Rynders climbs back into the carriage. "I *am* doing something. I'm not the person you think I am. In my own way, I am trying to make the world a better place. I've set up shelters; I create jobs; I supply food. I can't help everyone, as you can see, but we do help many of these people." He pauses. "The world is a messy place. When you help one person, you hurt another — give one man a job and starve another man and his family. It's tragic, but we trudge on, trying to make a difference."

Walt shakes his head. "The Blackwell proceeding remains unjust."

"Miss Blackwell will die," Rynders says.

"If you stay, you will die too. It's that simple."

"Three of my friends are dead," Whitman says, his hands trembling. "Am I supposed to just forget about them?"

"To be honest, Mr. Whitman, it does not concern me. People die every day, and I'm trying to reduce that number." He sighs. "Now, are you coming along? I'll drop you at the hotel where Miss Zakrzewska is staying. Or you can walk."

The mention of her name startles Walt. Rynders knows —

"Well?" Mr. Rynders says.

Whitman climbs into the carriage and shuts the door behind him.

Then Mr. Rynders taps the ceiling with his cane until the driver spurs the horses. "My guess is that you'll do something unwise and end up dead anyway. And then life will go on without you." He straightens in his seat. "The one mistake we all make is to think we're irreplaceable."

As the carriage rushes through the streets, Walt stares out the window. The buildings race by in a blur, the lights in the windows melting into one continuous stream. He has done everything he can, exhausted every idea. He failed Lena Stowe, he failed Henry Saunders, and now he can't save Miss

337

Blackwell, either. He remembers Lena's execution — the ropes around her legs, wrists, and waist. The minister read her last rites, but nobody in the crowd could hear because of the wind. Then the sheriff counted to three, and her body dropped.

The carriage slows as it approaches the front of the hotel.

"Remember you can't save the world, and no one expects you to, either," Mr. Rynders says. He taps on the ceiling again, and the carriage stops. "We'll be watching."

"You'll be watching," Whitman says. "Listen to yourself. You help some folks, yes, which means you hurt others. That's not a strategy. That's a justification. I've seen firsthand the damage you've done, and maybe one day you will too."

"Clearly, we share a difference of opinion."

"A difference of opinion? Who knows how many people are dead because of you? The Stowes. Henry. How many innocent people were shot the other night? And throw in Elizabeth Blackwell while you're at it. Jesus! Add to that what you've done to Azariah."

This seems to catch Rynders off guard.

"And he defends you. Disgusting." Whitman steps outside and the carriage speeds away.

He shivers and looks up at the moon — it

has rotated thirty degrees or so, which means it must be close to ten. There is only one other person he can ask for help. He takes a deep breath, and instead of going into the hotel, he walks the other way.

CHAPTER 32

Edgar Poe is drunk when he answers the door, and this fact, along with the late hour, leads to a predictable outcome: Mr. Poe slams the door in Walt's face. Walt knocks again. Nothing. And again. Nothing. And again. Mr. Poe is properly pissed off this time and engages in a one-sided shouting match until Walt shoehorns this in: "We met at the committee meeting tonight! You told me about the conspiracy! I need your help!"

The anger slips away now, and his voice softens. "Why didn't you say so?" He opens the door and steps aside so Whitman can pass.

The room is fastidiously arranged and sparsely decorated — a rug in the center of it, colored deep red and gold, a sofa and chair atop it that have been arranged perfectly, and between the sofa and chair, a table and a lamp. A fire flickers in a stone fireplace. Above the hearth is a portrait of

Virginia: her long black hair and eyes, and her pale skin. A writing desk sits in the corner near the fireplace. Each neat stack of books and the papers thereon suggest purpose, a trademark very much unlike his prose, Walt reflects.

Whitman sits on the red sofa, Mr. Poe in the indigo chair. He strikes Walt as a sickly sort, clearly intoxicated, and yet full of wit and intellect. His dark hair is wild, and his breathing is short and labored as if the man is out of breath.

"Nobody believed me," Mr. Poe says. "Nobody until you."

A voice calls out from the other room. "Edgar? Can you bring me my toddy?"

"But of course, dear — be right there!" Mr. Poe smiles at Walt. "I'll return shortly."

Whitman notices the spring in his step as Mr. Poe excuses himself. While he is gone, Walt stands and has a look around. He stops at Poe's desk, where he notices that among the papers and books lays a copy of *Franklin Evans*. He picks up the novel — his novel — and shakes his head. Henry was right. It is not good. He thought it was good — indeed, it was the best he could manage at the time, but he knows now he was simply trying too hard to write something that a lot of people would buy. As he holds the book, he feels ashamed of his efforts. And now the manuscript of his follow-up, *The Madman,* has burned up in the fire. Perhaps for the best.

He thumbs through the latest edition of Snowden's *Ladies' Companion* to Poe's third installment of "The Mystery of Marie Rogêt." In the story, C. Auguste Dupin, the main character from "The Murders in the Rue Morgue," never actually solves the murder; he only tells the reader how the murderer might be found, something Walt finds strange. He turns to the last page of the story and discovers handwritten notes on Abraham Stowe's innocence and a list of names including Mayor Morris and Isaiah Rynders. Walt sets down the magazine when Mr. Poe returns with a bottle of whiskey.

"She's comfortable now," he says, "the poor thing."

"I hope she regains her health soon."

Mr. Poe nods slowly. "You've read my 'Marie Rogêt.' You know what I believe." Mr. Poe appears more at ease now and sits down again in the indigo chair. "What is it that I can help you with?"

"You set out to solve the Mary Rogers murder with your story." Walt takes his place on the couch again.

"Yes."

"And yet the story offers no solution."

"I began that story thinking I knew enough to ratiocinate the solution, but the more I studied the murder, the more dead ends I encountered. I know Abraham Stowe did not kill Mary Rogers. Her body was staged at the murder scene to appear bludgeoned, but she died long before the bludgeoning. I consulted with a number of doctors who all confirmed my suspicions. We exhumed the body, and they reexamined it, and they all agree that the cause of death was likely a botched abortion. But the questions remain: Who ordered it, who performed it, and why is it so important to cover it up?"

"And that's why the story offers no solution?"

"I couldn't pretend," Poe says. "The story is my greatest failure. I promised the reader something I could not deliver. That's why I've followed the Lena Stowe story so carefully. That's why I had to be there tonight. You're clearly encountering the same obstacles."

"Isaiah Rynders told me the committee will not work. He said Miss Blackwell will hang despite her innocence, and he said I will die too if I don't leave this alone."

Mr. Poe pulls a small notebook and pencil

from his coat pocket, scribbles a few notes. "And why won't the committee work?"

Walt runs his finger along the sofa fabric.

Mr. Poe senses his hesitation. "I only want to know who it is *we* are up against, Mr. Whitman. If I'm going to risk my reputation, such as it is, I need to know."

"Rynders told me that the committee was just for show, that it has already been shut down."

"Ah." Mr. Poe nods. "So he told you this after the meeting?"

Whitman nods.

"Well, then — tell me everything you know."

Walt relates how he witnessed the sheriff's murder, how James Warren is being tried in Samuel Clement's place. He talks about Kenneth Barclay and Eli Quigley. He includes Henry Saunders's disappearance and murder, Frankie Clement's visit, and Walt's own encounter with Samuel Clement. Whitman spares nothing, hoping that Mr. Poe will indeed help him. He concludes with his meeting with James Bennett and the committee of safety. "And now I'm here with you. That's everything."

"You poor dear." Mr. Poe emerges from the chair, paces back and forth in front of the fire. He does this for what seems like several minutes before he turns to face Walt. "So you believe Mrs. Stowe did not kill her husband?"

"That's correct."

"Of course I agree with you," he says. "But let me play devil's advocate. They found the same arsenic on her person that killed Mr. Stowe, did they not?"

Whitman nods.

"Even if Mr. Stowe did not kill Mary Rogers, which I am most certain he did not, he had a history of being unfaithful to his wife, did he not?"

"So it seems, but —"

"Why, pray tell, do you think she is innocent?"

Walt considers his words carefully. "As I said at the meeting, his body was gutted like a deer and not dissected as suggested in the many accounts."

"Including the coroner's?"

"Yes."

"Was this reported by *anyone* but you? Because your voice, I hate to say it, has been discredited. But Mr. Saunders's dissection — that is interesting. As you know, I am no doctor, but I have been in dissection labs, and to gut a corpse like a deer, as you've put it, is not proper nor is it typical procedure. While that fact alone does not stand up in court as evidence for Miss Blackwell's innocence, it certainly casts reasonable doubt." He pauses. "Your friend Dr. Stowe, was his body found in a similar way?"

Walt nods.

"Suggesting —"

Whitman stands. "That the same person committed both murders, I know. It's obvious — but how do we prove it when it seems every important city official prefers to look the other way? What good is the truth if no one will act on it?" Walt is shaking now. He goes to the desk, points to the whiskey. "May I?"

Mr. Poe nods.

Walt pours himself a half a whiskey and drinks it down. "I feel I've proved innocence — starting with Abraham, then with Lena — over and over, but no one listens. I *saw* Samuel Clement murder Jack Harris."

"We have to force the mayor, the sheriff, and even Isaiah Rynders to act on the truth," Mr. Poe says. "If we demonstrate that the bodies were cut in the same manner, that the first autopsy was fraudulent, and then make those results public, city officials will have to do something. The citizens will demand it."

"It's the only play we have left," Whitman says.

Mr. Poe's posture is wobbly and unsure, a stark contrast to his words, which are resolute and clear: "I wrote a story about a man who disinters his —"

"You mean 'Berenice.' "

"Oh?" Mr. Poe raises his eyebrow. "You've read it? Well, then you know what I'm about to suggest."

"I'm afraid I do," Walt says, "because I came here tonight to suggest the same thing."

CHAPTER 33

The idea is crazy, but no crazier than the circumstances. At least that's what Walt Whitman tells himself as he steers the freight wagon north on Broadway, Mr. Poe leaning on his shoulder, clutching a bottle of whiskey. The farther north they travel, the quieter the streets and the nicer the buildings are. The trees are well groomed and part of an overall landscape design that Five Points residents have neither the time nor the resources to consider.

They had taken the freight wagon from a dairy farm a few blocks away from Mr. Poe's residence. They'd waited behind the two-story white house until the farmer disappeared inside the barn, before they hopped into the driver's seat and drove away, the farmer's voice ringing out behind them.

Outside the burial ground gates now, Walt stops the horses and listens. The only sound is the wind that brushes through him like a whisper. He lights the lantern.

From the seat of the wagon, he scans the headstones until he locates a grave, the name A. STOWE carved into stone above the years 1807–1843. His sight wavers, he is suddenly dizzy, and a sickness comes over him at what they are about to do. Edgar Poe sits up straight beside him, a great sweat upon his forehead, his cheeks bloodless as chalk.

"We've arrived, have we?"

Whitman lifts himself down from the driver's seat and stretches. His legs and arms are stiff already, and they haven't yet begun the real work. From the wagon bed, he gathers the pickax and shovel.

Walt turns to Mr. Poe. "Are you coming?"

Mr. Poe takes a drink from the whiskey bottle. "I will keep a lookout while you dig." Then he offers a drink to Walt.

Whitman shakes his head and sets the lantern on the gravestone.

Mr. Poe smiles and waves from the wagon seat. "Let me know if I can spell you in a while."

Walt begins by loosening the dirt with the pickax, and at first, the pointed end barely penetrates the frozen ground at all. With every swing, however, he moves more dirt, and he thinks he has made real progress, until he realizes it has taken over an hour just to break up the dirt enough to dig.

Mr. Poe, meanwhile, has crawled into the wagon bed, stretched out in the hay, and fallen asleep.

Whitman switches to the shovel. The deeper he goes, the easier the digging becomes, and while he works, he has a strange sensation that he is somehow outside himself, watching himself dig. He enjoys the monotony of physical labor, and he is able to settle his mind.

He reflects on the materiality of death, how his beliefs have altered because of it, and how naïve he had been before he experienced death firsthand. Indeed, not long ago, in his story "The Tomb Blossoms," he boasted how he does not dread the grave. *There is many a time when I could lay down, and pass my immortal part through the valley of the shadow, as composedly as I quaff water after a tiresome walk.*

As he moves the dirt with his shovel, awe spreads over him for the ubiquitous power of death. Not a moment passes without a body, and its flesh becomes one with the earth's flesh, a reminder of nature's fecundity, the boundless and endless growth and decay that encompasses them all.

The digging takes so long that Whitman wonders if Samuel Clement has already removed the body. When he hears the sound of metal on wood, he is both surprised and relieved. He stops and wipes his brow with his sleeve. His hands are torn apart, and his whole body aches. Despite the cold, he is sweating, a heat from the inside out, that almost burns in the wind. He glances around him. The horses stand still, Mr. Poe still sleeps, and beyond the lantern, all he can see is blackness.

Still, he can't shake the feeling that they are not alone.

In the grave, Whitman clears away the dirt around the casket. To get to the body, he has to remove the top half of the casket lid. With the pickax, he chisels around the edge and pries up the nails, just as he had seen Clement do. It takes all his strength to get the lid off. The force of it flings Walt against the wall of the grave, and from where he lands, he can't see into the casket, so he rotates forward and peers inside.

Abraham Stowe's skin is pasty gray. A shirt and tie constrict his bloated neck and body, and his dark suit is stretched tight from his arms to his legs. The body appears pumped full of air, as if a pin will make it explode. The body is Abraham, recognizable as the man Walt Whitman regarded as a surrogate father. But the form has changed. Walt remembers the night Abraham told him to mend things with his own father because *none of us knows when our time will come, when we will vanish from this earth.* Something has vanished from the man he knew, and it is crushing. This isn't the man who said those words to him. This is not Abraham.

Whitman wraps a handkerchief around his mouth and nose. Then, using his knife, he cuts off the buttons of Abraham's shirt one by one. Maggots swarm the insides of the body and buzz like fingernails on a chalkboard. Walt clears as many of the maggots away with the shovel as he can so he can examine the chest area. The incision, sewn together with black thread, runs up the middle of the corpse, from its navel to the base of its throat — the same as Henry's.

The smell has gotten to him, and so he crawls out of the hole and lies down until the nausea passes. Above him, the night sky is now framed by morning light. A house behind the cemetery has since become visible, along with a small church next to it. Exhaustion hits him, and if not so cold, he might fall asleep.

The horses don't sound like horses at first

— the rhythmic clomping dances along the wind like rustling leaves and shifting trees.

"Did you hear that?" Walt whispers. "Mr. Poe!"

Mr. Poe's head pokes up, looks around: " 'Tis the wind and nothing more."

But the horses only draw closer.

Whitman hurries back to the body and holds his breath while he threads the rope around the left arm twice, then around the neck and right arm. He climbs out of the grave, takes one end of the rope in each hand and ties them together around his waist.

In the distance, a lantern hovers.

The weight of Dr. Stowe's body surprises him. On his first try, the body doesn't budge at all. He takes a deep breath and readjusts his grip. He tries again. This time, he moves the body a few feet until Abraham Stowe's head pokes out of the ground, maggots pouring out of his chest.

The noises grow louder. Metal on wood. Breathing.

Walt pulls the rope again, and this time, he heaves the body out of the casket and onto the ground. He drags it to the wagon, where he hoists it in the back next to Mr. Poe. Walt covers the body with a tarp, then pulls himself up into the driver's seat and holds the reins ready.

Outside the burial ground, on the road, the voices have stopped.

Then footsteps on the frozen earth.

They have come for him.

All Walt Whitman can do is watch as the carriage rolls closer. He recognizes the sheriff in the driver's seat, his square jaw and broad shoulders highlighted by the hanging lamp. "I'm impressed," the sheriff says. "You don't give up easily."

"What makes you think I'm giving up now?"

"I know about the committee of safety and your conspiracy theories, but you're sniffing down a snake hole, son, and you're going to get bit." Petty spits on the ground. "Now, why don't you come with me and I'll go easy on you."

"If I go with you," Walt says, "we will all be complicit in the death of an innocent woman."

"Stop the bullshit, Mr. Whitman. Your reporting has done more damage to law enforcement credibility than anything I've ever seen," Petty snarls.

Mr. Poe's voice catches both men by surprise. It sings from the darkness, from an invisible space as if from the graves themselves: "We have put her living in the tomb," he calls out. "I now tell you that I heard her first feeble movements in the hollow coffin. I hear them even now."

The voice continues: "Have I not heard her footsteps on the stair? Do I not distinguish that heavy and horrible beating of her heart?"

Mr. Poe springs furiously from the wagon and charges the sheriff, who fires a warning shot in the air. The carriage lunges forward just enough to clear the way for Whitman. He doesn't hesitate, flipping the reins hard to make the horses go. The freight wagon races toward Petty, who has no choice but to scatter as it speeds past him and out into the street. Walt glances over his shoulder once, and he can't believe it: Mr. Poe is dancing in front of Petty, blocking his way, waving his empty whiskey bottle in the air, screaming "Madman! Madman! Madman!"

Walt needs to find Broadway, the most direct route south, so he takes a combination of streets southwest that will lead him there. The farther south he drives, the more people are out and about, and the more vehicles on the road. On one street, he gets stuck behind a milk wagon. He tries to go around it, but the traffic coming the other way is too heavy.

Whitman checks behind him and sees the sheriff's phaeton barreling toward him on the narrow cobblestone street. When Walt spurs his team into a gallop, his own wagon skids on the cobblestone as he drives around the milk wagon. An oncoming carriage drives onto the sidewalk to avoid him, and the horses kick up their legs, toppling the carriage. Whitman regains his spot on the right side of the road without causing any more accidents, but his actions have cleared the way for Sheriff Petty too.

Walt steers the freight wagon around the next corner and almost crashes into the stairway of the outermost row house.

The sheriff takes the same corner easily and closes the gap. The two vehicles drive side by side, Walt trying desperately to outmaneuver Petty.

"Pull over," Petty yells.

Swinging his phaeton almost into the wagon, Petty reaches for Whitman, narrowly missing him. He tries again, but this time, Walt kicks him in the side.

Whitman tries to speed up, but Sheriff Petty matches his speed. The sheriff's carriage swerves into the freight wagon again, and Petty stands up and makes ready to jump into the back of the freight wagon.

Walt checks his grip on the reins. He waits

until the last moment, right when Petty jumps, to throw the brake. When he does, the horses skid and the brakes screech. The sheriff flies past the wagon and hits the ground in a roll. The sheriff's phaeton tips over and scrapes to a stop, showering sparks along the street. Walt regains control of the freight wagon and navigates it around the sheriff and his wrecked vehicle.

He hopes the sheriff is not too seriously injured, but he knows he can't dwell. It is almost nine in the morning, and the streets are full of people — a tricky scenario for someone with a corpse in the back of his wagon.

CHAPTER 34

Walt Whitman brings the wagon to a stop in front of the row house at 104 Washington Street. The coroner's windows are dark, and there are no signs that anyone stirs at all.

He hastens up the front steps, pats his pocket for the pistol, and pounds on the front door. No one answers, so he knocks again, with increasing speed and intensity. Finally, a light comes on in the front window. Footsteps scrape in the entryway, and the door opens.

Kenneth Barclay comes to the door, wearing a robe and slippers. He frowns.

"Come with me," Walt says.

"Why won't you leave me alone, Mr. Whitman?"

"*Now.* Please."

The coroner staggers down the stairs after Walt to the wagon. Whitman lowers the endgate to reveal the corpse of Abraham Stowe.

"What have you done?" Barclay says, his

face turning white.

"Help me carry him inside."

He reaches underneath the tarp for Abraham's arms.

Barclay says, "Why in God's name would you do this?"

"Grab his legs."

Barclay hesitates, so Whitman grasps the pistol. "The legs."

"You don't need to point that at me." Barclay bends down, grabbing hold of the corpse's legs. "It's insulting."

Walt returns the gun to his pocket and takes up Abraham's arms again. The two men slide the bloated corpse out of the wagon, Barclay walking backward. He stumbles after a few steps, losing his grip on the body, which hits the sidewalk with a thud. Whitman waits for the coroner to gather himself, and the two men continue to transport the corpse up the stairs, through the front door, and into the morgue, laying it on an empty table.

The room is dark and cold. Walt looks around nervously for Henry's body and spots it, two tables over.

Barclay lights a lamp, revealing Henry in full view. Whitman's pulse quickens and a queasiness settles over him.

"I'm sorry about your friend," the coroner

says. "I know you were close."

Walt takes deep breaths to calm himself. The body has been scrubbed from head to toe. Henry's mouth is open, but unnaturally so, halfway between a yawn and a smile, and his head is tilted back. The skin is waxy and bleached. The area around and inside the bone saw's incision down the middle of his chest has been pulled apart, exposing the yellowish-gray insides. A thought strikes him: Henry is a thing now, nothing more.

"Mr. Whitman?"

Walt looks up.

"Why are you here?"

He takes a few more deep breaths. "I need to see the autopsy reports for Henry Saunders and Abraham Stowe."

Kenneth Barclay's expression falls flat. "Are you asking me or telling me?"

"Where are they?"

Barclay points to the desk.

"Get them."

Dr. Barclay shuffles to the desk, rifles through a stack of folders, and returns with a small bundle of papers, which he sets on the table next to Henry's body.

Whitman scans the documents. Both reports specify arsenic poisoning as the cause of death, and on the anatomical diagrams, the coroner has drawn the chest incisions in a square according to proper dissection protocol and not as they are: a gash down the middle of both bodies.

Incredulous, Walt looks up at the coroner. "How could you?" He has to fight to control himself. "Fix them."

"If only it were that simple."

In a smooth gesture, Whitman reaches for the gun and points it at Barclay. "This morning, I'm afraid, it is that simple."

Barclay grinds his teeth, his top lip tucked up under his gums. "I can redo the autopsy reports," he finally says, "but they won't hold up in court."

"Then do it."

The coroner reaches for a white apron stained with streaks of red, brown, and black. From the desk drawer, he removes two blank autopsy reports, a pen, and a bottle of ink.

Whitman instructs Barclay to write the word *amended* at the top of each form. Barclay does, and then gets to work.

"I don't know what Elizabeth saw in you," Walt says.

Barclay ignores him.

"And to think she's still in love with you."

The coroner looks up. "If I could stop it, I would."

"So you just let her hang?"

The two men stare at each other for several moments before Barclay shakes his head and returns to work. Whitman watches Barclay's hand as it writes, the very same hand that sealed Lena's fate. "Who told you to alter the autopsy results?"

"Why would I tell you?"

"Was it the new sheriff?"

Barclay doesn't flinch.

"Isaiah Rynders?"

Barclay shakes his head. "Once word gets out about these autopsies," he says, "then whoever it is will come knocking anyway. And then you'll know."

"Finish your work."

"There." The coroner slides the autopsy reports across the table to him. "I did everything you asked. But it doesn't matter," the coroner says. "The paperwork is only a formality. All the pieces have already been set in motion and nothing can stop it."

Whitman punches Barclay in the stomach, causing him to bend over in pain. "You're pathetic," he says. With the autopsies secure in a briefcase he finds on the desk, Walt rushes away.

Outside, on the landing, he stops abruptly.

Sheriff Petty leans over the freight wagon with his back toward him. Walt holds his breath as he takes a quiet step backward. But Petty flips around and, when he sees Whitman, rushes up the stairs.

Walt backs inside the coroner's house and slams the door. Behind him, Dr. Barclay appears. "What's the matter now?"

Whitman shoves Barclay aside and barrels toward the back door. Behind him, the sheriff enters the house.

With both men now in pursuit, Walt takes the six back stairs in one jump and sprints to the stone fence. He pushes himself up with his arms and almost clears the top, when Barclay grabs his left foot and, with the sheriff's help, pulls him to the ground.

Petty kicks him in the stomach. "I ought to shoot you."

Walt coughs.

Sheriff Petty towers over him. His forehead is scraped and bruised and his coat tattered from being dragged along the street.

He kicks Whitman again.

The pain is searing, and Walt struggles to catch his breath.

The sheriff bends down, rolls Walt over, and handcuffs him. "You are a real prick, Mr. Whitman."

"This man broke into my house," the coroner says. "Held me at gunpoint."

"I'm afraid I know all about Mr. Whitman's exploits." The sheriff prods Walt with his boot. "Now let's go." The sheriff pulls Walt to his feet, and the briefcase containing the autopsy reports drops to the ground.

Petty picks it up. "What's this?"

Barclay reaches for the briefcase. "That belongs to me."

The sheriff holds it out of the coroner's reach.

"Please, Sheriff Petty. I have a lot of work to do today." He attempts to take the briefcase again, and for the first time, it occurs to Whitman that the sheriff might not be a part of the conspiracy to frame Lena and Elizabeth for murder.

"Of course," Petty says. "But first tell me: What's in the briefcase?"

"Just some of my papers," he answers.

"What sort of papers?"

Barclay stumbles on his words now, and Petty turns to Whitman. "You know what's inside, don't you?"

Walt takes a deep breath so he can speak clearly. "The briefcase contains two sets of autopsies. Henry Saunders and Abraham Stowe. One falsified set, one corrected."

The sheriff stares past them now, as if he is putting it all together, as if he hasn't known the whole story until now. "That's why you dug up Abraham Stowe's corpse?"

Walt nods.

"Where are the bodies now?"

Whitman leads the way, followed by the sheriff and coroner. In a few minutes, Petty will know what Walt knows, and after everything that has happened, he can't believe his good fortune. He had not once stopped to consider that Sheriff Petty was not at the center of the conspiracy, and when the sheriff sees the bodies, he will have a powerful new ally.

Inside the morgue, the lamp still burns. Walt's stomach turns at seeing Henry again.

Petty sets the leather sheaf on the empty table nearest the two bodies. He removes the handcuffs, and Walt arranges the autopsy reports on the table.

Petty's eyes dart from one sheet to the other. When he reaches the anatomical diagrams, he holds them up in comparison with each body. "I can't believe it," he says.

Walt nods.

"Bravo, Mr. Whitman," Barclay says. "Looks like you've figured out how corrupt our world is."

Walt turns around to see his gun in the coroner's hand.

"Put the gun down, Doc," Petty says. "I know you didn't act alone."

"Quiet!" Barclay swings the gun back and

forth. His arm shakes. He's even less comfortable with the gun than Whitman was, and Petty knows it. "Let me think."

"We can still save Elizabeth," says Walt.

"I'm not responsible for that."

"Then who is?"

Barclay clearly doesn't know what to do. He is sweating, his breathing erratic. "I didn't think it would go this far," he says. "I didn't —"

The sheriff takes down Barclay in an instant, and for a moment, the two men struggle on the floor, but the sheriff's size is too much. He slides the gun to Walt, then handcuffs the coroner.

"You have no idea what's going on here," Barclay says.

"I've got a pretty good idea, thanks to you." Petty lifts the coroner by the collar. "Now let's go," he says. "You too, Mr. Whitman."

Walt says, "What about Miss Blackwell?"

The sheriff turns around. "She's safe where she is."

"I'm worried about the protestors."

The sheriff hands the briefcase to Whitman. "This is a good start, but we still have work to do," he says. "At the moment, Miss Blackwell is safer in jail."

In the freight wagon, Walt Whitman sits to

the right of Kenneth Barclay while the sheriff drives. The briefcase lies in his lap. The three men sit so close Whitman can smell Barclay's skin, see the black stubble on his chin and the gold ring he wears on his right index finger.

For a moment, Walt allows himself to enjoy the small victory. There remains work to do, and there have been many losses, but he knows now that he has the means to stop Elizabeth Blackwell's execution.

Chapter 35

Sheriff Silas Petty steers the phaeton down a narrow passageway to the rear entrance of the watch house. After he locks the brake in place, he pulls Barclay down by his handcuffs, then turns to Walt Whitman. "You have the briefcase?"

Walt lifts it into the air.

"Keep this between you and me for now."

Whitman nods.

Inside his cell, Kenneth Barclay breaks down. Of course he will testify in court, he says. He is ready to tell the truth.

Petty says, "Then tell us what happened with the autopsies."

The coroner sits on the cell bed, and Whitman and Petty stand opposite him. "Well," he begins, "Samuel Clement called on me the morning after Abraham's murder. He said he needed to tell me the truth, that Abraham Stowe had been murdered, then dissected by his own wife, Lena Stowe." He stops.

"Then what happened?" Petty says.

"I knew the Stowes, Sheriff Petty. At one time, they were like family to me." The coroner becomes emotional, and Petty and Whitman wait for him to regain control. "Abraham and I had a falling-out, but I will always be grateful to him for giving me my first post as a surgeon."

"A falling-out?" Walt can't believe it. He turns to the sheriff. "He despised Abraham for favoring Lena over him."

"Is that it?" the sheriff says to the coroner. "Don't you have anything useful?"

Barclay continues: "With Clement standing across the table from me, I conducted the autopsies. I told him that this was no dissection, and this was when he told me to make the autopsies match his story." He takes a deep breath, lets it out slowly. "So I did."

Hearing the words shakes Walt in a way he didn't anticipate. For so long he operated under assumptions and ideas, but now he has actual confirmation of his suspicions. He doesn't know whether to feel exhilarated or horrified. "And then you stood by," Whitman says, "and watched while the City of New York hanged an innocent woman.

Your rival."

"What was I supposed to do?"

Walt rushes the coroner, takes him by the collar. "You did *nothing.* You wanted it to happen!"

"Easy, Mr. Whitman." The sheriff pulls him back.

The sheriff turns his attention back to Barclay. "Tell us who sent Clement to you."

"There was nothing I could do." Barclay puts his head down. "I had to protect myself."

"Who sent Clement?" the sheriff says.

The coroner says nothing, and both Whitman and the sheriff understand that he will not implicate Rynders or the mayor. And why would he? Such an accusation will have no legal traction and only leave Barclay exposed in jail. No, the coroner will keep quiet, and then the powers that be will reward him for it with protection and a light sentence.

So Walt goes a different direction. "Did you alter Mary Rogers's autopsy too?"

Barclay's face drops at the mention of her name.

The sheriff turns to him. "Not now, Mr. Whitman."

But Walt ignores the sheriff. "You did, didn't you? She was pregnant. Someone

370

brought her to you to get an abortion. When she died during the procedure, you dumped her body. You made it look like a murder, fabricated the autopsy, and then you let Abraham take the blame."

"I didn't give Mary Rogers an abortion!"

Walt says, "But you altered the autopsy."

"Yes, but —" He knows he's been caught.

"Who told you to do it?" Whitman says.

The coroner puts his head down. "Let's say I know," Barclay starts. "What can you do for me if I tell you?"

"Who?" Petty says.

"What can you do for me?"

The sheriff takes the coroner by the neck, slams him against the wall. "Who told you?"

The coroner thinks for a moment. "Jack Harris."

That's when a copper bursts through the front door, shouting the word *mob.*

With Walt Whitman standing next to him, Sheriff Petty sends couriers out into the city and gathers those on duty, those at home with their families, and those in the bars. These men trudge the streets of the Lower East Side back to Sheriff Petty, who stands on his desk and tells the men how they will approach the prison and end the mob.

The men grab their bayonets and wait in

a line from the front door of the station to the back door — a line that winds around desks, chairs, tables, and jail cells. The men in the cells joke at the expense of the watchmen. "Like shooting fish in a barrel," they say. "Just the way you lawmen like it. Easy." The men ignore the prisoners — all but one watchman, who smacks the Irish man in cell five in the jaw with his rifle. The sound of wood against bone echoes through the watch house as the militia, the sheriff, and Walt spill outside.

Little Joe is careful not to pinch Elizabeth Blackwell's skin with the handcuffs, but insists they be tight. He fumbles with the cuffs. "Real sorry about that, miss." He is here to move her to a safer location to await trial. In different circumstances, Elizabeth might have found his awkwardness charming.

"Ready?" He opens the door and nudges her out into the hall, where the noises of the other prisoners echo. "Just ignore them."

She tries, but their jeers frighten her.

"That's right, you little cherry," the man nearest her calls. "Bring it right here," he says as he grabs her sleeve.

Little Joe raps the man on his knuckles

with the ring of keys until he releases Elizabeth.

At this, the other prisoners cheer. Their bodies press up against the prison bars, their tongues slither through their teeth, and they spit at her, the saliva hot on her skin. One voice croons, "One at a time, lads. I've already got my pants at my knees."

Little Joe unlocks the door that leads to the prison station, a small room separating the prison from the court.

"There you are, miss." He helps her sit on a bench against the wall. Goose pimples form on her arms and legs. "I'm real sorry about all that, what happened back there. Not a gentleman among them, I'm afraid."

Elizabeth nods, her eyes vacant. Since her arrest, it hasn't taken long for her life, and everything she has worked for, to slip out of her control and into the hands of men not much better than those on the other side of that door.

Beside the door leading back into the prison, there are three others — one to the court and another to the warden's office. The third, she guesses, leads to the street. Little Joe makes sure she is comfortable before he knocks on the door to the warden's office and waits. A man she can't see tells him it will be a few minutes yet. Little

Joe nods and stands with his back against the door, facing her.

Sitting there looking at Little Joe, she realizes he is even larger than she first thought — arms like pythons and even bigger legs, wider in the waist than in the chest, and a chin that blends in with his neck. He smiles when he catches her staring. "Not quite ready for you," he says.

She nods.

In the silence, they both hear shouting.

"They're out there, aren't they?"

Little Joe shrugs. "Don't know, miss."

Just then, the door to the court opens, and three men hurry through to the warden's office, a look of worry across their faces.

"What is it?" Little Joe says.

"Mob's getting riled up some," the last man says. "The warden wants us to be ready."

Mob.

The word is like a cannonball to her stomach. Images still fresh from two nights before play out in her mind — the smoke rising into the bedroom, the rocks through the window, and the building folding in on itself.

"I knew they'd come for me."

Little Joe starts to answer but stops himself, and the two of them stay silent. Elizabeth tries to think of happier times, but the moment is too big, and her thoughts drift to what might happen. Everybody knows there is only one way to stop a mob. She thinks of the handcuffs around her wrists, and her stomach turns.

The door to the warden's office opens again and the same men cross the room and go back through the door to the court.

"Don't you worry, miss," Little Joe says. "You're safe from them in here."

Just then, there is pounding at the door leading to the street.

The wood bows in the middle, and the daylight shines through the space around the door.

Their voices pour inside.

And then, both she and Little Joe hear it.

Her name. *Elizabeth Blackwell.* They are chanting her name.

The mob has backed down, and the prison is quiet. Little Joe has sat down next to Elizabeth on the bench, both of them unsure what to do next. He has unlocked her handcuffs, allowing her to move her arms from behind her back to the front before putting them on her again, a gesture she appreciates. Wearing the shackles in the front is not pleasant, but it is an improvement.

"You okay, miss?"

She turns to him. "I've been better."

One of her cuticles stings; a flap of skin has come loose enough to bleed. She nibbles at the skin, but it only bleeds more. "I didn't kill anyone," she says. "I want you to know that, no matter what happens."

"That's what the court's for, miss."

"It didn't work for Lena Stowe."

"The court says she killed her husband."

"What if the court was wrong?"

"That's not for me to think about."

She shrugs.

He says, "But I'd be mighty glad to find out you didn't kill nobody."

She touches his arm. "Thank you."

He fidgets with his own fingernails, trims them down to the skin with his teeth, then spits out the remnants onto the floor. He is a hulk of a man but, close up, has the face of a child. Still, the power in his arms and legs is not to be questioned, and his devotion to the law is both an asset and a liability. Lucky for her, he decided to protect her through this process, even if that process turns out to be corrupt.

The banging at the door startles them both. "What was that?"

The people from outside again lean into the door, the wood bowing.

Little Joe rushes to stop them but cannot hold them back. The door bursts open, and the mob streams inside, one giant mess of hands and arms led by two men wearing hoods. They say nothing; they only point at her.

Little Joe slings Elizabeth over his shoulder and rushes to the cell-block door. Her dress catches on a nail sticking out of the wall. The two men in hoods are nearly upon them now, and she screams. Little Joe yanks her hard, ripping a strip of fabric from her dress, and pulls her into the cell block, slamming the door behind them.

The prisoners bang against the bars of their cells.

"You've reconsidered, miss?" one prisoner yells.

"She's just as ripe as we thought," says another.

The metal handcuffs have cut into Elizabeth's skin, and she's crying. Little Joe picks her up and carries her down the hallway to her cell. "You'll be safer in here until this passes."

Only moments later, the mob breaks through to the cell block. The two hooded men motion for those behind them to slow down. Everyone knows they have her cornered. No reason to hurry now.

The prisoners back away in their cells and keep quiet, afraid to become leftovers.

When the mob is halfway down the hall, Little Joe joins Elizabeth in the cell, locking the door behind him. He has no choice. The two men in hoods appear at the cell door with the mob behind them. They crash into the bars, their hands and arms reach inside for Elizabeth. "Come out," they sing. "Or we'll come in."

From down the hallway, she watches a man push through the mob, his rifle raised in the air. Little Joe sees him too. "What do we do?" she says.

"Stay behind me."

The man points the gun at Little Joe. "Open the door."

Little Joe shakes his head.

"Give her up!"

"She has the right to a fair trial."

"I'll ask one more time."

The people behind the man turn silent while Elizabeth backs into the corner. Little Joe steps toward the man. "I will *not.*"

The shot echoes in the corridor, and Little Joe drops to the ground.

Elizabeth screams.

On the ground Little Joe thrashes. A tiny

spout of blood erupts from his mouth, drips down his cheek, and pools on the floor. He lifts his head, tries to speak, then his eyes turn glassy. His head drops to the floor.

The man points his gun at her. "You're next."

It is happening too fast.

She closes her eyes. "Please, God."

From behind him, a man yells, "I've got the keys." He works his way to the front of the crowd and unlocks the door. Inside, he steps over Little Joe's body and wrestles Elizabeth from the corner. He and the man who shot Little Joe lift her up and into the mob's hands. They convey her from one person to the next, out of the hallway and through the prison's front doors.

Outside the Tombs, the mob cheers when they see Elizabeth. They lift her above their heads and pass her down the street.

"God help me," she says over and over until her prayers are drowned out by her sobs.

The mob marches toward an oak tree, its branches scattered in all directions. As they get closer, the mob splits, encircles the tree, and delivers Elizabeth to the ground in front of it.

The priest's voice emerges out of the low hum that is the mob. He's running toward them, shouting for them to stop.

His appearance surprises all who can see him, and they quiet down to hear what Father Allen has to say. "Brothers and sisters." His voice is uneven as he catches his breath. "This is not the Lord's way."

"But she's a murderer," one of the men answers.

Father Allen stops near Elizabeth. His eyes meet hers to let her know he will do everything within his power to save her, and she believes him. "It is for God alone to judge his children," he says. "He who judges shall be judged."

A man standing nearest the priest says, "In the Bible, it is also written that 'every man shall be put to death for his own sin.' "

"All I'm asking of you is to allow the legal system to determine her guilt or innocence. We're not savages."

Jedediah Matthews, the antidissection follower of Father Allen, shakes his head. "Your timidity remains your weakness." He calls to the crowd. "Here is the woman!"

Down below them, the rumble rolls up through the masses. *Hang her. Hang her now. Hang her. Hang her now.*

Two men step forward from the crowd and hold the priest fast. He protests, but his voice disappears among thousands who chant for the woman doctor's death.

Then they pounce on her. They hold her arms and legs down while the same man wraps the rope around her neck three times.

"Please," she whispers. "Don't do this."

They lift her upright while the man tosses the other end of the rope over a high branch and pulls it tight.

Elizabeth can't hold it in any longer and cries again, her tears warm on her cheeks.

The man with the rope steps backward.

She stands on her tiptoes as her last breath fills her lungs. While they raise her off the ground, six inches at a time, she keeps her eyes open, the faces of the men, women, and children in front of her transfixed by the moment of her death.

She remembers walking along the East River with Kenneth Barclay, the sun on her face, the touch of his hand on her arm, their conversations of the future —

She concentrates on images of Lena, of Abraham, and of her father —

The last image is of her friend Jane. She comes to her, dressed in a black dress, her hair long and flowing, and takes Elizabeth into her arms, whispering that everything will be all right. Death, she says, is the start of something new. Something different.

"What is it?" she asks.

"You have come out of the great tribulation," Jane says. "You have washed your robes and made them white in the blood of the Lamb. Never again will you hunger; never again will you thirst. The sun will not beat upon you, nor any scorching heat. For the Lamb will be your shepherd and he will lead you to springs of living water. And God will wipe away every tear from your eyes —"

And then Jane vanishes.

The air runs out.

Elizabeth gags, and the rope tightens.

Sheriff Petty drives as far into the masses as possible before they have to get out and walk. The first thing Walt notices as they move through the people is that the mob is no longer a mob.

The second thing he notices is *her.*

Elizabeth Blackwell's body dangles from the oak tree, twirling in tiny circles, her feet pointed to the ground. Around her, thousands of her fellow New Yorkers stand in dumb silence at the spectacle they have created.

Walt's breath sticks in his throat when he attempts to call out her name. Devastation grips him tight, and his vision blurs.

The sheriff grabs his arm, snapping Whitman to, and they rush to Miss Blackwell.

To relieve the pressure from the rope, they hoist her body on their shoulders.

"How long has she been up there?" the sheriff calls out.

"Long enough," one of the two men says.

Then to Whitman, Petty says, "I've got her — you cut her down." The sheriff holds out his knife.

Walt lets go of the body and takes hold of the branch above his head. He swings his leg up and over, then scoots above the body and slices the rope in two. The body drops into the sheriff's arms, and he gently lays her on the ground.

Petty looks up. "We are too late."

Walt comes down from the tree and kneels next to her.

"Elizabeth, can you hear me?" He unwraps the rope from around her neck and winces when he sees the red welts. "It's Walt."

He presses his hand against her chest, then runs his fingers across her neck. He puts his cheek next to her mouth.

She has a faint breath.

Walt turns to the two men standing next to the sheriff. "Go for a doctor. *Now.*"

Miss Blackwell coughs.

Walt rubs her forehead. "That's it, take your time."

He looks up at those who have tried to kill her. Their faces stare back at him, blank and confused. One woman holds her daughter's hand and strokes her left knuckle with her right index finger. The girl's dark hair blows in the wind, and she meets his gaze with a smile, as if today is the most normal day in the world. How will she look back on this day? Another man braces his elderly father. Same stubby nose, same lanky frame, and same slouch. How did they come to participate in this? A glance in the newspaper, a conversation about God and dissection and justice until they foamed at the mouth — is that what made them leave their comfortable home on a cold winter day to help kill a woman they have never seen before?

Miss Blackwell whimpers.

"Doctor's on his way," he says.

"I'm a doctor," she whispers.

CHAPTER 36

Walt and Miss Zacky keep watch on Elizabeth while she sleeps. She looks peaceful — her face is clean and her hair combed. When Whitman and Sheriff Petty first arrived at New York City Hospital with Miss Blackwell two hours earlier, she was hysterical. Dr. Liston had administered laudanum, and she slipped into a daze that soon led to sleep. Just before she did, the doctor told her she would make a full recovery, and the welts on her neck were only a fraction of the damage that her near strangulation might have caused. "You're lucky," he told her. "Most people would have died going through what you did."

Miss Zacky arrived only minutes later. She hugged Walt, and it was different from before — he sensed a hesitation, a welcome development given his own ambivalence toward what happened in the hotel. She laid her head on his chest and cried.

Dr. Liston had dressed Elizabeth's wounds with a thick white pad, then cleaned her body with a sponge. He told them about a man hanged six times using the short-drop method. Each time, they assumed he was dead until reports trickled in that so-and-so had seen the man at this or that place. They called him the Resurrection Man.

Miss Zacky asked, "What happened to him?"

"They shot him," the doctor said. "No coming back from that one, I'm afraid."

Now, suddenly, Miss Blackwell yawns and opens her eyes.

Miss Zacky leans forward. "How do you feel?"

"Light-headed." She can only whisper because of the damage done to her vocal cords.

"Your neck?"

She traces her fingers along the white bandage, then looks at Walt. "You saved me."

"It was not I alone."

The doctor feels her head, then examines her neck. "Still doing well," he says. "I'll check on you again in an hour."

Miss Blackwell waits for the doctor to leave before she says in a hoarse voice, "What will happen now?"

Whitman recounts Dr. Barclay's confession and his willingness to testify, how once the sheriff heard that confession, he became more open to any other information Walt might have. "The sheriff is on our side now," he says.

"It's good news, but —" She stops.

"But what?"

"It's just that, to know that all these people died for nothing, well —" She can't finish.

Walt can only nod.

A knock at the door interrupts them. Isaiah Rynders and Sheriff Petty step in.

"The doctor tells us you will make a full recovery," Mr. Rynders says.

Mr. Rynders places his stubby hand on her shoulder. His deep-set eyes suggest genuine concern for Elizabeth Blackwell's welfare, but Whitman remains skeptical.

"On behalf of the mayor of the City of New York, I want to offer you an apology." The long scar on his oval-shaped head twitches when he speaks. "Nothing we can say or do will offset the damage of this catastrophe, but if you'll permit me to make an offering." He glances first at Miss Blackwell, then Walt Whitman.

"Mr. Bennett?" he calls.

The editor of the *Herald* limps into the

room. "Mr. Whitman. Miss Blackwell. Good evening. The committee has decided that you both should split the reward money. Five hundred twenty dollars apiece. That was the agreement, to give the money to those who helped apprehend Mr. Saunders's murderer."

"Did you arrest Samuel Clement?" Walt says.

"I locked him up myself," Petty says.

"And why should I believe he'll be prosecuted as he should?"

The men look at each other. "Allow me, gentlemen," Rynders says. "We regretfully acknowledge our mistakes, but you'll understand why we can't admit it publicly. I'm very sorry." He takes a deep breath. "Our justice system, for all its successes, does have its limitations."

"That's it?" Walt says. "After all the people who have died — that's the best you can do?"

Sheriff Petty steps forward. "*Mr. Whitman.* Please accept the reward money as a token of our appreciation."

"Rebuild your school, Miss Blackwell." Rynders steps forward. "This money gives you the means to do so, and you have our *full* support." He lets the words hang in the air before he continues. "This is the best any of us can do."

Whitman's face turns red, but he says nothing — he owes it to Elizabeth and Miss Zacky to hear what they have to say first.

Miss Blackwell closes her eyes.

Isaiah Rynders and Sheriff Petty face him.

Walt leans in. "What will happen to Clement?"

"He'll hang for sure."

"And James Warren?"

The sheriff nods. "Reduced sentence. Prison."

"Mr. Bennett has your money," Rynders says. "Now, if you'll excuse us, we have more work to do tonight."

After Rynders and Petty leave the room, Mr. Bennett hands both Walt and Miss Blackwell envelopes full of money. "This is the best we can hope for, Mr. Whitman."

"Maybe it's the best *you* can hope for." Whitman hands his envelope to Miss Zacky for safekeeping and leaves the room. He catches up to Isaiah Rynders and Silas Petty as they exit the hospital.

"Miss Blackwell might be satisfied, but I am not."

Rynders says, "Excuse us for a moment, will you, Sheriff?"

"I need to get back to the watch house, so

I'll say good night. Mr. Rynders. Mr. Whitman."

"No," Walt says. "I need to talk to the sheriff. Alone."

"Very well," Rynders says. "Then perhaps you'll give me a word?"

Whitman nods, and Rynders steps away to give them privacy.

"What is it?" Petty says.

"You know that Samuel Clement killed Abraham Stowe and Henry Saunders, and you know that Mr. Rynders was in on it. Possibly the mayor."

"What would you have me do?"

Walt has no answer.

The sheriff continues. "We've done all we can do. I'm sorry innocent people have died, but bringing down Rynders, or going after the mayor, won't fix it. Your good work proved Clement is a murderer. He will get what he deserves, and life will go on."

"Not for Henry. Not for Lena and Abraham. Not for Mary Rogers. Not for their families."

"I'm sorry about your friends," Petty says, "and I'm not saying you asked for it, but those articles you wrote about us —"

"But they were true!"

"Truth is a funny thing. How many more people are dead for it?"

Whitman scowls.

"Oh, and I almost forgot," the sheriff says. "The body of that Runkel girl is at the New York University Medical College. They put her back together as best they could and are waiting for you to pick her up. Her parents are anxious to get her back, I'm sure."

"You found Maggie Runkel?" Walt can't conceal his surprise.

"I'm not all bad, Mr. Whitman."

"The Runkels will be relieved. Thank you."

"I'll say good night, then." Sheriff Petty tips his hat and leaves.

Whitman pauses before he turns to Isaiah Rynders.

"I know you don't think much of me," Rynders starts, "and I can't say that I blame you — but try to understand the larger implications of what has gone on here. If we announce that we hanged an innocent person, we lose all credibility, and that won't change what's happened to your friends. Clement will hang, and that has to be sufficient. The end result is the same."

Walt shakes his head. "You covered up what really happened."

"This city has many more problems. The majority of citizens fear anatomical dissection, for one. It doesn't matter what the *truth* is — they believe that dissection keeps them out of heaven. And how can anyone convince them otherwise? At the same time, every medical professional in the country understands that dissection is necessary for medical progress. In the future, medicine can prevent disasters like the cholera epidemic a few years back."

"Until then, the city will hang innocent citizens?"

"Mr. Whitman, please. Body snatching has become an industry that supplies jobs, placates the public, *and* helps medical progress. You're intelligent enough to see what's at stake here. The Bone Bill would eliminate the industry so abruptly that it would take the city half a century or more to recover. Abraham made a choice, and all that has happened in the past three weeks is unfortunate but necessary, given that choice. Your friend Henry didn't die in vain, and maybe one day —"

"In a few days, I will see his parents at the funeral. What do I tell *them*?"

"The truth."

"That he died to protect the traffic of dead bodies?"

"Tell them he believed in his job as a journalist enough to expose the injustices of a business that disproportionately hurts the poor, and that in doing so, he made progress in clearing the way for legislation that will one day end that business."

"But nothing has changed."

"The Bone Bill *will* pass someday, but it will take time."

"What about Mary Rogers?"

Rynders seems surprised. "What about her?"

"I know Barclay altered her autopsy report to hide the botched abortion, and I know Sheriff Harris ordered him to do so," Walt says. "What I don't know is who botched the abortion. Or who the father is."

Rynders sighs. "What changes if I tell you the mayor had an affair with Rogers? What changes if I tell you that he *and* Miss Rogers went to Quigley for help? And what changes if I tell you that when the procedure failed, the mayor told Harris to look away while Clement cleaned it up?"

"What changes?" Whitman says. "Everything changes. The truth comes out. Victims are vindicated. Justice is served."

"But how many more people are hurt in the process?"

"All of New York believes that Abraham killed Mary Rogers and that Lena killed him."

"Mary Rogers is dead, Abraham and Lena Stowe are dead, and nothing will bring them back."

Whitman starts to speak, then stops. Rynders is not wrong, but he is not completely right, either. The gap between truth and narrative can be wide and deep, Walt knows, and should he allow himself to live in *that* world, everything around him might fall away — the hospital, the carriages lined up out front, the streetlamp, the cobblestones, Elizabeth and Miss Zacky, his family, the Stowes, the women's college, his time with Henry — all of it slipping away into nothingness. Walt cannot let that happen, and so he looks Mr. Rynders in the eye and says, "The truth is the truth."

"I'm very impressed by you," Rynders says. "If you turn some of that idealism into action, you will accomplish great things. If there's anything I can ever do for you, please let me know. Now, good night."

"There is something else," Walt calls out.

Rynders stops, turns. "Oh?"

"Azariah Smith."

"What about him?"

"Azariah needs a family, Mr. Rynders. He has done everything you asked."

"I will think about it."

Whitman watches until Rynders disappears around the corner before he returns to the hospital. In the hall, he passes Mr. Bennett.

"If you ever need a job," Bennett says, "come see me. I know a newspaper in New Orleans that might need an editor. Great experience for a young writer who needs to work on his prose."

Whitman pauses only a moment. "You are as bad as they are."

Back in the room, Walt sits down with the two women. "Don't waste your voice on those men," he says.

"But we can rebuild the school with the reward money."

"But how can you trust the likes of Rynders?"

"God oversees all," Elizabeth whispers. "Abraham and Lena understood the importance of the college, and the only way to honor their sacrifices — and Henry's — is to make the college relevant and part of something larger." She looks at Miss Zacky. "With your help."

"Of course."

"You know something else?" Elizabeth's eyes have that spark again, evidence of an inner strength Walt envies. "You are part of this too. God has preserved you for a reason."

Whitman counts out one hundred dollars of his own money and hands it to her. "For the college."

"Are you sure?"

"Absolutely."

"Thank you for everything." She puts the money in her envelope. "And now I'll be resting — I'm so tired."

Walt sits back in his chair and plans what he will do with the rest of his money. Two hundred to the Runkels and another hundred to August and Edie Saunders — that's what Henry would have wanted. The last hundred is for his family.

Across from him, both women have fallen asleep.

Whitman closes his eyes, and the blackness closes in on him until he slips out of consciousness. He dreams that Henry is there with him, dressed in his striped pantaloons and black jacket, clean-shaven and smiling, his chest put back together.

"Walt." Henry pulls him close and whispers: "Every one that sleeps is beautiful, every thing in the dim light is beautiful, peace is always beautiful, the soul is always beautiful." Henry recedes now, the dimple in his chin, his black hair and eyes, and white teeth. "The wildest and bloodiest is over, and all is peace." He smiles and nods,

then vanishes.

And Walt is left alone.

CHAPTER 37

The double rows of beds of the Women's Medical College of the New York Infirmary are filled with women sleeping, and three or four children, flushed and fevered. Karina Emsbury and Patricia Onderdonk change sheets and compresses while Elizabeth Blackwell walks briskly between the rows, giving orders to the young women, and to Miss Zacky, who is trailing behind. "It's stifling in here," she says. "Miss Onderdonk?"

"Yes, ma'am." Patricia hurries to the windows, opens them. "I told Miss Zacky you wanted them open, but she —"

Elizabeth waves her off. "Miss Zakrzewska is a formidable woman, and not to be trifled with, Patricia. It's quite all right."

"How amusing," Miss Zacky says.

Miss Blackwell stops and feels the forehead of an elderly woman who's asleep. She takes the woman's chart from the hook over the bed, flips the pages.

"One hundred and two this morning."

"I suspect yellow fever," Miss Zacky says. "Should we quarantine?"

Elizabeth pulls the woman's eyelids down, shakes her head.

"Her pupils are distended," Miss Zacky says, "her skin is turning blue."

"Cholera! Miss Onderdonk, help me turn Mrs. Skory!"

As Patricia hurries over, Elizabeth gently shakes the old woman awake. "Mrs. Skory? We're going to change your bedding now, all right?"

Elizabeth nods to Miss Zacky; she and Miss Onderdonk roll the tiny woman to her side, then Miss Emsbury pulls the sheets and gathers them into a ball. As she turns around with the sheets, Elizabeth takes them from her.

"I'll take them down, Miss Emsbury."

Miss Zacky says, "You shouldn't be handling those, Lizzy."

"I need to remind the laundry maids to double the chlorine in the washtubs anyway."

"But if anything were to happen to you —"

"Then the infirmary will be in your capable hands. Now, mind you both scrub yours, then get a pint of salt water and sugar into Mrs. Skory."

A scream sounds from across the room.

Seated by an open window, Azariah Smith squirms as Miss Perschon holds an eyedropper over his upturned face. "Hold still, Mr. Smith! This will only take a moment."

She manages to get several drops in his eye before he shrieks again.

"Quit being a baby!" Miss Perschon puts a compress on the boy's eyes, pats his shoulder, then walks over to Elizabeth. "He is in better health for sure, but he is no better at being a patient, I'm afraid."

"No, indeed." Elizabeth smiles. "Mr. Whitman will arrive at any moment to retrieve him." She surveys the room, allowing herself to take it all in. The hustle and bustle of a hospital morning. Medical students chatting with their patients. She feels the losses of recent events deeply, but for now she will cling to gratitude for the present and hope for the future.

Someone approaches from the front.

"There he is now."

Mr. Walt Whitman strides into the room dressed just like Mr. Henry Saunders. He twirls a walking stick and wears his floppy-brimmed hat tilted to the side, a shirt with its collar open, and a jacket with a boutonniere adorning his lapel. Elizabeth Blackwell cannot help but smile at the beauty of the gesture. *Mr. Saunders will live on through him.*

"Good morning, Mr. Whitman."

"Elizabeth." He takes her by the hand, kisses her cheek. "Congratulations! This is a magnificent place to continue your work. Abraham and Lena would be proud."

"Mr. Smith has been making life challenging for Miss Perschon here, but he's as healthy as he's been in quite some time."

At the sound of Walt's voice, Azariah Smith removes the compress. "Am I glad to see you. I've had a hell of a morning with these doctors."

"Come now," Whitman says. "The Runkels will be expecting us."

Azariah gets out of bed and joins him. "I don't know about this, Mr. Whitman."

Walt puts his hand on Azariah's shoulder. "The Runkels are wonderful people, and they can't wait to meet you."

Azariah frowns. "What about you?"

"I'll visit often. I promise."

Azariah takes a deep breath. "Okay, then, I'm ready."

"Are you not forgetting?" Walt asks him.

The boy approaches Elizabeth. "Ma'am, I wish to thank you."

401

"You're very welcome," she says. "Don't forget to visit. Both of you." She watches as Walt and Azariah disappear down the stairs, and she takes a moment to whisper a short prayer: *Thank you, God, for helping us keep the college going. Thank you for returning the students. May thy servants, Abraham, Lena, and Henry, find peace in your kingdom.* She opens her eyes to find the other students staring at her. "What is the matter, ladies?" Elizabeth Blackwell says. "Back to work!"

Twelve inches of new snow have blanketed the city, and the frozen top layer cracks under Walt Whitman's feet. The air is thick and gray.

The Runkels' new apartment is in a two-story tenement building that floats up in the distance, its red brick shiny in the haze, a long piece of black cloth draped over the doorframe. The Runkels used some of Walt's reward money to move into these larger and safer living quarters. In only a few days, Whitman has helped Ned Runkel find employment at city hall as a bookkeeper, and Harriet Runkel will soon begin seamstress work at home.

Last night, when Whitman returned from a long day at the *Evening Tattler,* his new employer, Azariah Smith waited at his door with a small bag of his belongings and a deed of trust, signed by both Rynders and his solicitor, transferring the boy's indenture from Isaiah Rynders to Walter Whitman.

Now, after his checkup at the infirmary, they are on their way to the Runkels for Maggie's re-interment service. The communal response to Maggie Runkel's return has been wide and supportive. All of New York City is shaken by the past month's events and Maggie has become a symbol of the city returning to normal, if such a thing is possible, as documented by Walt in his front-page article in the *Tattler*.

When Walt and Azariah step into the entryway of the new building, the first thing they hear is singing. Children and elderly folks, and everyone in between, raise their voices together in tribute to Maggie Runkel. And as the two make their way to the stairway, these same people recognize Whitman as *that* reporter. They all want to say hello, and they jostle and crowd him.

Walt has never experienced anything like this before, and part of him loves it and wants to soak up the attention as much as he can, but today is not the time. Instead, he thanks them, shakes their hands, and continues to press toward the stairs.

On the second floor, Whitman straightens

his boutonniere before he raps on the door with Henry's cane.

Harriet Runkel, dressed all in black, answers the door. "Mr. Whitman! And you must be Azariah. My, you are as handsome as Mr. Whitman reported."

"Ma'am," Azariah says. "Nice to meet you."

"Don't you ma'am me," she says. "It's Mrs. Runkel or Mum." And she takes him unto herself, hugs him tight. The gesture makes it clear that Azariah is *her* son now, and this is just as it should be. Some things do work out.

Mrs. Runkel releases Azariah. She wipes her eyes. "Come in where it's warm. I'll take your coats." Inside, the room is a mixture of smells — cakes, roasted meat, flowers, and perfumes. "Here are your black armbands." She helps Azariah slide on the symbol of mourning first, and then Walt.

She kisses Whitman's cheek. "Ned and I are so grateful. Thank you for everything." She breaks down, crying now. "You'll have to forgive me. This is the second time we've mourned her, and . . ."

"I can't imagine how difficult that must be."

Walt turns, and that's when he sees Maggie's body for the first time since the night of the grave robbery. The pine casket lies at an angle in the corner, propped up to make her visible from anywhere in the room, framed on either side by candles, which make her glow. Her tiny body appears even smaller in the casket. A mortician from the other side of the city volunteered his services. With the combination of makeup on her face and the beautiful burial dress, Maggie looks like a life-size porcelain doll, and the perfumes help cover the smell, which would otherwise be overbearing. They will bury her after a short graveside service later this afternoon.

Mrs. Runkel gathers herself. "We are so thankful to have her back."

Walt nods. It occurs to him that Henry's body has arrived at the Saunders' farm in northern Manhattan. He'll be traveling there next to say good-bye.

Ned Runkel appears, shuffles toward them. "Mr. Smith?" He dabs his eyes with a handkerchief.

"Mr. Runkel," the boy says, and they shake hands. "I'm sorry for your loss."

"Thank you, son. Welcome to our home."

Azariah's smile returns.

And then she appears, tentative at first, mindful of Azariah. Abby runs across the room and leaps into Walt's arms. "You did it, Mr. Whitman. You found my sister."

From his pocket, he pulls the small bag of horehound candy he picked up for her earlier that day, places it in her tiny hand.

"Oh, thank you," she says. "Maggie and I both love horehound." Before she does anything else, she slides down from Walt's arms and walks over to her sister's body. She removes a piece of candy and places it in Maggie's hand. Then she takes one for herself and pops it into her mouth. "It's delicious." Whitman admires the young girl's frankness about death. She is young, yes, but she has had to face what death is, unadorned with the rhetorical flourishes of age.

Now she turns to Azariah for the first time. She's nervous, Walt can tell, but she gathers herself, curtsies. "My name is Abby," she says, "welcome to our family."

Azariah smiles, of course, and reaches out his hand. "It's a pleasure to make your acquaintance, Miss Abby."

Abby, suddenly overcome with the enormity of what's happening, wraps her arms around her new brother. "I'm so happy you're here." She releases him, then takes his hand. "Come. I'll show you where you'll be staying."

Whitman sits on the bed next to Maggie's

casket and studies her. In one way, she looks normal — all the parts are in the right place and they have covered up the damage done to her chest by the medical students. At the same time, however, Maggie doesn't look like a person at all. More than anything, it is the stillness that makes Maggie not Maggie. No breathing, no blood, no life. Walt has had enough death for now. He touches her cheek with his index finger. The skin is taut and warm from the wood-burning stove.

"Hard to believe, isn't it?" Mrs. Runkel stands behind him now.

Suddenly, Walt is overwhelmed with sadness. "A dead body has no hope," he says.

"Oh, Mr. Whitman," Mrs. Runkel says, turning emotional. "When I look at her, all I see is hope."

After his wife disappears around the corner, Mr. Runkel pulls a pipe from his suit pocket. "The others will be here soon. Why don't you have some dinner? Harriet has baked some delicious breads and cakes, and the meat's almost done." He pours the tobacco with his right hand, clutching the pipe in his left.

Walt sets the piece of paper on the mantel. "This is Azariah's deed of trust. He was indentured to Isaiah Rynders, and now he is legally indentured to me. Keep this, and we will visit a solicitor to have this changed at a later time."

Ned nods. "Yes, of course."

"He's a good boy."

"We'll take care of him." Ned struggles to strike a match on the fireplace. "You're from Long Island?"

"Born in West Hills," Walt says, taking the match from Ned. "but my family lives in Brooklyn." He lights Ned's pipe for him.

"We heard about your friend Mr. Saunders. Please accept our condolences."

"Thank you, Mr. Runkel," Walt says. "Tomorrow, I leave for his funeral in northern Manhattan."

"We've all had our share of grief," Ned says.

Walt can only nod. He feels exhausted from the inside out, and he can't fathom a future without feeling this way.

"How is Miss Blackwell recovering?"

"Azariah and I just left her. She's already moved into another building for the Women's Medical College, and she has more students and patients than they can handle."

"And in only a few days," Ned says. "Good news indeed."

Abby returns without Azariah. In the kitchen, Mrs. Runkel is already teaching him how to peel potatoes, and Walt knows that this is where Azariah belongs. Whitman had briefly considered keeping the boy himself, but he's not set up for this yet, and upon hearing about Azariah's plight, the Runkels offered, without pause, to take him in.

"Your friend is in heaven with Maggie," Abby says to Walt. "I bet they are having a grand time together. Don't you think?"

Walt smiles. "I imagine you're right."

"Of course I am," she says. "Where else would they be?"

"You're always welcome here," Mr. Runkel says.

The three of them sit together in silence around Maggie's body, until Mr. Runkel finally speaks. "When you're ready to eat, come into the next room."

Then Mr. Runkel leaves him alone with Abby. Walt Whitman leans back against the chair and cries.

Abby climbs into his lap and puts her arms around his neck. She squeezes and holds him for what seems like minutes, and when she lets go, she whispers into his ear, "You and me are the same, Mr. Whitman. We've both lost important people in our lives."

Walt wipes his eyes with his handkerchief.

"We are a lot alike, aren't we?"

"I told you when you first arrived that God sent you to us."

"I remember."

"Do you want to know how I knew that?"

"How?"

"At night, when everything is quiet and the only sounds are my parents breathing, sometimes God talks to me. The night before we met, he told me he would send you to us, and then two nights ago, he told me you would be coming back, and you would bring me a new brother."

"He did?"

"Yes, and he wants me to give you a message."

"What is it?"

"God wants me to tell you that everything is going to be okay." After she says this, Abby leans into him so that her head rests under his chin. Her legs dangle on either side of his right leg and her breathing slows down as if she is asleep. To their left lies Maggie in her casket. He again thinks of Henry, wondering what he will say when he meets August and Edie Saunders for the first time.

His thoughts unspool into the future, two months from now when winter has gone, and spring has conquered. A splash of green pasture, red flowers, and yellow sunlight against the blue sky. Robins and sparrows zipping through the warm air. Children scampering about the streets in their shirt-sleeves, women meandering through the market without their petticoats, and the men ignoring it all from their desks on the third floor — all while Henry's body, deep in the dirt, dissolves into itself.

It's there, in the future, that he's able to confront the loss of his friend, and so he takes what's left of his memories and reconstructs Henry: The leg muscles gather together in the air, the skin closes in a series of buckles before they shoot back into the torso. The heart and the liver drop inside the chest from the sky, and the two sides close like stage curtains —

The head turns —

and Henry waits —

but when Walt opens his eyes, Henry vanishes, and Walt perceives the multitudes of his loss, that he will carry images and impressions and memories of Henry, but that his friend is gone forever —

So Walt returns to the present, to Abby on his lap, to the mourners in the other room, to the chorus of voices rising from the street, to the materiality of the real, and he holds on tight.

AUTHOR'S NOTE

In 1842 New York City, Walt Whitman was the twenty-two-year-old editor of the *Aurora.* He was just about to publish a temperance novel, *Franklin Evans,* and he would begin work on the follow-up, *The Madman,* only a fragment of which he ever published, in January 1843. His short fiction, poetry, and editorials were being published in newspapers all over New York City. He already had a sense of himself as a famous author and was a ruthless self-promoter, but his writing was overwrought, sentimental, and derivative. Whitman himself called *Franklin Evans* "damned rot — rot of the worst sort" (Traubel 93). Indeed, the most striking thing about the 1842 Whitman is just how average he was.

Only thirteen years later, Whitman would become *the* American poet, the one who abandons the strictures of classical form and meter for long lines of free verse, the creator of a literature distinctly American in *Leaves of Grass*. These poems comprise an important historical map of a century that saw mass immigration, industrialization, enormous technological advances, and a Civil War that tore the country in two. Whitman documented slavery before, and after, the amendment that abolished it; and he memorialized Abraham Lincoln after his assassination. Whitman wrote that *Leaves of Grass* "arose out of my life in Brooklyn and New York . . . absorbing a million people . . . with an intimacy, an eagerness, an abandon, probably never equaled" (*Walt Whitman's America* 83).

How did the average Whitman of 1842 become the genius Whitman of 1855? Of course this is a question without a real answer, and Whitman's trajectory as a writer, and his genius, owe us no explanation. Thirteen years of writing is a lot of time for a writer to develop, and yet I can't help but wonder at the gap. The quality of his writing is not only different in technique but in scope and understanding. The broad impetus for *Speakers of the Dead* was to imagine what might have happened to change Walter Whitman the journalist and temperance novelist into Walt Whitman, *the* American poet.

Walt Whitman left home in 1831 when he was only twelve years old to work for the *Long Island Patriot.* The editor of the paper, Samuel E. Clement, was "a tall, hawk-nosed Quaker of Southern antecedents who walked the village lanes in long-tailed blue coat with gilt buttons and a leghorn hat" (Kaplan 75). Whitman admired Clement, and "went along for the ride and for the company when the editor drove out to Bushwick and New Lots delivering papers to country subscribers." It is easy to imagine how Whitman might have viewed Clement as a father figure — his own relationship with his father was strained, and he was living away from home for the first time.

So when Clement was arrested for digging up the body of Walt's spiritual mentor, the Quaker prophet Elias Hicks, Whitman was shocked. Samuel Clement and the noted sculptor John Henri Browere made a plaster cast of the corpse's head and face. The plan was to sell busts made from the cast to Hicks's admirers, a venture that would have made them hundreds of dollars had they not been caught. So affected was Whitman by the grave robbery that he wrote "a newspaper article about the incident in the *Brooklyn Daily Times* in 1857, included both prose and pictorial portraits of Hicks in *November Boughs,* and perhaps reworked his adolescent, gruesome experience in the surreal poem 'The Sleepers' " (*A Historical Guide to Walt Whitman* 155):

> A shroud I see and I am the shroud, I wrap a body and lie in the coffin,
> It is dark here under ground, it is not evil or pain here, it is blank here, for reasons.
> (It seems to me that every thing in the light and air ought to be happy,
> Whoever is not in his coffin and the dark grave let him know he has enough.)

Whitman's experience with grave robbing turned out to be a pivotal moment in the evolution of *Speakers of the Dead.* This is when I first began to think about Whitman as a person instead of "the poet." The fact that he came face-to-face with grave robbing at so early an age would undoubtedly shape his identity, and might be one way of explaining the theme of death that is present in *Leaves of Grass.* And, on a more practical note for my own writing, it meant that a young Whitman would have certainly been aware of the resurrection men.

RESURRECTION MEN

With no legal means of acquiring cadavers, medical students and their instructors had to rely on the illegal body trade run by resurrection men. These businessmen would troll the obituaries, then dig up the recently deceased and sell them to medical schools for anatomical dissection. Stealing a body was illegal, but "at $5 to $25 per body, grave robbery was too lucrative to resist: a skilled journeyman in the mid-1820s might only earn $20 to $25 for an entire week's work. And when body snatchers were caught, the statutory [five-year prison sentence] was rarely enforced" (Sappol 113–14). At a time when jobs were scarce and the demand for cadavers high, body snatching became a legitimate career choice.

The year 1843 was an exciting and frustrating time in the medical field: Anatomical dissection had opened the door for new discoveries and possible cures, but those in the medical profession had a serious PR problem. "In the eighteenth and nineteenth centuries, pranks involving body parts were common. Students courted disaster by throwing pieces of their dissections at visitors, displaying severed limbs in windows, or taking bodies or body parts home" (Sappol 84, 104). Indeed, an entire collection of photographs exists in which medical students prank the bodies. This, along with the religious belief that dissection prevented resurrection, made it almost impossible for doctors and medical students to win public support for a legal cadaver supply. Riots and medical-school mobs became commonplace, and human dissection a dangerous enterprise. Legislation called the Bone Bill would give the medical community a way to procure these bodies, but the bill would not pass until 1854.

ELIZABETH BLACKWELL

My research into the illegal body trade and the importance of anatomical dissection led me to Elizabeth Blackwell. In 1847, when women did not study medicine, Blackwell became a student at Geneva Medical College in upstate New York after the other 150 medical students, who believed the application was a joke, voted to accept her. Her interest in becoming a doctor came from watching a close friend die from a painful disease. Blackwell came to believe that women patients would benefit from a woman doctor. After graduating from Geneva in 1849, Blackwell moved to Paris to pursue her dream of becoming a surgeon. There, while treating an infant with ophthalmia neonatorum, she lost her sight in one eye when some of the contaminated solution squirted in her eye. Blackwell returned to New York City, where she opened her own clinic. Her sister, Emily, along with Marie Zakrzewska, both MDs, joined her in 1857 to help run her newly established New York Infirmary for Indigent Women and Children.

Blackwell's appearance in *Speakers of the Dead* imagines a time before she attended Geneva Medical College. The Women's Medical College of Manhattan is my creation, as are its founders, Abraham and Lena Stowe. It seemed a good way to bring Elizabeth to New York City in 1843 (when she was actually in Cincinnati) and have her rub shoulders with Walt. The Stowes' work on behalf of women in the novel also seems a good way to represent the real work both men and women did at the time on behalf of women's rights. Blackwell's story, as far as I can tell, has not yet been adequately told, and I make no claim to have done so here. I only hope that readers will be persuaded to learn more about her life and work after reading this novel.

MARY ROGERS

Walt Whitman spent much of the 1840s jumping from newspaper job to newspaper job, with a few failed teaching jobs in between. He had a reputation for being difficult, and he was often walking the streets of the Bowery when he should have been typesetting at the printing press. Not only would Whitman have reported on body snatching and anatomical dissection, but he also would have known about the Cigar Girl Murder.

In his book *The Beautiful Cigar Girl,* Daniel Stashower writes that the Mary Rogers murder "became a catalyst for sweeping change" in 1840s New York City (4). Law enforcement was exposed as inadequate. The sensational details gave rise to sensationalism. And murder became "a bankable commodity" (5). Edgar Allan Poe decided to take on the murder in a desperate attempt to restart his career. "The Mystery of Marie Rogêt" was his fictional attempt to solve the real murder of Mary Rogers. The problem for Poe was that, by the time he published the trilogy of stories, new theories about the death of Rogers had emerged, rendering Poe's own theories useless.

A novel about 1843 New York City cannot ignore the impact of the Mary Rogers murder. Rogers's death exposed a city mired in corruption, power plays, and incompetence. Isaiah Rynders was a Tammany Hall boss who manipulated the truth to his benefit, who really could start and stop a mob, and who was a middleman between the upper and lower classes. James Gordon Bennett used the Mary Rogers case to further his own career and to promote the *New York Herald,* and he was involved in a committee of safety organized to find Mary Rogers's murderer. The medical establishment was condemned when the rumor emerged that Rogers died from a botched abortion. And the public was dragged through it all: From the moment the body washed up on the banks of the Hudson River, through the various theories of her death and the sensationalist reporting, to the case's ambiguous conclusion, New Yorkers watched the drama unfold.

Speakers of the Dead is first and foremost a mystery novel, and I have played fast and loose with the details in service of the genre. One big change I made for the sake of the novel's chronology is to set the novel in 1843. Whitman enthusiasts will recognize, for example, that Whitman worked at the *Aurora* in spring 1842 and not winter 1843. That said, I have tried to be as accurate as possible within this fictional framework, and while I have leaned on a lot of secondary sources to create this story, the mistakes are mine.

J. Aaron Sanders
Columbus, GA

ACKNOWLEDGMENTS

I am grateful beyond words to my agent, Jeff Kleinman, whose brilliance and generosity carried me through, and he continues to make me look good. I wish also to thank the team at Folio Literary Management for their work on my behalf.

Infinite thanks to my editors, Kate Napolitano and Denise Roy, whose expertise and guidance pushed this book to new heights and depths. Thanks also to the team at Plume: publisher David Rosenthal, VP/ associate publisher Aileen Boyle, managing editor LeeAnn Pemberton, cover designer Samantha Russo, associate director of marketing Christina Hu, executive publicist Marian Brown, publicity assistant Alie Coolidge, and editorial assistant Joanna Kamouh. Their vision for the novel has been a thrilling complement to my own, and I am forever indebted to these folks for their wisdom and generosity.

Thanks to PR masterminds Rich Kelley, Ron Koltnow, and Bridget Marmion of Your Expert Nation.

Thanks to Robert Palm, mentor and genius writer; and to Carey Scott Wilkerson, poet and playwright and the most well-read person I know.

This book has benefited from the many friends and colleagues who read and commented on working drafts: Chris Dowd, Joshua Eyler, Stone Gossard, Matthew House, Patrick Jackson, Molly McVey, Rae Meadows, Morgan Lamberson, Nick Norwood, Heidi Packard, Anthony Rand, Dan Ross, Lauren Sarat, Jenny Spinner, Jonathan Vogler, and Matthew Williams. Their insights and encouragement have been invaluable.

A thank-you to those gifted writers and teachers with whom I had the pleasure to study: Douglas G. Bonzo, Scott Bradfield, Karen Brennan, François Camoin, Katharine Coles, Margaret Higonnet, Marisa Januzzi, David Kranes, Ellen Litman, Brenda Miller, Marilyn Nelson, Jacqueline Osherow, V. Penelope Pelizzon, Samuel Pickering, Wendy Rawlings, and Melanie Rae Thon.

Boundless thanks to my good friends who have been there for me on page and off:

John Aldous, Alf Alver, Ken Cormier, Matt Dixon, Tom Ingram, Mariko Izumi, John McCann, Eric Palmer, Matthew Simpson, Henna Smelhoven, Lange Taylor, Markus Weidler, and Lenny Zbyk.

I want to thank my family for their love and support: Joseph Sanders, Lana Sanders, Chad Sanders, Jared Sanders, Nicole Holm, Jordan Sanders, Jake Holm, Amy Sanders, Ashlee Sanders, William Sanders, Edith Sanders, George Poulsen, and Orlene Poulsen.

Last, I salute my sons, Gareth and Eliot, who have spent countless hours in libraries, coffee shops, and bookstores helping me become a better father and a better writer.

WORKS CONSULTED

"Visit to the Red Light District, 1843." Eye-Witness to History. www.eyewitnesstohistory.com (2006).

Allen, Gay Wilson. *The Solitary Singer: A Critical Biography of Walt Whitman.* New York: Macmillan, 1955. New York University Press, 1967.

Anbinder, Tyler. *Five Points: The 19th-Century New York City Neighborhood That Invented Tap Dance, Stole Elections, and Became the World's Most Notorious Slum.* New York: Plume, 2002.

Asbury, Herbert. *The Gangs of New York: An Informal History of the Underworld.* New York: Thunder's Mouth Press, 2001.

Cantor, Norman L. *After We Die: The Life and Times of the Human Cadaver.* Washington, D.C.: Georgetown University Press, 2010.

Dana, Richard Henry, Jr. *The Journal of*

Richard Henry Dana, Jr. Vol. 1. Edited by
Robert F. Lucid. Cambridge, MA: Harvard University Press, 1968.

Emerson, Ralph Waldo. "The Poet." Published in *Essays: Second Series,* 1844.
http://www.emersoncentral.com/poet.htm.

Kaplan, Justin. *Walt Whitman: A Life.* New
York: Simon & Schuster, 1980.

Lamb, Martha J. & Mrs. Burton Harrison.
*History of the City of New York: Its Origin,
Rise, and Progress.* Vol. 3. New York:
The A. S. Barnes Company, 1896.

Loving, Jerome. *Walt Whitman: The Song of
Himself.* Berkeley: University of California
Press, 2000.

Myers, Gustavus. *The History of Tammany
Hall.* 2nd ed. New York: Boni & Liveright,
1917.

Overstake, Jillian Amber. *A Most Earnest
Plea: Pregnant Women Facing Capital
Punishment in the American Colonies.* MA
thesis. Wichita State University, 2012.

Reynolds, David S. *Walt Whitman's America:
A Cultural Biography.* New York: Vintage,
1996.

———. *A Historical Guide to Walt Whitman.*
Oxford: Oxford University Press, 2000.

Richardson, Ruth. *Death, Dissection and the
Destitute.* 2nd ed. Chicago: University of

Chicago Press, 2001.

Roach, Mary. *Stiff: The Curious Lives of Human Cadavers.* New York: W. W. Norton, 2003.

Sappol, Michael. *A Traffic of Dead Bodies: Anatomy and Embodied Social Identity in Nineteenth-Century America.* Princeton, NJ: Princeton University Press, 2002.

Scheick, William J. "Whitman and the Afterlife: 'Sparkles from the Wheel.' " *Walt Whitman Quarterly Review* 20 (Fall 2002), 80–86.

Stashower, Daniel. *The Beautiful Cigar Girl: Edgar Allan Poe, Mary Rogers, and the Invention of Murder.* New York: Dutton, 2006.

Traubel, Horace. *With Walt Whitman in Camden.* Vol. 1. Boston: Small, Maynard, 1906.

Warner, John Harley, and James M. Edmonson. *Dissection: Photographs of a Rite of Passage in American Medicine: 1880–1930.* New York: Blast Books, 2009.

Whitman, Walt. *Franklin Evans.* New York: Random House, 1929.

———. *Leaves of Grass.* New York: W. W. Norton, 1973.

———. *The Early Poems and the Fiction.* Edited by Thomas L. Brasher. New York:

New York University Press, 1963.

———. *Walt Whitman of the "New York Aurora": Editor at Twenty-Two.* Edited by Joseph Jay Rubin and Charles H. Brown. State College, PA: Bald Eagle Press, 1950.

Wilson, Dorothy Clarke. *Lone Woman: The Story of Elizabeth Blackwell, the First Woman Doctor.* Boston: Little Brown, 1970.

ABOUT THE AUTHOR

J. Aaron Sanders is associate professor of English at Columbus State University, where he teaches literature and creative writing. He holds a PhD in American literature from the University of Connecticut and an MFA in fiction from the University of Utah. His stories have appeared in the *Carolina Quarterly, Gulf Coast, Quarterly West,* and *Beloit Fiction Journal,* among others. This is his first novel.

The employees of Thorndike Press hope you have enjoyed this Large Print book. All our Thorndike, Wheeler, and Kennebec Large Print titles are designed for easy reading, and all our books are made to last. Other Thorndike Press Large Print books are available at your library, through selected bookstores, or directly from us.

For information about titles, please call:
(800) 223-1244

or visit our Web site at:
http://gale.cengage.com/thorndike

To share your comments, please write:
Publisher
Thorndike Press
10 Water St., Suite 310
Waterville, ME 04901